CoVid

By Richard Van Anderson

The Final Push: a short story
The Organ Takers: a novel (McBride #1)
The Organ Growers: a novel (McBride #2)
CoVid: a novel (McBride #3)

CoVid

A novel of surgical suspense

Richard Van Anderson

WHITE LIGHT PRESS
SEATTLE

Publisher's Cataloging-in-Publication Data

Anderson, Richard Van, author.

CoVid : a novel of surgical suspense / Richard Van Anderson.

Seattle : White Light Press, 2020. | Series: The McBride trilogy, bk. 3.

LCCN 2020909946 (print) | ISBN 978-0-9907597-7-5 (paperback) | ISBN 978-0-9907597-6-8 (hardcover) | ISBN 978-0-9907597-8-2 (ebook)

Subjects: LCSH: Physicians--Fiction. | COVID-19 (Disease)--Fiction. | Viruses--Fiction. | Biological weapons--Fiction. | Conspiracies--Fiction. | BISAC: FICTION / Thrillers / Medical. | FICTION / Thrillers / Suspense. | GSAFD: Medical novels. | Suspense fiction.

LCC PS3601.N54486 C68 2020 (print) | LCC PS3601.N54486 (ebook) | DDC 813/.6--dc23.

For Jackson Streeter—
former flight surgeon US Navy/TOPGUN training program,
master plotter, character development specialist, and friend.

Author's Notes

Surgery is a technical endeavor. As such, this story is laden with surgical terminology. Taken in context, the meaning of these terms should be clear. If, however, you are interested in expanded definitions, photos of surgical instruments, X-rays and CT scans of pertinent pathologies, please visit the glossary on my website: rvananderson.com. I encourage you to take a look. Gaining familiarity with the subject matter will enrich your reading experience, and the glossary is interesting in its own right.

Regarding the use of "Native American" in this book: the first inhabitants of America were referred to as Indians, and later as American Indians. The term Native American grew out of the civil rights movements of the 1960s and '70s as a way to avoid the negative historical context of Indian or American Indian. The latest edition of the *Chicago Manual of Style* states that American Indian remains the preferred reference among many tribes. When researching this book I learned that there is not a one-size-fits-all terminology for referring to native peoples. Many Native Americans use a range of words to describe themselves, including Native or Indian, while others, if not most, prefer to be known by their tribal affiliation. In this story, the non-native characters use the term Native American. Nova Featherstone, a member of the Fallon Paiute-Shoshone tribe, uses Native and American Indian, as well as Shoshone, the tribe with which she identifies. All of these references are appropriate.

In November 2002, individuals in China's Guangdong Province develop an unusual respiratory syndrome. Researchers determine the infectious agent is a coronavirus carried by horseshoe bats and link the outbreak to a local wet market. The World Health Organization designates the pathogen SARS-CoV and classifies the medical condition as Severe Acute Respiratory Syndrome. In March 2003, the WHO issues a global alert warning of an atypical pneumonia spreading throughout the world by people using air transport. In April, the WHO issues warnings asking people to postpone all but essential travel to affected areas, including Hong Kong, Toronto, parts of mainland China, and Taiwan. On July 5, the WHO declares the SARS epidemic contained. Before disappearing, SARS-CoV infects 8,439 people, including seventy-three in the United States. Worldwide it kills 812.

In September 2012, scientists report that a new coronavirus, designated MERS-CoV, has been isolated from a patient in Saudi Arabia. Within the next month, the number of Middle East Respiratory Syndrome cases rises to nine, with five fatalities. Since 2012, twenty-seven countries have reported cases of MERS, but around 80 percent of those have occurred in Saudi Arabia. According to the WHO, contact with dromedary camels is the most common route of infection. To date, MERS-CoV has infected 2,519, including two in the US. It has killed eighty-six.

In December 2019, an acute respiratory syndrome is identified in Wuhan, China. Although similar to SARS-CoV, scientists classify this pathogen as a novel coronavirus and designate it SARS-CoV-2. Within weeks, Coronavirus Disease 2019—or COVID-19—rapidly spreads around the globe.

- 1 -

An isolated airstrip in an unnamed desert
Fifty miles from the Kazakhstan-China border
0200 hours
The inaugural mission of the Night Fury

Beyond the halo of multiple floodlights, nothing but black-ink darkness. Within the halo of the floodlights, a single UAV, or Unmanned Aerial Vehicle, commonly referred to as a drone. But this was not a run-of-the-mill surveillance or armed tactical drone. This was the most advanced UAV yet to be conceived: the HoQA50 Night Fury.

Like its namesake from the kid's movie, the Night Fury was all about stealth. Its outer skin was coated with carbon black—a material that readily absorbs radar waves. Its shape and profile were that of a manta ray with a thirty-foot wingspan. The fuselage was no more than a slight convexity in the middle of the aircraft, housing a liquid hydrogen fueled jet-propulsion system that allowed it to stay aloft for two weeks and fly at altitudes higher than sixty-five thousand feet, more than twice that of commercial airliners.

The Night Fury's inaugural mission would barely test its full capabilities. Its target was three thousand kilometers away, had a population of eleven million, and covered an area of nine thousand square kilometers, or three thousand square miles. With a top speed of 220 kilometers per hour, the Fury would reach its target in thirteen hours, drop its payload in a single pass from an altitude of one thousand meters, and return to the airstrip, all without being detected. As weapons systems go, however, the Night Fury was a World War

I biplane compared to the simple white powder contained within its cargo bay. Even if loaded with American Hellfire missiles, or forty-five hundred pounds of conventional ordnance, the killing power of the Fury paled in comparison to the nanometer-size virions it now carried.

Before its eradication in 1979, the smallpox virus killed more than five hundred million people. Influenza, also a viral disease, is estimated to have killed one hundred million throughout history, and if one were to ask the leading biomedical researchers studying past and present pandemics, they would tell you the next big killer will likely be a mutation of a known coronavirus—a new variant of SARS or MERS—which spread through the air and enter the body via the lungs.

In recent decades, a group of viral diseases has emerged that have captivated the social conscience. Although they've had minimal impact compared to smallpox and influenza, they kill their victims in a much more terrifying fashion. They are members of the "viral hemorrhagic fever" family and include the Ebola, Marburg, and Lassa viruses. Each of these pathogens cause multiple organ failure, internal bleeding, and hemorrhaging from mucosal membranes— eyes, mouth, and GI tract. All three are classified as biosafety level-4 pathogens, but fortunately, intimate contact between individuals is required to pass the virus, thus limiting their ability to rapidly spread beyond borders.

If the lethality of smallpox was combined with the airborne spread of influenza and the dramatic mode of death seen with the viral hemorrhagic fevers, you would have what the world will soon come to know as the Wuhan Supervirus.

There were many things to admire about the supervirus. First, its simplicity. Its creation was complex—a noninfectious strain of the coronavirus upregulated by splicing twenty-three new genes into its existing genome—but it was still just a virus, a particle consisting of a single strand of RNA inside a protein envelope. Its lifecycle was simple as well. Find a host. Enter the host's cells. Insert its RNA into the host's DNA and then wait as the host cell's machinery creates millions of new viral particles. When the host cell has completed its duties, it bursts open, releasing the newly created virions, which move on to the next cell—invade, replicate, repeat.

The second admirable quality of the supervirus was its ease of production, delivery, and propagation. The virus was easily mass-produced, grown by the ton in giant bioreactors, then purified and dried into a simple white powder. The viral powder was then exposed to two basic elements, silicon and oxygen, forming silicon dioxide, or glass—or more specifically, superfine glass known as silica nanopowder. As the name implies, the silica particles are nanometers in size, small enough to coat individual virions. This process makes the virus "smooth" and "slippery" and gives the white powder an ultrafine consistency like bath talc. It is creamy to the touch and readily dissipates into the air, quickly becoming invisible and drifting for tens if not hundreds of miles, carried on the slightest currents and slipping through the smallest openings in any surface—through cracks in walls, gaps in windowsills, down chimneys, and along ventilation ducts—behaving more like a gas than a solid. In summary, this glass-coated virus could go anywhere and everywhere. And it could sit for days, or even weeks, on any object or surface, waiting for a breeze or gust of wind or for someone to simply walk by and kick up an invisible cloud of viral particles that could then be inhaled by unknowing victims.

And the third admirable quality of the supervirus? In animal studies it had a mortality rate of 100 percent. You breathe it in, you're dead.

- 2 -

One year before the inaugural mission of the Night Fury
Washington, DC
Basement, West Wing of the White House
The Situation Room

"Gentleman, I have come here to discuss, and plan for, the greatest threat mankind will ever face. Within a matter of months we will be exposed to a new viral pandemic whose lethality and ability to spread are magnitudes greater than the CoVid19 coronavirus that is now sweeping the globe."

The man speaking was Colonel Jonathan Neville, United States Army, director of DARPA—the Defense Advanced Research Projects Agency—and commander, biosafety level 4 laboratory, Fallon, Nevada. The men to whom he was speaking included the national security advisor, the director of homeland security, the director of national intelligence, the secretary of defense, the director of the CIA, the secretary of the navy, the White House chief of staff, and the president of the United States.

Wearing his impeccably tailored "dress greens," Neville stood tall and fit at the head of the table with two stacks of file folders in front of him and an array of screens mounted on the wall behind him. The president sat at the far end, slouched in his chair, already looking distracted and fidgety.

The colonel circled the table, placing folders titled WUHAN SUPERVIRUS, with CLASSIFIED stamped in red ink, in front of each attendee. "In these files," Neville said, "is a report compiled by a trusted colleague of mine in the KIBR."

"The KIBR?" asked the idiot chief of staff, who had neither the experience nor the synaptic capacity to run the White House.

"The Korean Institute for Biological Research," Neville replied. "It's the equivalent of our USAMRIID, the United States Army Medical Research Institute of Infectious Disease."

Each of the officials shared looks of concern, then opened their folders and thumbed through the pages.

"This report," Neville continued, "contains credible evidence that China has developed, and plans to use, a bioweapon of unprecedented destructiveness. The South Korean National Intelligence Service recently secured a weaponized strain of the CoVid19 coronavirus, which they have classified as CoVid23. The NIS believes the Chinese are going to release CoVid23 in countries already affected by the current pandemic. They fear the mortality rate could reach as high as eighty percent, compared to the one percent we're currently seeing. And they believe the Chinese will claim that this new, more deadly strain is a natural mutation of the CoVid19 L strain we are presently dealing with."

CIA Director Mike Kelly closed his file, scrutinized the front and back covers, then tossed it onto the table. "What the hell is this?" he said. "Nobody comes into the president's daily brief and presents classified material that has not been called to the attention of, and vetted by, the Central Intelligence Agency."

All eyes moved from Mike Kelly to Jonathan Neville. Neville took a moment to savor his position of authority over the president's hand-selected group of buffoons and yes-men. Then he calmly said, "The president has already seen it."

"Mr. President," Kelly said, "with all due respect, you've allowed a colonel in the United States Army to circumvent the well-established channels for handling materials with national security implications."

The president sat up straight. "Jonathan and I go way back. He's as much a trusted advisor as any of you."

"In spite of that, this report has not been—"

"Let him finish," the president said sharply.

"But Mr. President, between myself and the director of national intelligence, sixteen intelligence agencies are represented at this table. Don't you think the Korean NIS would have passed this on to anyone other than an army colonel who works with germs?"

"Passing a potential bioweapon to someone that spends his days studying bioweapons makes perfect sense to me," the president replied, "so let him finish."

"Thank you, sir," Neville said. "My colleague in the KIBR has performed preliminary animal studies to confirm the virulence of the agent, and it turns out to be a very bad actor. Within seven to ten days of airborne exposure, the mammalian species tested— everything from mice to monkeys—experienced rapid enlargement of certain lymphoid organs."

"Layman's terms?" said General Harold "Harry" Beckwith, secretary of defense.

"Some lymphoid organs, such as the thymus and bone marrow, produce immune cells, while others, like the lymph nodes and spleen, filter the blood and lymphatic system, removing toxins and invading microorganisms. In the preliminary animal studies, the pulmonary lymph nodes and the spleen rapidly enlarged and either ruptured, causing massive hemorrhage in the case of the spleen, or impinged on and damaged surrounding structures, in the case of the lymph nodes in the chest. In all studies, the mortality rate was one hundred percent."

"And this is an airborne agent," said Admiral Bill Richards, secretary of the navy.

"Yes," replied Neville.

"Christ," said Joseph Steadman, director of homeland security.

"Mr. President," Kelly said, "this must be confirmed."

"I've already confirmed it," Neville replied. "I have the virus. I repeated the Korean experiments. I achieved the same results. That, Mr. Kelly, is the scientific method."

"That, Colonel Neville, is not how matters of national security are handled," Mike Kelly said. "You don't acquire a potential weapon of mass destruction from an enemy state, dick around with it in a high school biology lab, then go straight to the president without telling anyone else."

Neville stood stoically, his calm expression revealing nothing while internally he was scoffing at the CIA director's idiocy and ignorance. With perhaps a couple of exceptions—the general and the admiral—everyone else seated at the table were ignorant idiots, handed cabinet positions not because they earned them or were uniquely qualified, but because they had donated to the president's election campaign or had gained his favor in some other way.

"Okay," said National Security Advisor Rex Masterson, "let's say we confirm the Chinese are engaging in an act of biowarfare. What's our next move?"

"I'd like to fast-track a program to further classify the agent, determine its potential modes of human transmission, develop a vaccine to prevent infection, and devise treatment protocols for those who become infected," Neville said.

"What kind of time frame are we dealing with?" Masterson asked.

"Korean intelligence believes the attack will happen within six months, if not sooner."

"Is it realistic to think," Admiral Bill Richards said, "we can go from classifying an unknown bioagent to finding a vaccine that will kill it and widely disseminating that drug in six months? The pharmaceutical companies are struggling to come up with a vaccine for the current coronavirus."

"That's the consequence of being tied down by myriad FDA regulations. We have also been working on a vaccine, but because we've been playing by the rules, we are not even close to human testing. So yes, the six-month time frame is a daunting prospect, but if we devote the full resources of the US military, and bend or even bypass a few regulations, we can get it done."

Jonathan Neville walked around the table, handing each of the men a second file folder. This one had OPERATION GENE MIST printed across the top with CLASSIFIED stamped below. "Inside you will find maps and pages of data, demographics, statistics, et cetera, but let me summarize the major points."

Neville returned to the head of the table and tapped his laptop. A map of the state of Nevada filled the largest of the monitors hanging on the wall behind him. "This," the colonel aiming his laser pointer at a speck in the western part of the state, "is Fallon, Nevada—home to Naval Air Station Fallon and the TOPGUN training program. It is also the site of a biosafety level 4 USAMRIID laboratory, or a BSL 4 lab. Four is the top biosafety designation, meaning BSL Fallon, which I command," Neville directing his comments at Mike Kelly, "is designed to contain and study nature's most deadly and contagious pathogens, unlike your local high school biology lab. With BSL Fallon, we already have the infrastructure in place to develop and manufacture a vaccine and treatment. As we speak, the proteins coating the virus are being sequenced. When this is complete, we will proceed with the development and testing of potential vaccines."

General Beckwith said, "I suppose the testing phase is where the bending and breaking of regulations is going to occur."

"Yes." Neville tapped his laptop, pulling up a detailed map of western Nevada. "The town of Fallon is a well-circumscribed community of eighty-five hundred people, and by circumscribed, I mean the town proper is surrounded by pastures, crops, the desert, and mountains. The nearest population centers are Reno and Carson City, both sixty miles up the highway," Neville highlighting the cities with his laser pointer, "and more importantly, sixty miles upwind. It's important to note the prevailing winds coming down out of the Sierra Nevada are relentless. Hardly a day goes by that they haven't kicked up by the early afternoon, and downwind from Fallon is little more than sagebrush, abandoned mines, and deserted buildings." The colonel turned and faced the room. "Once we have a vaccine, we will vaccinate the local population, then expose them to the CoVid23 virus."

"Without their knowledge," Admiral Richards said.

"Yes," Neville replied. "We don't have the time—"

"C'mon," Mike Kelly said, lurching forward in his chair. "Do you hear what you're saying?"

"Unfortunately," Neville replied, "we find ourselves in the position of possibly sacrificing a few for the benefit of many. If we adhere to the FDA regulations for new vaccine development, including lengthy animal and human trials, and we get bogged down by ethics protocols, millions of Americans will die before we even complete the paperwork."

Rex Masterson said, "What is the average failure rate of all vaccines?"

"Six to eight percent," Neville replied.

Masterson tapped the screen of his phone, then looked up at Neville. "So somewhere between five and six hundred US citizens may develop this one-hundred-percent-fatal lymphoid disease."

"During the early stages of testing, we'll use progressively sophisticated animal models until we achieve a failure rate under two percent. Only then will we test it on humans."

"That still calculates to one hundred seventy deaths," Masterson said.

"Look," Neville replied, "I know this sounds quite unsavory—"

"Unsavory?" Kelly said. "How about illegal and immoral?" He turned toward the president. "Mr. President, please, this conversation is absurd and should be shut down right now. Let me verify the intelligence before we proceed with such a ridiculous plan."

Speaking slowly and deliberately, Jonathan Neville said, "With regard to the CoVid19 pandemic, it is my opinion that we have dodged a huge bullet. Ten million cases? Hundreds of thousands of deaths? We can recover from those numbers. A new pandemic with a mortality rate of eighty percent instead of two will cause many millions of deaths, blow up what's left of the health-care system and the economy, and result in the collapse of the Unites States. Therefore," Neville now speaking directly to the CIA director, "urgent drug development must get done, and somebody has to bear that burden."

"And if your CoVid23 plague doesn't materialize, society remains standing, and we're left with a bunch of dead people in a tiny town?" Kelly said.

"We blame the cluster of unusual deaths on an environmental toxin, or contaminated drinking water, or a virus unique to western Nevada."

"You implied that the prevailing winds will protect Reno and Carson City," said Joe Steadman, "but all it'll take is one vaccine nonresponder to drive sixty miles, make human contact, and the virus will spread beyond your containment zone."

"Or someone gets on a plane and flies to LA or San Francisco," added Harry Beckwith.

"To be effective, a bioweapon requires human-to-human transmission," Neville explained. "An infected person arrives in Reno or Carson City, coughs and sneezes and shakes a bunch of hands, and within weeks ninety percent of the population has contracted the same infection. Regarding the Wuhan bioweapon, it is an airborne virus, but we don't yet understand its mode of transmission. If it is not transmitted by human-to-human contact, if someone has to throw handfuls of it into the wind or drop it out of a plane, it will kill many people, but it will fail as a large-scale weapon. If indeed the virus is passed from human to human, this will prove to be the deadliest infectious disease ever faced by mankind, and we'll need to impose a draconian lockdown on the people of Fallon while we vaccinate the rest of the country."

- 3 -

Following the meeting in the Situation Room, the colonel and the president moved upstairs to the Oval Office. After removing their jackets—Neville smoothing and hanging his, while the president tossed his onto a nearby chair—they each sat on one of two opposing sofas. Neville noted how the man had declined physically since their days at Yale. He had a potbelly. His face and neck had thickened, while his once-dark hair had thinned and taken on a gray hue. His complexion was pale and thin as if he were secreting too much of the stress hormone cortisol. Twenty-five years had passed, and with that came the ravages of time, not to mention the chronic stress of running the country, Neville figured. Jonathan had done his best to avoid a similar fate. His hair had taken on a salt-and-pepper tint, but he kept it cropped short, and he'd forced himself to maintain a level of fitness commensurate with his college days. In the midst of a global crisis, health and fitness were paramount.

"I don't know if you're looking for approval from those guys," the president said, "but they're never going to green-light the use of American citizens as subjects for secret biowarfare experiments. Just saying it out loud sounds very Nazi-ish, if that's even a word."

"It definitely is, Mr. President, and here's another word, four actually: savior of the world. When a deadly virus is racing around the globe and it's the United States—your country, your administration, you specifically—that is responsible for not only the vaccine to stop it but also a treatment to cure it, you will be a hero. You will be the savior of the world. You will be a titan among historical figures."

The president leaned back in the sofa and rubbed his chin, the wheels turning, the words "savior" and "world" and "titan" undoubtedly swirling around and stoking the fires of his narcissism. He then sat forward. "And what if a hundred farmers mysteriously die and it's linked back to us?"

"There *will be* a cluster of suspicious deaths, which is why I presented my plan to those six men this morning. With their help, we can manipulate any investigation that may arise. We can control any narrative that gains credibility. We can assign blame to whatever environmental agent, toxin, or microorganism we see fit. Those six individuals are the most powerful men in your administration. They can see to it that not a single dead farmer is linked to this office."

"If they'll go along."

"That's going to be your job. You are the president of the United States. You will see to it that they go along."

"You're describing a conspiracy, Jonathan—a conspiracy that starts with me—and you're sounding a bit demanding. Maybe you should remember who you're talking to."

"Maybe you should remember how you got here, Silas."

"I know," the president said wearily. "Your father-in-law."

"And who introduced you to my father-in-law?"

"We both know how we rose to our current positions. Without Jack Prescott and his billionaire-boys-club advisory council, neither of us would be sitting in the Oval Office."

Indeed, Silas Dixon Bell, current president of the United States and former Yale roommate of Jonathan Neville, was right. Although both men hailed from dissimilar backgrounds, their paths had taken them straight through Jack Prescott.

During his first year at Johns Hopkins, Jonathan began to see himself not as someone who would simply exist in the world and have a traditional career, as his father—a telecom CEO—had done. Instead, he wanted to shape history, and not just a single event that might land him in a news archive or textbook. He wanted to shape events that would resonate with humankind for both the near and far future. While his classmates partied and squandered their free time, Jonathan spent his Friday and Saturday nights reading classic works like Sun Tzu's *The Art of War*, Adolf Hitler's *Mein Kampf*, and the collected works of Machiavelli. He devoured the historical texts and biographies of history's great leaders—Alexander, Jesus Christ,

Martin Luther, Julius Caesar and Marcus Aurelius, Gandhi and George Washington—and its great innovators and thinkers—Da Vinci and Galileo, Curie and Pasteur, Edison, Franklin, Jobs and Gates, Einstein and Feynman. And as Jonathan Neville read and studied and broadened his mind, he came to understand that many who changed history had done so from a position of power. But in what form? A life in politics was considered but quickly rejected. The two-party system didn't work. Nobody was getting anything done. Instead, Jonathan decided true power could only be achieved with money and lots of it, but he also knew capital by itself would not be enough to shape history.

Next, he considered where he should deploy his considerable intellect. He ultimately settled on biotechnology, not only because he had always favored the life sciences, but the prospect of redesigning and manipulating living systems held a seductive power of its own. Thus, after graduating with honors from Johns Hopkins, Jonathan entered the MD/PhD program at Yale, and while he focused on his medical and scientific education, he began to court a young economics major of the billionaire class—Miss Amy Prescott—whom he viewed as a potential mate. But, in order to win her hand, he would first have to go through her father Jack.

Jack Prescott was a self-made Texas oilman who grew up with "both fists flying," as he liked to put it. After he made his fortune in the West Texas oil fields, he diversified his holdings into a multi-national conglomerate that included commercial real estate projects focusing on large warehouse distribution. His timing was perfect, as his company became the leading developer of the massive infrastructure supporting the burgeoning e-commerce sector. At over six feet tall, and with the rugged appearance of someone who'd spent most of his life outdoors, his aura was that of a man who tolerated zero bullshit. The one soft spot in Jack Prescott's life was his youngest daughter Amy, and Jonathan Neville knew how he would play his hand.

A few months after he began seeing Amy, Jonathan had asked for her father's phone number. He then called the man. "Mr. Prescott," Neville had said boldly. "I would like to introduce myself, and I hope we can meet in person soon. I am Jonathan Neville, and I'm dating your daughter, Amy."

"Who the hell are you?" Jack Prescott had replied, and after a brief conversation, he flew his Gulf Stream G650 from Dallas to New Haven to meet Jonathan. As soon as Jack walked into Amy's living room, Jonathan stood up, looked him in the eye, and gave a firm handshake. By the end of the night, Jack Prescott was more than impressed with Jonathan Neville.

Jonathan's relationship with Jack became his top priority—fishing trips to Alaska, football games at Cowboy Stadium, and finally what Jonathan truly sought, a position on Jack's corporate advisory board. Since New World Corporation was a private entity controlled solely by Jack Prescott, when he gave the word, Jonathan was in. New World's board included a former president of the United States, a former prime minister of the United Kingdom, two former secretaries of state, several former members of the Joint Chiefs of Staff, and former directors of three intelligence agencies, as well as selected leaders of finance and industry. The annual meeting for this "billionaire boys club" took place at Jack's estate in Aspen and was legendary for inviting speakers from the cutting edge of science, technology, business, and politics. Even though there was much wining, dining, and entertaining, one piece of business received the highest priority. Politicians with presidential aspirations, or perhaps those who could be persuaded to run, were summoned to appear before the board. It was during the fall retreat that decisions were made as to whom the council would support and whom they must thwart and never allow to attain a position of real power.

At Jonathan's first council meeting, a discussion had ensued regarding a popular young governor from Ohio. The governor's message of free health care for everyone, free college for everyone, universal worker's rights, and dismissal of all student debt was starting to take hold, and serious talk about a run for the presidency had gained traction. This was not acceptable to the board, and a few months later the governor was forced to resign in disgrace when his dalliance with a transgender Washington, DC, escort made the front page of the *New York Times*.

With Jonathan's graduation from Yale nearing, it came time to decide what to do with his MD/PhD degree. One of his favorite quotes was by Wayne Gretzky, who said, "I skate to where the puck is going to be, not to where it has been." While at Yale, Jonathan had become familiar with the Human Genome Project and had a prescient feeling that this area of biotechnology was where the world-changing advancements in science and medicine would occur. That was where the puck was going, he told himself, and he was right.

For his post-doctoral work, Jonathan joined the laboratory of Nathan Rothberg, PhD, at the Broad Institute of MIT and Harvard. "The Broad" was founded to take the results of the Human Genome Project to the next level. Even though the human genome had been decoded, scientists needed to translate that knowledge into a clear understanding of the genetic basis of disease and then develop preventative, diagnostic, and treatment regimens for the most critical challenges in medicine. During his two years in Boston, Jonathan became Nathan Rothberg's star protégé, was the lead author on multiple groundbreaking scientific publications, and—along with his Broad Institute collaborators—pioneered advanced gene-editing techniques that were quickly adopted by the rest of the world. These techniques enabled scientists to easily and rapidly edit the genetics of any targeted cell in any living organism.

Dr. Nathan Rothberg, aside from being one of the great minds in the field of genomics, was also on the scientific advisory board for the Defense Advanced Research Projects Agency. DARPA is buried deep within the Department of Defense, and its mission is simple: to keep the United States ahead of the world in the development of new technologies that will protect and advance national security. Most DARPA projects are unclassified. However, a significant number are highly classified with funding lines so convoluted that many sensitive "black projects" escape the prying eyes of the United States Congress.

While in Rothberg's lab, Jonathan obtained a security clearance allowing him to work on a DARPA-funded classified project. He quickly realized the agency represented an opportunity unparalleled in academia or industry, and this led to Jonathan's second major insight regarding his career: DARPA was the epicenter of scientific power, and one day Jonathan Neville would run it.

Since the head of DARPA had to be an active duty military officer, Jonathan took the highly unusual step of joining the United

States Army as an MD/PhD. Although the army did have a few doctors with Ivy League backgrounds, nearly all of them entered the service as a means to pay for medical school, and after their four-year obligations were complete, they signed their discharge papers as fast as possible and joined lucrative private practices. Having someone with Jonathan's academic prestige made him an instant sensation in the army medical command.

In many ways, Silas Bell was Jonathan Neville's opposite. Neville enjoyed an upper-class childhood, growing up inside the Beltway in McClean, Virginia. Bell grew up outside of Columbia, South Carolina, the only son of a single mother who worked as a licensed practical nurse. Both boys were raised primarily by their mothers—Neville senior traveled often and was not very attentive when home—and Mrs. Neville constantly reminded her boys to never regard themselves as ordinary, like the people in line at the DMV or queuing up for general admission at a Nationals game. By contrast, Silas Bell's mother offered her son a roof, clothing, a K–12 education and little more. As a result, Silas knew from a young age that if he wanted to escape a life of low-wage poverty he would have to do it himself, and he did just that, graduating at the top of his high school class, then on to college with an Army ROTC scholarship. After four years of active duty as an infantry officer and two tours of duty in Afghanistan, which earned him a Bronze Star, he entered Yale School of Law. It was during his time in New Haven that he met Jonathan Neville.

With law degree in hand, Silas Bell's rapid rise to power was no less impressive than Jonathan's. Following a short-lived career as a corporate lawyer in Charlotte, North Carolina, Bell returned home to Columbia, South Carolina, to run for Congress in the second congressional district. Running as a right-wing populist war hero, Bell easily won his seat in a district that is 70 percent white and predominantly Republican. His firebrand message of conservative values and protectionist foreign policies resonated particularly well in this poor, rural area of the Deep South.

After serving two terms in the House of Representatives, Bell set his sights on the US Senate. But prior to announcing his run, Jonathan Neville had secured for Silas an audience with Jack

Prescott's advisory council. Well coached by Jonathan, Silas delivered the message the board wanted to hear: an ongoing commitment to conservative principles, free market protectionism, and a promise to secure the southern border against the hordes of illegal immigrants "invading our country." Bell received the full backing of Jack Prescott and his board, support that would propel Silas Dixon Bell into the Senate, and eventually the presidency. And thanks to Prescott's far-reaching influence, Bell was given choice assignments on the Senate Intelligence and Armed Services committees. As is the case in politics, one good turn deserves another, and Jonathan Neville directly benefitted from having an ally on the powerful Armed Services Committee.

After joining the army medical corps as a captain, Jonathan received early promotions on three occasions and was a full colonel within five years. Jonathan's rapid rise rankled many of his colleagues for whom a promotion to full colonel may never happen, even after twenty years of service, let alone after just five. But Jonathan's severest critics had to admit he was scientifically brilliant, and before long, with help from the Senate Armed Services Committee, Jonathan Neville landed what he wanted most: the directorship of DARPA and commander of USAMRIID's level 4 laboratory in Fallon, Nevada, the latter having left more than a few people scratching their heads.

"You know what?" Jonathan Neville said to Silas Bell. "Every man in that room will support, and ensure the success of, Operation Gene Mist, because every man in that room is under the thumb of Jack Prescott. Well, all but one—and we can handle him."

- 4 -

When CIA Director Mike Kelly arrived back at his Langley office, the first order of business was a dossier review. He called his secretary, had her call a secure number on a secure line and relay two names to the person who answered. Thirty minutes later, three dossiers were placed on his desk by a nondescript man in a gray suit.

"You were given two names," Kelly said. "There are three folders here."

"There's a third player who is an integral link between the first two," the man said.

Mike Kelly checked the file folders: Jonathan Neville, Silas Bell, Jack Prescott. He set the Neville and Bell files aside, opened the Prescott file, and started reading through the pages. "Can you summarize the key points?"

The gray-suited man sat down. "The first part of Prescott's story is fairly typical, West Texas oil money parlayed into a multinational conglomerate of companies—warehousing, mining, construction, telecom infrastructure, large public works projects here and abroad."

"One of the richest men in the world," Mike Kelly added.

"And one of the most powerful."

"Money *is* power," Kelly said, looking up.

"Yes, but Prescott's source of power goes beyond just money and the influence that comes with it. The advisory board of his parent company, New World Corporation, includes a former US president, a former UK prime minister, two former secretaries of state, several former members of the Joint Chiefs of Staff, and former directors of three intelligence agencies. The sphere of connections, influence, and access to data and intelligence by a civilian group such as this is unprecedented and almost limitless."

Kelly sat back in his chair. "And his connection to Silas Bell and Jonathan Neville?"

"Neville and Bell were roommates at Yale. Neville married Prescott's daughter while in New Haven, then introduced Bell to Jack Prescott when Bell was making the jump from the House of Representatives to the Senate, and after that, Bell's rise to the presidency was meteoric. As a member of the Senate Armed Services committee—also acquired with Prescott's influence—Bell helped Neville mount his own meteoric rise, first to the rank of colonel and then to the head of DARPA and commander of the USAMRIID lab in Nevada."

"So Neville marries the right girl, taps into his father-in-law's power and influence, advances his career, and lands his buddy in the White House. You've got one hand washing the other, which is how things get done inside the Beltway. Nothing new here."

"Yes," said Gray Suit, "but there's another dimension to Jack Prescott. This guy is the darling of the alt-right and New World Order conspiracy theorists. They believe Prescott and his advisory board, along with a vast network of others in similar positions of power, make up a shadow elite with a globalist agenda."

"Also nothing new," Kelly said. "There are theories that Tom Hanks and George Clooney are plotting to take over the country and confiscate all the guns."

"There's no question that the overwhelming majority of New World Order conspiracies are crackpot, like the rise of the Fourth Reich or that aliens and reptilians have assumed human forms and can only be detected by the Men in Black, but those are fringe elements. The serious students of conspiracy theory see Jack Prescott as someone who could actually pull it off."

"And having his son-in-law's Yale roommate in the White House is throwing fuel on that fire."

"Exactly. Think about the policies this president has enacted or proposed—build a wall, stop all Muslims from entering the country, severely restrict immigration as a whole, gut all the social reforms put in place by his predecessor, bolster the ruling elite, make false promises to the middle class, insult the lower class at every turn. Nothing but isolationist and protectionist policies."

"And how does that translate into a new world order?"

"It's a bit of a stretch, but one can almost view the Bell administration as the rise of the Fourth Reich. First, revive nationalism. Hitler blamed the Jews for all of Germany's problems. Bell has blamed all our problems on the immigrant class and nonwhite Americans. Second, Hitler touted the Aryans as the master race. Bell has made no attempt to distance himself from white nationalists. Third, Hitler built a massive military-industrial complex. We already have one. Fourth, use it. Hitler invaded Europe. All we need is a provocation to invade or nuke someone, then build it into a larger conquest—perhaps a false flag conspiracy."

"Like the theory that the United States government perpetrated 9/11 against itself," Mike Kelley said, "then used it as an excuse to invade Afghanistan and Iraq, increase surveillance against its own citizens, and restrict civil liberties. But how would Jack Prescott fit into something like this?"

"He and his shadow elite would dictate policy and strategy from behind the scenes and eliminate any nonaligned entities. The theorists claim he already has the plans drawn up, he just needed the right man in the White House, and now he has him."

"Sounds like you're a believer."

"I believe the false flag scenario could be used successfully to justify going to war. I don't think it could be used to restructure the world order unless other events, like a total collapse of the global economy or some other international catastrophe—"

"A deadly pandemic?" Mike Kelly suggested.

"Yes," said the man in the suit. "A viral pandemic causes a breakdown of the world's health-care systems, wreaks havoc on its economies and financial markets, forces countries to close their borders and stop trusting each other. What better time for a false flag implementation of a conspiracy theory. The US claims China is building a bioweapon and set it loose on the world. China counters that the US released the deadly virus inside China's borders. Then the blame game escalates into an international crisis."

"Or worse," Mike Kelly added.

After the dossier specialist left his office, Mike Kelly used the CIA's internal communications channel to send an encrypted message to one of his top section chiefs: "I want to know what Jack Prescott and his advisory board are up to these days. Top priority. Top secret."

- 5 -

Six months before the inaugural mission of the Night Fury
Churchill County, Nevada
The base of Table Mountain
Fifteen miles from downtown Fallon

Gary Kinghorn parked his sunbaked rattletrap of a pickup truck off the side of the dirt road, stepped out of the cab, looked up at the star-filled sky, and said, "Time to kill some 'yotes." Earlier in the day he'd been in the area scouting for coyote sign when he came across a dead cow up in the canyon. He knew that tonight the coyotes would come out to feed on the carcass, and if he quietly approached from downwind, he'd get two, maybe three clean shots before they scattered. At twenty-five bucks per pair of ears, the current bounty paid by the local ranchers, that translated into a much needed fifty or seventy-five dollars. Gary took his rifle off the gun rack, put on his 'yote-killing hat—a baseball cap with a trio of green LED lights clipped to the bill—and set out tromping through the sagebrush.

As he approached the mouth of the canyon, he turned on the LEDs. This provided just enough light for him to see where he was going and to spot the coyotes, but the coyote brain did not process the color green, and therefore they would not see him coming. They did, however, possess keen senses of smell and hearing, so Gary was happy to feel a light wind blowing down the canyon.

He passed an outcropping of rock he had noted earlier that afternoon, putting him less than a hundred yards from the dead cow, then continued up the canyon, one quiet step at a time. Now about fifty yards away, he smelled the stench of rotting flesh. He tied a bandana around the lower half of his face and carried on. About thirty yards out, he heard the rustling and yipping of a coyote feeding frenzy. At twenty yards the rustling stopped, and eight pair of glowing green eyes stared right at him. They heard him but couldn't see him. He slowly raised the rifle to his shoulder, aimed the crosshairs of the scope between the eyes of one of the coyotes, and then he coughed. The animals scattered, and he coughed again, a metallic taste in his mouth. He switched the green LEDs to white, pulled the bandana off his face, and spit into the dirt. Blood. And then a fit of violent coughing erupted, blood spraying onto his coat, covering his hands. He tried to catch his breath but choked on the thick fluid caught in the back of his throat. More coughing and choking, the blood pouring out now. He strapped the rifle over his shoulder and ran down the hill—coughing, choking, spitting up blood—and just as he passed the rocky outcrop, Gary Kinghorn collapsed onto the desert floor.

Ron Ellison maintained his horse at a slow but steady pace. He was riding along the base of Table Mountain in the midday sun, searching for a missing cow, when he spotted a dark-colored heap lying in the sagebrush about twenty yards ahead. It looked like a balled-up blanket or tarp, but he was several miles from the road. It was generally odd to find trash or other discarded junk way up here. He slowed the animal as he approached, then pulled up on the reins when he realized the heap was a man. Ellison climbed off the horse, heart thumping as he circled around to where he could see the man's face. Dried blood was caked around his mouth, all over his hands, and pooled in the dirt near his head. Ellison got down on one knee to check for a pulse. The skin was cold and gray, the guy clearly dead, so no need to go pushing around in his neck or handling his bloody hands. Ellison took off his cowboy hat to get a close look at the man's face, then he drew back. He knew the guy. Gary Kinghorn. A Paiute Indian from the Paiute-Shoshone reservation just outside of Fallon. Ron had been paying Gary a twenty-five-dollar bounty for every pair of coyote ears Gary brought to him. They'd see each other every two or three weeks, knew each other's wives and kids.

"Shit, man," Ron Ellison said to the deceased Gary Kinghorn. "What happened to you?"

Kinghorn's rifle lay in the dirt a few feet away from his body. Ellison wondered if Gary had tripped coming down the hill, and maybe the gun went off and shot him in the gut. But that was a lot of blood for a gut shot, and there was no exit wound in the back. The rifle was high powered. The slug would have gone right through him. Whatever happened, Ron knew better than to disturb the body. He slipped the phone out of his coat pocket and dialed the Churchill County Sheriff's Office.

"Hello, Jenna," Ron said to the gal that answered. "Is Lou in? I got something urgent to talk to him about."

The secretary put Ellison through.

"Hey, Ron," the Sheriff said. "You okay? Jenna said it was urgent."

"Yeah, I'm fine, but I just found a dead body out here at the base of Table Mountain. It's Gary Kinghorn, one of the Paiutes from the reservation."

"You sure he's dead?" Lou Smith asked. "I don't need to send an ambulance out there?"

"Hold on," Ellison said in a raised voice. "I got two F-18s coming up the valley about three hundred feet off the deck."

Ellison shoved his phone in his pocket and clamped his hands over his ears as the TOPGUN F-18s passed directly over him, the twin jet engines roaring, the afterburners spewing cones of flame, the ground shaking and the horse getting skittish. Ron Ellison had grown up in this valley and had experienced these low-altitude flyovers countless times, and still he was blown away every time. He retrieved his phone from his pocket. "You there, Lou?"

"Yeah. Sounded like they were gonna take your head off."

"They must have just gone wheels up and had their afterburners on. Never gets old."

"No, it doesn't," Lou Smith said, "but as I was saying, you sure Kinghorn is dead? You don't need an ambulance?"

"Cold and gray. Looks like he was hunting coyotes last night and fell coming down the hill. His rifle is nearby. I'm thinking it went off and shot him in the gut or the chest."

"Okay," Smith said. "Tell me where you are, and I'll head straight out there."

Gary Kinghorn's body had been delivered to the Churchill County Coroner's Office, which resided in the basement of the Fallon-Churchill Community Hospital, and he now lay on a stainless steel table in the autopsy room. Most hospitals have their own pathology department, and all but the most sparsely populated counties in the US have independent coroners or medical examiners. Churchill County was, by any measure, sparsely populated, so the hospital pathologist and county coroner were one and the same—Dr. Susan Preston.

Preston, a former navy lieutenant, made a Y-shaped incision that started at Gary Kinghorn's shoulders, met at the base of the sternum, then continued down the midline of his abdomen to the suprapubic region. The midline abdominal fascia was divided, the ribs snipped, and the anterior rib cage removed, thus exposing the entirety of Kinghorn's thoracic and abdominal organs.

The first finding of note was massive enlargement of the spleen, or splenomegaly. The organ had its usual reddish-brown coloration, but a normal spleen would fit in the palm of Preston's hand. This one was the size of a football. Moreover, it was pulpy and appeared on the verge of rupturing.

The second finding of note was even more remarkable. The hila of both lungs—the area where the bronchi and pulmonary vessels entered and exited—were encased in baseball-size masses that she presumed were lymph nodes. Normal lymph nodes were generally less than a centimeter in length, the size of a kidney bean. With lymphomas and some benign diseases, lymph nodes often grew to two or even three centimeters, perhaps the size of a golf ball, but these were massive, and red and angry looking. In her report she would refer to them as inflamed. But whether angry or inflamed, merely enlarged or massive, these were not the findings associated with malignancy, allergies, granulomatous diseases, infection, or chronic illness. This was something she had never seen personally or in the medical literature.

Once Gary Kinghorn's organs were dissected free of their attachments and removed from their respective cavities, Susan Preston sat down at a back table with the heart and lungs, and scissors and forceps. The thoracic organs had been excised en bloc, thus maintaining the anatomy as seen in situ, or within the body. Based on the amount of blood reported at the scene, and the earlier findings of clotted blood in the trachea but not in the esophagus, Susan Preston was sure the answer to Gary Kinghorn's death resided in the block of organs lying before her.

She began her dissection by trying to separate the abnormal lymph nodes from the lungs and the heart, but the rampant inflammation had caused the nodes to adhere to one another and had bound the surfaces of the lung and the pericardium of the heart into a matted mess of distorted nodal, cardiac, and pulmonary tissue. Taking great care not to destroy the integrity of the organs, she eventually made her way to the hilum of each lung.

The human lung serves as an interface with the outside world. Air is inhaled, oxygen is extracted, carbon dioxide is exhaled. But along with the air comes contaminants—dust, allergens, toxins, and microorganisms. The pulmonary lymphatics do a good job of collecting these contaminants, but something needs to be done with them once they're sequestered. Enter the lymph nodes, the body's oil filters. These bean-size structures are packed with immune cells ready to attack, kill, and dispose of foreign invaders, and the chest is full of them. On occasion, however, the nodes will overreact. The immune cells within get overstimulated and multiply at an exponential rate, causing the tiny structures to enlarge, and that's what Susan Preston believed she had found. But enlarged lymph nodes did not explain Gary Kinghorn's death. Somewhere within reach of her scissors and forceps was a connection—a fistula—between the trachea, or a bronchus, and a large cardiac or pulmonary vessel, a connection that had allowed blood to travel up the trachea, out the mouth, and onto the desert floor where Gary Kinghorn bled to death.

A few snips later she found it. Where the main trunk of the pulmonary artery passed over the left mainstem bronchus, an enlarged, inflamed node had eroded into both structures, creating a dime-size communication between a large vascular structure carrying a massive amount of pressurized blood and a hollow tube that provided a direct conduit out of the body. Cause of death: exsanguination secondary to a bronchopulmonary artery fistula.

Dr. Preston performed an en bloc excision of the fistulized bronchus and artery and placed it in a jar of formalin. She collected several lymph nodes of varying sizes and put these in additional jars of formalin. Then she cut wedges of tissue from other nodes that would serve as fresh, unpreserved specimens. All these tissues would be subjected to microscopic and histologic study. She then turned her attention to the remainder of Gary Kinghorn's organs, specifically the enlarged spleen.

Once she had completed her postmortem exam, Preston returned to her desk and called Colonel Jonathan Neville on a secure line.

"Neville," he said, answering on the second ring.

"This is Preston. I just finished the autopsy on patient zero. I found splenomegaly, massive enlargement and inflammation of the pulmonary and mediastinal lymph nodes, and a bronchopulmonary artery fistula that proved to be the terminal event."

"Did you find any viral particles in the tissue samples?" Neville asked.

"Histology and microbiology are pending."

"If the subject had made it to a hospital and was rushed into surgery, would there have been any chance for survival?"

"No," Preston said. "There's too much inflammation of the tissues and distortion of the anatomy. Surgical access to the fistula would be difficult, and repair would be impossible. If what I've seen here today represents the norm, anyone infected with this virus will exsanguinate and die with or without surgical intervention."

- 6 -

In the weeks and months following Gary Kinghorn's demise, nineteen more people coughed themselves to death. About a third were old. About a third were young. The remaining third, somewhere in between. Some were found dead, some died in front of family or friends, two made it to the hospital. One of them, a nine-year-old girl, died on the operating room table. The other, a thirty-two-year-old man, exsanguinated in the med-evac chopper before he could be transferred to a larger hospital. Also of note were three patients who died with ruptured spleens. The autopsies of the splenic-rupture patients demonstrated inflammation of the lymph nodes in the chest in addition to splenomegaly. There was no question in Sheriff Lou Smith's mind that the deaths of all twenty-three people were related.

"This is a goddam epidemic," he yelled into the phone. "It has to be related to the coronavirus." He was speaking to Dr. Josh Brannigan at the Nevada State Board of Health.

"Look," Brannigan said, "I understand your alarm. The numbers are beyond coincidence, and the unusual mode of death is disturbing, but the pathophysiology of the disease process is completely different from what we're seeing with the coronavirus. Besides, every resident of Fallon has been tested and retested. You are all negative. Churchill County is the only county remaining in the United States that hasn't had a case of CoVid19. The army has been drawing your blood, looking for a novel antibody or some other explanation as to why a whole town is immune while the rest of the country keeps reporting hundreds of thousands of cases, and the county coroner has not found evidence of viral infection in any of her autopsies."

"I don't trust the army or the coroner. She's navy, you know," Smith said. "I think the army lab and the brass at the navy base know something we don't. And Preston? She's stonewalling us."

"I've spoken with Dr. Preston. As soon as she receives the pathology reports from the Armed Forces Institute of Pathology, we'll send an investigator to review those results with her."

"In the meantime, we could rack up another five or six deaths."

"The study of disease clusters is slow and tedious work, and often there are no definitive results. The department has reviewed all the pertinent documentation—including patient histories, Dr. Pennington's operative reports, and Dr. Preston's autopsy reports—but until we have the microbiology, cytology, toxicology, and histology results, there is nothing more we can do. We need to have some idea of what we're looking for before we just show up and start looking. I'm sure you understand."

"Right," Smith said.

"Okay then," Brannigan replied. "Please keep the department informed of all new cases, and pass along any other information you deem important."

- 7 -

**Five weeks before the inaugural flight of the Night Fury
Biosafety Lab Fallon, Nevada
Sublevel 4, Negative-Pressure Room 1
10:46 p.m.**

Colonel Jonathan Neville entered the anteroom of NP 1 and began
the laborious undertaking of donning a positive-pressure suit. Having
already changed into scrubs, he selected a suit from the rack and
closely inspected the garment, looking for rips, tears, punctures, or
failed seams in the body of the suit, the outer gloves, the integrated
boots, and the head cover. With the visual inspection completed,
Neville connected an air hose to the breathing line, zippered the suit
closed, inflated it, and examined it for leaks. None were detected,
so he leaned the inflated garment against the wall and turned his
attention to himself. He pulled his white athletic socks over the
cuffs of his scrub pants and duct-taped the gap between the socks
and the pants, then slipped into a pair of nitrile gloves and taped
the gap between the gloves and the cuffs of the long-sleeved scrub
shirt. The inflated suit remained erect against the wall, indicating air
had not leaked out, so Neville deflated it and stepped into it. After
slipping into the outer gloves and taping the cuffs to the sleeves of
the suit, he added a Kevlar glove to his right hand.

   With the suit zippered and fully sealed, Neville again connected
an air hose to the breathing-air line that entered on his right at waist
level. He filled the suit with oxygen, disconnected, passed through
the air-locked doors of the chemical shower, then into the lab. Once

inside, he reconnected to one of the many air hoses hanging from the ceiling and gave his suit a moment to fully inflate.

Captain Mark Wallace stood with his back to Neville, working with cultures of the CoVid23 virus under a ventilation hood. Neville had not put on a radio-frequency headset, and the captain's head was near the strong fans of the hood. He did not hear Neville enter.

The colonel went over to the supply shelves near the entry door and carefully removed a pair of two-liter glass bottles. One contained an aqueous solution of sulfuric acid, the other an aqueous solution of potassium cyanide. Neville came over behind Wallace—the captain still unaware of the colonel's presence due to the bulkiness of the positive-pressure suit and the noise from the strong, negative-pressure fans.

Neville smashed the bottles at Wallace's feet, then grabbed a shard of glass off the floor using his triple-gloved right hand. The captain turned, wide eyed and confused. Neville used the piece of glass to gash open the plastic face shield of Wallace's suit. Mark Wallace was stunned, slow to react, and then it was too late. The potassium cyanide had reacted with the sulfuric acid to form a cloud of cyanide gas around him. He gasped for air. For good measure, Neville reached down and disconnected the captain's breathing-air line. Wallace reached for Neville, but the effort was feeble. Neville took a step back as the captain's gasps turned to spasms, and seconds later, Captain Mark Wallace collapsed on the floor.

Neville flipped the captain's body into the prone position so he didn't have to look at the dead man's purple lips and bulging eyes. He then dragged Wallace into the chemical shower chamber where he doused both his and Wallace's pressure suits with Lysol disinfectant. Leaving the captain face down on the shower floor, Neville returned to the ante room, changed back into his desert-camo army combat uniform, and picked up the phone receiver hanging next to the exit door. "We have a code red, sublevel four, negative-pressure room one," he quietly said into the phone. "Handle the body per the Ebola protocol. I'll take care of the incident report. I don't want anyone else to know about this."

Neville returned the phone to its cradle, left the main laboratory building, and headed for the vaccine-manufacturing facility.

- 8 -

A five-minute walk up a gently sloped gravel road took Jonathan Neville from the main laboratory to the vaccine production plant. Built within the last year specifically for this mission, the plant—along with its sister facility farther up the canyon—was the size and shape of a Home Depot. Other than the glassed-in entrance at the far eastern corner, the facade consisted entirely of a series of roll-up metal doors, cargo bays, and loading docks illuminated by flood lights lining the top of the structure.

Neville passed through the empty front offices and entered the dimly lit control room, which even at this late hour was fully staffed with technicians and scientists in long white coats, tending to digital displays and CCTV monitors.

"Colonel on deck," shouted one of the army scientists.

The staff members who were military snapped to attention and saluted Neville. The private contractors did not snap to attention, nor did they salute, but they did stand tall and greet him with slight nods of the head.

"At ease," Neville commanded, and as the men and women returned to their duties, he called out to the operations manager. "Lieutenant Rayburn, anything to report?"

"Yessir," replied an African American man wearing a white coat over green surgical scrubs. "We are on pace to complete twelve million new doses of vaccine this week, as per your directive, sir."

"Very good, Lieutenant."

The results of the Fallon vaccination trial had exceeded all expectations. Never before had such an elegant experimental design been implemented—an entire town vaccinated, then exposed to a deadly pathogen, and their blood collected at regular intervals to quantify antibody titers and monitor the immune response, all under the guise of protecting the public health. To date, the aerosolized vaccine had been 99.7 percent effective—the highest rate ever achieved by a vaccine, or by any medical intervention, for that matter—and this was more than sufficient to proceed with mass production and round-the-clock operations. Unfortunately, a meager twenty-three deaths among a population of eight thousand would be enough to draw unwanted attention, but as he had told the president, once CoVid23 was spreading across the globe, and all three hundred million Americans had been vaccinated, these twenty-three deaths would be quickly forgotten.

Neville walked over to the plate glass windows that loomed above the production floor. Sprawling out below him was the most sophisticated and efficient vaccine-manufacturing system ever devised. Row upon row of sixteen-ton, gleaming steel, stirred tank bioreactors filled the area. A vast latticework of tubing and pipes carried nutrient broth and oxygen to the reactors and carried away concentrated viral particles for purification and drying. A system of fans, vents, and ducts maintained an airflow nearly free of contaminants. The vaccine, of course, was the real star of the show, born of techniques that would revolutionize the development and administration of all future vaccines, thus the tragedy of what just occurred in Negative-Pressure Room 1, Sublevel 4, Biosafety Lab Fallon.

Captain Mark Wallace was largely responsible for the research and development of the vaccine that would protect the United States and its allies from the worst bioweapon attack—the worst pandemic—mankind would ever experience, and it all started with llamas. Llamas are mammals, and they make antibodies to fight off invading microbes just as humans do, but their antibodies are much smaller than those in the human. Therefore, the DNA sequences coding for those antibodies are much shorter—small enough to fit in a virus. Mark Wallace knew this and decided to exploit the interesting variation between man and animal. First, he exposed a group of llamas to an attenuated version of the Wuhan bioweapon. He then isolated the antibodies formed in response to the infection, bioengineered a replica of the gene responsible for the llama antibodies, and inserted that gene into the DNA of a harmless mammalian respiratory adenovirus. The adenovirus was then sprayed into the noses of mice. Two weeks later the mice were exposed to the full-strength version of the Wuhan Supervirus and, as predicted, they were immune. The mechanism of action? The adenovirus had inserted its DNA, including the sequence for the llama antibodies, into the DNA of the respiratory tract cells of the mice. The mouse respiratory cells detected the presence of the supervirus, produced the designer antibodies, and killed the invader before it had a chance to enter the lungs.

The real brilliance of Mark Wallace's vaccine was the delivery system: an adenovirus "gene mist" that could be sprayed into the air ducts of schools, shopping malls, restaurants and office buildings, or dropped from military jets or drones, all of which had been performed in Fallon, although Fallon's shopping mall was a Walmart. And if that wasn't enough to spread the vaccine throughout the population, adenoviruses are unusually stable to chemical or physical agents and adverse environmental conditions, allowing for prolonged survival on inorganic surfaces such as door handles and knobs, books and grocery bags, tables and countertops. If you wanted to give an entire town a cold, this would be the way to do it, except in this case the townspeople were exposed to a harmless adenovirus carrying a life-saving gene. And two weeks later, that life-saving designer gene was tested when the town was exposed to the deadly Wuhan Supervirus.

Although Mark's vaccine was a landmark success, for him the twenty-three deaths were unacceptable, particularly the nine-year-old girl. The people of Fallon had not signed up to be subjects in a medical experiment, no informed consent had been granted, and this weighed heavily on him. His crisis of consciousness ultimately got the best of him. He went AWOL from the lab and flew to Washington, DC, for a clandestine meeting with an NSA agent, which resulted in the events of twenty minutes ago in Sublevel 4.

Neville was profoundly disappointed that such a brilliant mind had to be silenced, but military doctrine dictated that the mission take precedence over any of its subordinate parts. If Mark Wallace had only stayed true to that doctrine, he would have been revered as the man who saved the world from total annihilation. He would've had a Nobel medal placed around his neck. He would have been a hero. Instead, his unceremonious death will be blamed on the accidental exposure to the deadly Ebola virus. His cremation will be quickly undertaken as a matter of public safety and military policy. His family will be presented with an urn full of ashes, a medal or two, and the gratitude of the United States Army, the president of the United States, and the American people. If he had just put the mission above all else.

- 9 -

Six days before the inaugural flight of the Night Fury
1624 S. Kedde Street
Fallon, Nevada
1:37 a.m.

Dr. David Aaronson—formerly known as Dr. David McBride, fugitive from multiple law enforcement agencies in the Northeast United States, wanted for the murders of two men and the theft of three kidneys, currently occupying a prominent spot on the FBI's most wanted list, motherless, fatherless, no wife, no children, only a false identity and a surgical practice in Fallon, Nevada, to keep him sane—Dr. David Aaronson, partner of Dr. Thomas Barner Pennington, awoke to the shrill ring of the telephone. He quickly silenced the phone, hoping Cassandra had not been awakened, but when he looked over to see if she had been, he was reminded that she wasn't there, and never would be. He picked up the phone and said hello.

"I need you in the OR," Pennington said. "Massive hemoptysis."
David threw on a pair of scrubs and rushed out the door.
As he drove to the hospital—less than ten minutes—he thought about the differential diagnosis of hemoptysis, which literally translated to coughing up blood. Most of the time it was caused by bronchitis, bronchiectasis, tuberculosis, or lung abscess. Necrotizing pneumonia was also on the list, as was bronchogenic carcinoma—lung cancer originating in a bronchus. And severe congestive heart

failure could cause high pressures in the pulmonary circulation and bleeding into the lung tissue.

Considering the dry climate and sparse population, he doubted TB was prevalent in western Nevada. He did recall from his med-school microbiology course that the Hantavirus was endemic to the Desert Southwest. The virus, carried by rodents, was shed in their urine, feces, and saliva. When inhaled, such as after sweeping up dried droppings and creating dust born particles, the virus resulted in a sometimes-fatal pulmonary infection, but he couldn't recall if these patients coughed up blood, and he didn't know if western Nevada was considered part of the Southwest.

He also didn't know Pennington's definition of massive hemoptysis. The textbooks would tell you that coughing up more than one hundred milliliters of blood—five of those cups from a children's Tylenol bottle—over the course of a twenty-four-hour period qualified as massive. On the other hand, there were cases where the bleeding was so profuse, patients drowned in their own blood. With such a wide spectrum of possibilities, there was no telling what might be waiting on the third floor of Fallon-Churchill Community Hospital.

10

David went straight to the locker room and changed into clean scrubs, a hat, and shoe covers and now stood outside OR 4, peering through the window as he tied a mask over his face. The patient—a thin white male, probably early twenties—lay supine on the operating table. An endotracheal tube protruded from his mouth. The respiratory tech bagged him while the anesthesiologist hung two units of blood from an IV pole. Gina—a tall, dark Native American woman who served as the senior scrub nurse—was cutting off the young man's clothes with shears. A second nurse was slipping a catheter into his penis while a third was starting another IV.

The patient's vital signs were dismal. Systolic blood pressure 79. Heart rate 160. Oxygen saturation in the low 80s. The EKG monitor was pinging, the O2 sat monitor was chirping, and everyone in the room was painfully aware this kid could arrest at any moment.

David stepped into the room as a tech wheeled a bronchoscopy cart to the head of the bed. Pennington slipped into sterile gloves and took a flexible bronchoscope from the cart. David examined the chest X-ray displayed on a thirty-two-inch computer monitor. "Jimmy Miller, 22yo male," read the identifier on the screen. The film was remarkable for massive bilateral hilar lymphadenopathy. The lymph nodes in the hilum of each lung had enlarged greatly, obliterating what would normally be the sharp borders between the heart and lungs. This was consistent with lymphoma and sarcoidosis, but neither of these disease processes typically presented with hemoptysis. David went over to the table and positioned himself next to Pennington.

"We got some serious bleeding here," Thomas Pennington said. "I need to get him sucked out or he's gonna die on us. We may have to go with a rigid bronchoscope if we can't adequately clean him out with the flexible. Ever used a rigid scope?"

"A handful of times on bleeding TB patients."

"So you're no stranger to blood-filled airways."

"I have a little experience."

"Well, you're gonna get a lot more if you're around here for very long."

That was an odd statement, David thought. Only large academic institutions and level-one trauma centers typically dealt with significant volumes of massive hemoptysis. He would not expect a place like Fallon, Nevada, with a population of eight thousand, to be a hotbed of hemorrhagic pulmonary disease.

Evan Mitchell, the anesthesiologist, hand-ventilated the patient until he got the oxygen saturation into the low nineties, then gave Pennington the go-ahead. Pennington inserted the bronchoscope through the endotracheal tube and advanced it into the trachea, suctioning blood as he went. The oxygen saturation immediately dropped back into the eighties, the scope taking up space within the tube, thus diminishing air flow.

"He's not liking this," Evan said.

"I know," replied Pennington, "but I need to see which side the bleeding is coming from so we can get a double-lumen tube in him."

"Sat's 81."

Pennington ignored the anesthesiologist and advanced the scope. Both David and Pennington watched the television monitor mounted on the bronchoscopy cart. Nothing but red. Then the field of vision cleared for just a moment, and the division of the trachea came into view. The right mainstem bronchus was clear, the left pouring blood. Pennington quickly removed the scope and told one of the nurses to get him a double-lumen tube. Evan Mitchell vigorously bagged the patient, trying to raise the O2 sat.

A double-lumen endotracheal tube was what the name implied— one tube, two lumens, the end terminating in an angled segment that can be advanced into one lung or the other. In this case, Pennington advanced the tube into the left bronchus, then inflated the balloon at the end, which isolated the left lung and blocked further blood flow into the trachea. He then inflated a second cuff higher up, isolating the right lung, allowing the anesthesiologist to ventilate the non-bleeding side. As the oxygen saturation improved, the blood pressure stabilized, the heart rate slowed, and the alarms stopped pinging and chirping.

"Let's position him for a left thoracotomy," Pennington said.

Gina went out to the sink to scrub her hands. Maria and Lori, the circulating nurses, started retrieving instrument trays, suture packs, and other equipment.

The anesthesiologist stabilized the endotracheal tube as David and Pennington turned the patient onto his right side. David added a slight bend to both legs and placed pillows between the knees and under the ankles. Pennington padded the arms, straps were placed to secure the patient to the table, and Gina started painting the left side of the chest—from sternum to spine, armpit to pelvis—with iodine solution.

Pennington said he needed to step out for a moment and asked David if he could help drape and then get started. "Treat this like an ER thoracotomy," he said. "Make a big incision and move fast. This isn't plastic surgery." And he left the room.

David quickly scrubbed, gowned and gloved, then draped the patient with Gina. After Evan Mitchell gave the go-ahead, Gina handed David a scalpel. He made a curvilinear skin incision starting at the left border of the sternum and extending around past the tip of the scapula. He then exchanged the scalpel for an electrocautery device and used it to cauterize the major skin bleeders and divide the muscles overlying the fourth intercostal space. David glanced at the window over the scrub sink, hoping to see Pennington out there washing his hands. He wasn't.

"Where is he?" David asked Gina, as if she knew.

Actually, she did know. She turned her thumb into the neck of a bottle and pretended to drink from it, tipping it to her mouth.

"Really?" David said. "Right before a case?"

"Particularly before a case. Steadies his nerves and helps him concentrate."

"And you guys are all right with this?"

"Before you came along, he was the only surgeon in town. There isn't exactly a long line of qualified applicants clamoring for the position. Besides, he does a good job."

David buzzed through the muscles of the fourth intercostal space and entered the pleural cavity, and as he placed the rib spreader and cranked it open, Pennington came through the OR door, wet hands raised in front of him. While Gina helped him gown and glove, David used some laparotomy sponges to push the lung down toward the diaphragm and out of the way, but the lung was not as mobile as it should have been. The hilum was encased in the lymph nodes David had seen on the X-ray, and they were bigger and more inflamed than anything he had ever seen.

As Pennington approached the table, David draped a moist lap sponge over the apex of the lung and again tried to retract it downward—then something tore. The operative field quickly filled with dark, deoxygenated blood. The pulmonary artery had torn.

"Suckers to each of us!" Pennington called out.

Gina handed each surgeon a suction catheter, but the blood was rising too fast.

"Lap sponges. Quickly. And keep 'em coming."

Both surgeons shoved wads of laparotomy sponges into the pool of blood, trying to pack off the operative field, but the effort was futile, and despite more packing and more suctioning the bleeding wouldn't stop.

All the monitors sounded at once.

"He's coding," Evan Mitchell said.

The cardiac monitor showed ventricular fibrillation.

The blood pressure was undetectable.

Pennington stopped what he was doing and just stood there, nodding his head and staring blankly into the chest cavity.

"Shouldn't we be trying to resuscitate him," David said, "cross-clamp the aorta, extend the incision across the sternum, start internal cardiac massage?"

"No. There's nothing more we can do." Pennington stripped off his gown and gloves, threw them toward the trash bag, and stepped away from the table. As he reached for the OR door, he turned. "David, if you'll close, I'll go talk to the family."

11

After Jimmy Miller had been tagged, bagged, and transported to the hospital morgue, David grabbed a Diet Coke and a bag of peanut M&Ms from the vending machines near the cafeteria and headed for the surgeon's lounge.

Even though Fallon-Churchill Community Hospital was small, and the surgical service consisted of two surgeons, the lounge was of reasonable size. A couple of old leather recliners occupied the corners at one end of the room. A desk with an out-of-date computer was tucked into the opposite end. A round table with four chairs filled the center, and a flat-screen television was mounted on the wall—the TV always turned on and always tuned to CNN. David put the Diet Coke and M&Ms on the table, went to the locker room to change into clean scrubs and wash up, then returned to the lounge. He sat down at the table, his shoulders slumped, his head falling forward. He had been in Fallon for only three weeks and had lost his first patient.

David heard the click of the doorknob and quickly sat up straight. Pennington entered, passed through to the locker room, then reentered the lounge. After tossing his disposable surgeon's cap and mask into the trash, he grabbed two paper cups from the coffee machine, took a silver flask from the pocket of his white coat, and filled each cup halfway.

Dr. Thomas Pennington was about five inches shorter than David, which would put him at five feet six, but what he lacked in height he made up for in girth. He wasn't exactly obese, but he did need to wear extra-large scrub tops, and he had to undo the buttons on his white coat before sitting down. Despite his advanced age—late sixties was David's guess—Pennington still had a full head of silvery gray hair, the grandfatherly hue patients like to see on their surgeons.

"Fancy some Maker's Mark? Dull that edge a little?" Pennington sliding one of the cups across the table.

"Uh, okay," David replied. "You sure this is a good idea, seeing how we are the only surgeons serving Churchill County?"

"We're just sippin' tonight, but if you ever plan to tie one on, do it when I'm on call."

"Duly noted," David said. The bourbon had a soft bite as it rolled over his tongue but turned warm and silky as it slid down his esophagus. "How did it go with the family?"

"Not well." Pennington took a sip from his cup. "One minute this strapping kid is tossing around sixty-pound bales of hay, the next minute he's bleeding to death. Doesn't make sense to the family, or to me for that matter, but don't beat yourself up. The kid didn't have much of a chance going in."

"What were we dealing with in there? I'm guessing broncho-pulmonary artery fistula, but what were those huge masses in the hilum of the lung? They were the size of baseballs."

"Lymph nodes."

"That's what I thought when I looked at the X-ray and opened the chest, but I've never seen nodes that big."

"Neither had I until a few months ago." Pennington finished the whisky and refilled his cup. "Back in August we got a patient in the ER with the same presentation. Massive hemoptysis. Unstable. Bleeding to death. I wanted to transfer him to Reno where they have angiography capabilities and could embolize whatever's bleeding."

"That's the standard of care," David added. "It's well documented that emergency surgery in these types of cases has a very poor outcome."

"That was my logic, but before the chopper even got off the ground, the patient was dead. They wheeled him straight from the landing pad to the morgue. Then, two weeks later we get another case. Same presentation, too unstable to survive the flight to Reno, so I rush her to the operating room." Pennington stared into his cup as he swirled the whisky, a painful memory shrouding his face. "I was thinking …" He paused again, the words caught in his throat. "I was thinking if I could get her to the OR, open her chest and clamp off her hilum, maybe I could find the bleeding vessel and ligate it."

"Same outcome, I'm guessing."

"She was nine goddamned years old. Nine-year-old kids don't grow massive lymph nodes in their chest and die from hemoptysis. Hell, twenty-two-year-olds don't either. One case like this is an outlier. Two is an epidemic. And now I've seen three."

"Is this a variant of the CoVid19 respiratory syndrome?"

"No. The coroner tested both patients for the virus postmortem. Both were negative."

"What have the pathology reports shown?"

"They've been inconclusive. Nobody has seen anything like this. The nodes are packed with granulomas."

"Like sarcoidosis," David added.

"Yes, but sarcoid is a benign, noninvasive disease. The nodes we're seeing are much more aggressive, adhering to and invading surrounding tissues and organs."

"Like a malignancy."

"Exactly, but there are no malignant cells in the specimens. It's more of a benign granulomatous disease behaving like a cancer."

"What about tuberculosis? It's a granulomatous disease, and it's extremely destructive."

"You know how indolent TB is. It takes years for the granulomas to result in widespread tissue destruction."

"Have you reported this to the state?" David asked.

"I've spoken with Susan Preston, the hospital pathologist slash Churchill County coroner. She has seen seventeen hemoptysis cases that died outside the hospital and went directly to her office. So counting tonight's case, that's twenty over a six-month period. She contacted the state board of health, as did the sheriff."

"What was their response?"

"The state doesn't know what it is, but they've determined it's not CoVid19. When the microbiology and toxicology studies are done, they'll take a look, if they can spare someone."

"That doesn't make sense. Sarcoid is rare to begin with, so twenty cases of a sarcoid-like disease with malignant tendencies occurring in a town of eight thousand people? That screams environmental etiology. There's something in the air, or the water. This is a public health crisis until proven otherwise. What about the CDC?"

"Like the state, they're up to their asses with the pandemic. They just don't have the manpower."

David leaned back and sipped his whisky. "So we're on our own," he said.

"Yes," Pennington replied.

- 12 -

As David passed through the ER waiting room on the way to his car, the admissions clerk called out to him. "Dr. Aaronson? Dr. Aaronson. They'd like to see you in the back."

David kept walking.

The security guard, a lanky black man named Robert, stepped toward him as he neared the door. "Hey, Doc. They need you in the back."

"Hmm? What?" David said.

"The ER doc wants to see you. The clerk was tryin' to get your attention."

"Oh. Sorry. Guess I was—"

"Don't sweat it. We all know you had a rough time up there."

"Yeah, thanks."

It *had* been a rough couple of hours, but in reality David simply had not grown accustomed to his new name. Although he'd been Dr. David Aaronson for eight months now, his spotty contact with other humans during that time had prevented his new surname from becoming ingrained.

"Bed two," the clerk said as David walked by the desk.

"Thank you," he said, then mumbled, "Ah shit," as he passed through the automatic doors. He'd been sipping Maker's Mark up in the surgeon's lounge, and it would be poor form to answer a consult with whisky breath. He pulled the bag of peanut M&Ms from the pocket of his white coat and popped a handful into his mouth.

At the nurse's station, a doctor in scrubs and a long white coat approached. He was close to David's age, early thirties, and about the same height. His hair was short and black, close-cropped military style. "Dr. Aaronson," he said. "Lieutenant Vince Strahan. I'm the flight surgeon for the TOPGUN squadron over at the naval air station. I moonlight here a couple nights a week."

"Good to meet you," David said.

"Likewise," Strahan replied. "I'm sorry to hear about the kid. What did you find?"

"A bronchopulmonary artery fistula, I think. His mediastinum was full of massively enlarged lymph nodes, and I suspect the inflammation created a fistula between his pulmonary artery and the left mainstem bronchus. I was mobilizing the lung when something ripped. We couldn't keep up with the bleeding."

"Unfortunate," Strahan said. "Anyway, I hate to bother you after a tough case, but I have a twenty-eight-year-old male with a facial fracture. I'd appreciate it if you'd take a quick look."

"No problem," David said.

Lieutenant Strahan led David down the hall to a large X-ray viewing monitor, where a series of facial X-rays were displayed.

David noted immediately that the arch of bone that forms the left cheek was broken in three places and displaced inward. There was also a linear fracture of the superior orbit—the top of the eye socket—also on the left. He turned to the flight surgeon. "Let me guess, a right hook to the left side of the face."

"In all probability."

David scrutinized the rest of the facial films and the skull series. "Any other injuries?"

"No."

"C-spine is okay?"

"Yes."

"Loss of consciousness?"

"Yes, but unclear for how long. CT of the brain was normal."

"Bar fight?" David asked.

"I'm thinking sucker punch, but yes, there was alcohol involved, along with a hooker and her pimp. It's an interesting story if you have a moment."

"I'm always up for a good ER tale."

"The patient and his buddy," Strahan began, "they grew up in Reno, went to college together, then their careers take them to different parts of the country. Our guy becomes a fiction writer and decides to set his next novel here in Fallon, and he invites his friend to join him so they can brainstorm the plot together. They end up at the Big Brown Beaver over on Main Street, yellow legal pad on the bar, pencils in hand, and they decide every time they have a breakthrough they'll do a Range Fire."

"A Range Fire?" David said.

"A shot of tequila mixed with Tabasco sauce. The Tabasco settles in the bottom of the shot glass, so after the tequila goes down, it's chased by a bolus of Tabasco."

"Tequila, hookers, and pimps, oh my."

"Exactly. Anyway, after several *breakthroughs* they become a little boisterous, the local gentry becomes interested in what they're doing, and a crowd forms. Enter Miss Ruby Mae Parker, one of Fallon's resident hookers. This girl is a tiny blonde, maybe five feet tall with heels on and no more than ninety pounds, so her pimp is never far away. Miss Parker pushes her way through the crowd, bellies up between these two guys, and proceeds to offer her opinions as to the direction the story should take. Now, our former Reno boys can tell she's a hooker, so the writer's buddy slips two one-hundred-dollar bills down her shirt—solely as a tribute, he says. Well, the writer, he doesn't think she's earned this money, so he reaches into her shirt and takes it back."

"With the pimp looking on," David said, slowly shaking his head.

"Yes, and after a couple more breakthroughs, including several good ideas from Ruby Mae, the writer takes a bathroom break. He disappears down a poorly lit hallway, and when he doesn't come back, his buddy goes to check on him and finds him in a heap on the floor, left eye swollen shut, the two C-notes gone."

"Sounds like good material for the novel."

"I'd put it in if I were the writer."

"All right," David said. "Let's go meet Fallon's Hemingway."

The patient was propped up on the gurney, holding an ice pack to the left side of his face.

David introduced himself. "Dr. Strahan tells me you had a run-in with an unhappy pimp."

"That's the prevailing theory."

"Mind if I have a look?"

"Do what you need to do."

David gently gripped the patient's head, turning it slightly one way, then the other. The left eye was swollen shut by a blood-filled knot of contused tissue. Also of note, four knuckle-size abrasions on the temple and cheek that correlated perfectly to a large fist.

"I'm going to look in your left ear," David said as he took the otoscope from its cradle on the wall. He was checking for hemotympanum, or blood behind the eardrum, the hallmark sign of a basilar skull fracture. Basilar skull fractures were hard to detect by X-ray or CT scan but were easy enough to rule out simply by looking in the ear. The eardrum was normal.

"You have a displaced fracture of your zygomatic arch—your cheekbone—and a nondisplaced orbital-rim fracture. That's your eye socket. The orbit does not require treatment, but the fractured zygoma might need to be surgically elevated—put back into its normal position—so I would recommend you see a maxillofacial surgeon. We don't have one here in Fallon, but I can refer you to someone in Reno."

"Is this urgent?" the writer asked.

"No. Surgery would only be offered for cosmetic reasons, and nothing would be done until the swelling resolves."

"Then I'll pass on the referral. I just want to get out of this godforsaken town and never come back. If my appearance has been altered, I'll see a surgeon when I get home."

"Okay," David said. "We'll make copies of your films, and you can be on your way."

The two doctors returned to the nurse's station to finish up their paperwork. When they were done, the flight surgeon swiveled his chair toward David. "Thanks for the consult," he said.

"Not a problem," David replied.

Strahan swiveled away, then turned back. "Hey, you want to grab a beer sometime?"

David almost reflexively said no but changed his mind. "Sure, but under three conditions: no Big Brown Beaver, no Range Fires, and you have to promise we'll steer clear of Ruby Mae Parker and her enforcer."

- 13 -

David grabbed a beer from his refrigerator, went out back to the patio, and sat down to watch the sun set behind a featureless mountain range rising several thousand feet above the desert floor. It was a beautiful October evening, the temperature quickly dropping as the sun disappeared, but the day had been nice, low seventies—warm for this time of year, according to the locals. Before his death, Richard Whitestone purchased David a modest two-bedroom house in a development on the edge of town, complete with a patio that filled half the backyard. The yard was otherwise appointed with artificial turf bordered by multiple varieties of cacti and other succulents that thrived in the water-starved moonscape of western Nevada. Beyond the white post-and-rail fence bordering the yard lay an endless expanse of sagebrush, interrupted by nothing but a craggy range of treeless mountains ten miles off in the distance. Such uninhabited vastness was about as different from New York City as the surface of Mars, but David embraced the isolation. He'd been in Fallon for three weeks now, and things were falling into place. He had formed a comfortable working relationship with Thomas Pennington, and for the first time in a long time he felt as though he no longer had to run and hide. Of course, he was on the run, and he was hiding, but this would be the end of the line. He'd stay put, assimilate himself in the community, and if his past reared its malignant head, so be it. He would surrender to whatever forces caught up to him and accept the consequences. He was done running, and he was done fighting.

He fought back once before, and his efforts resulted in a trail of carnage. He'd lost his wife and unborn child, and to avenge the loss he executed a man who'd been a father figure and mentor. The fallout resulted in the murder of a Russian corporate spy and the death of Richard Whitestone—known to David as Mr. White—the NSA spook who had entered David's life as an adversary but later, out of necessity, became an ally. As a result of those three deaths, both the NYPD and FBI, and probably the NSA, were looking for him.

On the upside, he had grown a human kidney in the laboratory, thus saving the life of Richard Whitestone's daughter Heather, and he anonymously shared that knowledge with the rest of the world, which would someday save hundreds of thousands like her. But despite this, something was still missing—his fate, and his identity. These were necessary to restore balance to his life. Restoring the latter would be the easier of the two. His identity was that of a surgeon, he who would open body cavities, lay hands on the diseased organs contained within, and restore health to the sick and dying. Through his new position as partner in a thriving surgical practice, he would touch the lives of those in the community every day, and that would allow him to atone for past transgressions and redeem himself.

Controlling his own fate? Out of his hands. He had a new name, a new past, and a slightly altered physical appearance—all courtesy of Mr. White—but homeless men in New York City had been robbed of their kidneys, a New Jersey man and a Russian spy methodically executed, a rogue NSA agent found dead in a penthouse in upper Manhattan. There was no way the FBI, Manhattan South Homicide, and detectives from the Passaic County Prosecutor's Office were going to give up the hunt because the trail had gone cold. Nonetheless, all David could do was go about his business, blend in, avoid doing anything stupid that might raise suspicion, and with each passing day perhaps the trail leading to David McBride would grow colder, while David Aaronson became increasingly assimilated.

But first things first. It was Saturday night, and he'd agreed to meet the flight surgeon for a couple of beers. He had mixed feelings about this. There was a deadly virus racing around the globe, and even though Fallon and Churchill County seemed immune and businesses remained open, he was still uncomfortable exposing himself to crowds, large or small. But more importantly, the thought of putting himself into a social situation made him feel ill at ease. Although confident in his new appearance—cheeks and chin slightly enhanced, eyes a darker shade of brown, hair shorter and darker than when he left New York, plus he had recovered the weight he'd lost while on the run and during his stay at the Manhattan Detention Complex, otherwise known as the Tombs—he still felt he was being scrutinized whenever someone looked at him for more than a few seconds. In addition, the descent of his life into chaos started eight months ago with the death of Cassandra, his unborn child, and his father, and he'd been living a life of self-imposed isolation since then.

Cassandra had been the center of his universe, but he was certain he'd never made her feel that way. He knew he had never said it, and now he would never get the chance. While living near UCSF in San Francisco to develop his surgery residency backstory, he thought about her every day. And while living near UNR in Reno to build up his medical school background, he thought about her every day. And as he walked the streets, studied the neighborhoods, observed the locals, and had taken in the major sights—alone—he thought about her every minute of every day.

There had been social encounters, in the diviest of dive bars with people who had no interest in who you were, where you were from, or where you were going, as long as you were buying. Then came the coronavirus lockdown and the endless days spent sitting alone in a dark apartment, imagining the things he would be doing to protect his wife and his baby and his father from the pandemic. And now he was here. The Nevada State Board of Health had tested him for the coronavirus, proclaimed him negative, granted him a medical license and permission to move into the county. So yeah, eight months after Cassandra's death, and after eight months of self-imposed isolation—and of feeling rootless, unanchored, and disconnected—he was about to embark on his first social outing, and to say he was a little nervous would be a gross understatement.

- 14 -

The Stockman's was the nicest and newest of the Fallon casinos. It was small, as were the others in town, but it was clean and appeared to have a respectable clientele. The casino proper was the size of two basketball courts sitting side by side, but despite its lack of size, it hummed with the same action and sensory stimulation as the bigger establishments. The myriad bells, whistles, and chimes were accompanied by flashing lights, strobes, and neon of every color. The patrons sat on stools, either hunched over slot machines or leaning on one of four blackjack tables, their cocktails and cigarettes within arm's reach. And there were no concerns about a global pandemic in this place—no social distancing, no masks, no worries.

Beyond the boundaries of the casino floor were a steak house on one side and a bar on the other. At one end of the bar sat eight round-top tables. David claimed one of the tables against the wall and sat down facing the casino. The cocktail waitress seemed to be working the floor by herself, so David went over to the bar to order.

The bartender, a plump middle-aged woman who already looked tired even though she was only halfway through her shift, spotted David and ambled over. "What can I get ya, hon?"

"How about a Maker's Mark on the rocks and a Miller Genuine Draft."

David was not out for a night of hardcore drinking, nor did he want to give that impression, but he did want to imbibe a little social lubrication. He was twenty minutes early. He'd be able to finish the bourbon before the flight surgeon arrived. And just as David put the empty tumbler on the bar, Vince Strahan walked in. David ordered him a beer.

"Doctor," Strahan said.

"Lieutenant," David replied.

"What do you think of our humble little place?" Strahan asked. "Not quite in the same league as the Reno casinos and not even in the same universe as Vegas."

"I'm not a gambler, so good enough for a couple of beers."

"Speaking of Reno, I know you attended medical school at UNR, but are you from there originally?"

"No. I grew up in Lakeview, Oregon, which is a small farming community very much like Fallon," David said, "but how did you know I went to the University of Nevada?"

"Everyone at the hospital knows your background—medical school in Reno, surgery residency in San Francisco, and the younger nurses are all excited you're single—but the one thing nobody can figure out is why you would come here to practice. UCSF is a top-tier program. You could have gone anywhere."

"So this is a fact-finding mission?" David said with a smile.

"No, and I don't mean to pry, it's just that you're an oddity here. All of us navy guys, we're told where to go. But a well-trained surgeon, young and single, why would you set up shop in a tiny town in the desert?"

David sipped his beer, then gave his scripted answer about having elderly parents in Lakeview, how that would have been his first choice but the two surgeons in town are young and not retiring anytime soon, and it's only a four hour drive should his parents need him. "But the real reason I accepted this position," David added, "is the unique opportunity to take over the practice in three years."

"We heard Pennington is phasing himself out," Strahan said. "So you'll become sole proprietor? Not a bad deal."

"Exactly. In most private practices you'd wait five years before they even offer a partnership. That means taking an inordinate amount of call, covering the holidays, draining all the perirectal abscesses."

Strahan smiled at the abscess reference.

"And the best thing about a small hospital in a small town? There are no surgical subspecialists. If I want to take out a colon, remove a thyroid, or perform vascular or thoracic procedures, I don't have to wage a turf war with colorectal, endocrine, vascular, or thoracic surgeons. I can practice old-school general surgery."

"Sounds pretty good," Strahan said. "When I leave the navy, maybe I'll complete my residency training and join you."

"So flight surgeon is a misnomer?"

"I've completed a one-year general internship along with specialized training in aviation medicine, but no formal surgery training."

"And you moonlight in the ER to broaden your skill set?"

"Sort of," Strahan said. "I may have torpedoed my naval career, no pun intended, so whatever civilian experience I can pick up, the better."

"How does one go about sinking their naval career?" David asked. "No pun intended."

"Three words," Strahan said with a slight grin.

"I hope you're not going to say hookers, tequila, and pimps."

"Something even more dangerous. The admiral's wife."

"You mean the admiral's daughter."

"No," Strahan said. "His wife."

"Jesus," David said as he leaned back and sipped his beer. "Not sure I want to hear this."

"It's not what you think."

"Right now, I'm thinking Dean Wormer's wife from *Animal House*."

"Uh, you're not too far off."

"All right," David said. "Let's hear it."

"Late one afternoon I was staffing the hangar clinic near the flight line, which is for active duty personnel only. This apparently meant nothing to one Mrs. S. J. Smith." Strahan went on to explain that Elaine Smith was the wife of Vice Admiral S. J. Smith, the highest-ranking naval officer for the entire Pacific region, also known as Commander-in-Chief US Pacific Fleet, or CINCPAC. "We recently opened a Naval Air Support Command Center here at the base, and CINCPAC and his wife, Elaine, were going to join the governor for a ribbon-cutting ceremony, then travel to Carson City for dinner at the governor's mansion. Now, Mrs. CINCPAC forgot to stock her travel bag with its customary supply of Xanax, which she allegedly takes for an anxiety disorder, and she thought she'd drop by for a quick refill."

The clinic was about to close for the day, Strahan explained, and he was looking forward to getting in nine holes before dark with a couple of the pilots, then settling in at the clubhouse for spades and liar's dice. "I've got my feet on the desk, and I'm thumbing through an ESPN magazine when I hear my petty officer Michael Rubio trying to convince someone that the clinic is for active duty only. Before I can drop my feet to the ground, this woman barges into my office and demands to see the doctor immediately. It takes me a microsecond to size up the situation—an attractive woman, early fifties, thin bordering on gaunt with high-end makeup, hair, and clothing. A senior officer's wife. The visiting admiral's wife. And, of course, she fully understands the power equation of the military. Her husband, a three-star admiral, outranks the commanding officer of this godforsaken airbase in the middle of nowhere by three levels, and outranks me by five, so she's going to get what she wants."

"Sounds like a no-brainer," David said. "Just write the scrip and send her on her way."

"That was the plan, but procedure mandates that prescription renewals get their vital signs checked, and while Petty Officer Rubio is signing her in and checking her vitals, which she vociferously objected to, I pulled up her records and perused her prescription history."

David shook his head disapprovingly. "I'm all for reeling in the overmedication of the populace, but the power dynamics are not in your favor."

"I knew that going in, but when I saw the amount of Xanax numerous navy doctors had been prescribing for the woman, I wanted no part of it. When I told her I thought she was being overprescribed and would not honor her request, she went ape shit on me, screaming, 'Do you know who I am, Lieutenant?' Then she calls her husband, right there in front of me, and makes it sound as if I'm some yokel from the sticks, and within minutes my base commander calls me and tells me to stop fucking around and fill the prescription."

"Okay," David said, "you decide it's time to forego the procedures and ethics and just give the admiral's wife what she wants so you can get to the golf course."

"That's what I should've done, but goddammit I'm a commissioned officer in the US Navy, and if it wasn't for my piss-poor vision, I'd be flying F-18 Hornets every day instead of swabbing sore throats and doing pap smears in the Dependents Clinic. And then to get bullied by some substance-abusing waif of an admiral's wife?" Strahan paused and sipped his beer, then said, "Sorry. I didn't invite you here so I could piss and moan about my career."

"Don't worry about it," David said, recalling that just ten months ago he was in the same position, sewing rat aortas together instead of operating on humans and complaining about it to Cassandra every chance he got. "What about the base commander?" David asked. "Didn't he give you a direct order to prescribe the Xanax?"

"He did, but as a medical officer I have the authority to refuse writing a prescription I deem medically unjustifiable."

"Wow," David said, leaning back and grinning. "I butted heads with a few surgical attendings, but your base commander, the commander-in-chief of the pacific fleet, and his wife?"

"Yeah, well, seemed like the right thing to do at the time, but I'm sure any day now I'll be getting orders from CINCPAC to report for coronavirus-screening duty in Okinawa."

David glanced past the flight surgeon and noticed three attractive young women crossing the casino floor and coming straight for them. Two were blonde, dressed in tight jeans and blouses, both too tall to be Ruby Parker. The third was shorter and darker than the other two, her skin a light shade of bronze, her eyes a deep shade of brown, and she had a flood of straight black hair cascading down to the small of her back. The short sleeves of her blouse revealed a dream catcher tattoo on her right upper arm. She appeared to be Native American, and she was the most beautiful woman David had ever laid eyes upon.

One of the blondes said, "Hello, Dr. Strahan."

The lieutenant turned around. "Hello, ladies. How are you on this fine evening?"

"We're good. We'd love it if you introduced us to the new doctor in town."

"Of course," Vince Strahan said, turning toward David. "Dr. David Aaronson, this is Bethany Sims, Victoria Kaiser, and"—he gestured toward the Native American girl—"Nova Featherstone. She's the quiet one of the group."

Nova smiled and looked down, her slight embarrassment quite alluring. David stood and shook hands with Bethany and Victoria, saying hello to each of them. When he took Nova's hand in his, her shyness seemed to melt away as she smiled again, and for a fleeting moment they held each other's gaze. *Absolutely stunning* was the only thought in David's head at that moment. Then he gathered himself. "It's nice to meet you, Nova," he said.

"Nice to meet you, Dr. Aaronson," she replied, still smiling, her teeth as white as pearls and luminescent against the beautiful hue of her bronze skin and perfect complexion.

"What are you ladies up to tonight?" Strahan asked. "Do you have time for a drink?"

"Wish we did," Bethany replied. "Will you guys be here later?"

"We're not sure, but if you're passing by, stop in and check."

After the girls left, David went to the bar for two tumblers of Maker's Mark.

"Trying to douse the flame, Doctor?" Strahan said when David returned. "The way you and Nova Featherstone were staring at each other? I thought we were going to have to hose the two of you down."

"No. I mean, she is definitely a beautiful girl, but I'm not—"

A burst of chimes and lights and hooting and hollering. Someone had hit a big jackpot.

When the clamor subsided, David said, "I'm probably ten years older than her."

"She's twenty-six. I'd say you're only five or six years older, but it's just as well. I would advise you to give that one a wide berth."

"Don't tell me she's one of Ruby Parker's coworkers."

"Quite the opposite. Sweetest girl you'll ever meet. It's her father you want to stay away from. Have you heard the name Two Feathers since you've been here?"

"No," David said.

"That's his tribal name. His real name is Billy Jack Featherstone, and he is the supreme overlord of the northern Nevada meth trade. He has cooks, he has enforcers in the form of a motorcycle gang, and he has the reservation on which to cook his product and bury his bodies."

"That shy, beautiful girl is the daughter of a drug trafficker and killer?"

"Yes, and that shy, beautiful girl is also a flame that draws naval aviators to their demise. You've seen the movie *Top Gun*, right?"

"Of course," David replied.

"And you remember how arrogant and cocky Maverick and Iceman were? That's pretty much an accurate depiction, and when you get all these hotshot pilots assigned to Fallon for TOPGUN training, and they see this beautiful, exotic Shoshone woman, they try like hell to get her attention. But then they come up against this tall, massively built, dark-skinned man with black hair as long as his daughter's, and he's wearing faded jeans, cowboy boots, a biker vest with 'The Branded Few' stitched across the back, and all he has to do is say 'Boo' and they're scurrying back to the base with their tails between their legs. He doesn't need his crew. He doesn't need to flash the ten-inch Buck knife that hangs from his belt. It's just him."

"Sounds like you have a man crush."

"Not at all. It's just fun to see 'the best of the best' get shot down once in a while."

"Your warning is duly noted," David raising his tumbler of bourbon in a salute. "Perhaps one might be safer in the company of Ruby Mae Parker."

"Perhaps," said Strahan.

After the lieutenant excused himself to answer a call from the base, David polished off the rest of his Maker's Mark and tried to suppress the guilt rearing its ugly head. His wife had been dead for only eight months, and he felt shame for getting all googly eyed over a young woman, but damn, he was lonely.

- 15 -

A woman wearing only a hospital gown crashed through the glass door, cutting her arms, legs, and feet. A crescendo-decrescendo air raid siren pierced the desert air. Swirling spotlights turned darkness into day. She ran down the hill through sagebrush and dry rocky dirt, her bare feet getting torn apart, and in the dark space between swipes of the spotlight, she ran into a fence built from stacked coils of razor wire. She struggled to free herself, becoming more tangled with every movement, the wire slicing the flesh of her arms, hands, and legs. And then she began to cough.

- 16 -

Vince Strahan's ringing phone snapped him out of a deep sleep. He glanced at the clock. Two thirty in the morning. "Lieutenant Strahan," he said, somewhat annoyed.

"Sorry to wake you, sir, but we need you at the army biolab ASAP. A woman is trapped in our razor wire perimeter fence, and she's panicking. The more she moves, the more cut up she's getting."

Strahan needed a moment to process what he was hearing, thankful that he and the surgeon had not made a late night of it. The only women on the base were active duty, the wives of active duty, and support staff, none of whom had any reason to go near the lab—a dark site that even he, as an officer, did not have clearance to enter. "Is she base personnel or civilian?"

"Civilian. A patient here at the facility."

Strahan was not aware the lab treated patients. He had always thought of the place as a labyrinth of subterranean rooms full of test tubes, petri dishes, and moon suits. "If you treat patients, isn't there a physician on the premises, or at least on call?"

"It's complicated, sir. We would just really appreciate it if you could help us out."

"Do you have heavy gloves and wire cutters?"

"We're getting them, but she's panicked and thrashing around. We may need you to sedate her."

"Okay," Vince Strahan said. "I'm on the way."

He slipped into his service khakis, grabbed his jacket and medical bag, and hopped into his Jeep.

The only connection between the biolab and the naval air station was the use of US Marines for security at both installations. The facility—a subordinate laboratory of USAMRIID—was nine miles from the air base, with the final four miles consisting of a graded dirt road terminating in an isolated desert canyon. Strahan had never seen the lab, and as he approached he was struck by its non-descript appearance. In the depths of a dark, steep-walled canyon sat a dimly lit single-story redbrick building that could pass for a 1950s elementary school. In contrast to the unimpressive structure stood a twelve-foot perimeter fence made of rows of coiled razor wire stacked one upon the other. The entrance was secured by an iron gate backed up by anti-ram bollards—ten inch-diameter steel columns that rise up from, and lower into, the ground. After exchanging salutes, Strahan showed his ID to the marine sentry manning the post.

"They're waiting for you one klick in that direction, sir," the guard pointing to the lieutenant's right.

Strahan followed a dirt road paralleling the perimeter fence. After six tenths of a mile, which roughly equaled a kilometer—or one klick—the road climbed from a gully, and at the top of the rise he came upon a bizarre and grisly scene. A brown-skinned woman, Native American by all appearances, was deeply embedded in the coils of razor wire. Her hospital gown was shredded and bloody. Her arms and legs, also shredded and bloody, were tangled in the fence. She was illuminated by the headlights of two vehicles, and the look on her face was pure panic, an animal caught in a trap. A pair of men in white hazmat suits and respirators were talking to her, trying to calm her, but it wasn't working. She was gripped by fear, arms and legs flailing despite the slashing barbs of the razor wire.

Strahan climbed from his Jeep and approached two Asian men in white coats standing near the vehicles. They were almost as panicked as the woman in the fence.

"Lieutenant Vince Strahan," the flight surgeon said. "Who's in charge?"

"We're civilians," one of them replied. "The men in the suits are the ranking officers."

"Who is the woman?"

"A patient. She's been quarantined with an unidentified viral disease. She just went crazy tonight and escaped."

"Are you guys medical doctors? Who's responsible for this woman's care?"

Headlights crested the same rise Strahan had driven up moments ago—a black Escalade coming in fast, dust flying, gravel crunching. It skidded to a stop, sending a cloud of chalky dust over Strahan and the other men. From the passenger door exited a high-ranking army officer wearing his camo ACU, or army combat uniform.

"It's Colonel Neville," one of the Asian men said. "This is his lab. He's in charge."

Neville and his driver came toward them at a fast clip. The colonel was tall, six one or two, with close-cropped graying hair under his cap. His features were sharp, the skin over his temples and along the angle of his jaw taut, his eyes probing and alert. He looked more like a marine colonel than army. Strahan had crossed paths with many high-ranking officers during his eight-year career, and his initial assessments were generally accurate. His impression of Colonel Neville? This was the kind of guy who would beat his little brother bloody for control of the TV remote. Steer clear and be glad you didn't have to report to him every day.

Strahan stood at attention and saluted the colonel.

Neville gave Strahan a half-assed salute in return, then said, "Who the fuck are you?"

"Lieutenant Vincent Strahan, Flight Surgeon, NAS Fallon, sir."

"We don't need you here."

"It's my understanding that there is not a physician assigned to this facility, and once the woman is extracted from the fence, she's going to need one."

"We'll handle it," Neville said, "so get back in your vehicle and return to base. And forget what you just saw. You are not authorized to be here. You are not authorized to treat this patient. Any discussion of what you witnessed tonight, even with your superior officers, will result in grave consequences. Is that understood, Lieutenant?"

As the word "lieutenant" left the colonel's mouth, the woman in the fence began to cough violently, and then she coughed up about a cup of blood, and the coughing became more violent as she started to gurgle and fight for air.

Strahan moved toward her.

"Stay back, Lieutenant," Neville commanded. "She's infectious."

The colonel ordered the men in the hazmat gear to stand down. "Do not risk tearing your suits on the razor wire," he told them.

"We can't just let her hang there and bleed to death," Strahan said.

Neville did an about-face and glared at Strahan. "I am a colonel. You are a lieutenant. And even though I am army and you are navy, if you do not leave immediately you will be court-martialed for insubordination. Is that clear, Lieutenant Strahan?"

Vince Strahan came to attention, saluted, and said, "Yes, sir. Loud and clear."

As Strahan drove away, he looked in his review mirror just before dropping down into the gulley, and what he saw repulsed him—six men, including a colonel in the United States Army, doing nothing as a woman bled to death in front of them.

- 18 -

Lieutenant Vince Strahan would not sleep tonight, not after what he had just witnessed. It was a scene right out of a Stephen King movie—a pitch-dark night, an isolated military lab hidden deep in a desert canyon, a woman in a hospital gown illuminated only by headlights, hanging from razor wire as if she'd been crucified, her extremities gashed open, bleeding from every laceration, and then she starts to cough, spewing columns of blood onto the desert floor, and a high-ranking army officer—a colonel—ordering his men to stand down as the woman bleeds to death. This would be a nightmare if he were asleep, but he wasn't, so he went to the kitchen, grabbed his bottle of twelve-year-old scotch, and filled a tumbler three quarters of the way.

He was well into the third pour, a nice buzz coinciding with the orange glow of dawn, when he heard a loud knock on his front door. He turned an ear toward it, wondered if it was an auditory hallucination spawned by the unshakeable image of the woman in the fence, then he heard a car drive away.

Strahan went over to the window, pulled back the curtain, saw nothing unusual. He opened the door and grabbed the rolled-up newspaper sitting on the porch.

Back in the kitchen he sipped his scotch and unrolled the paper. A cheap flip phone clattered onto the table.

It rang.

Strahan flipped it open. "Hello?" he said confusedly.

"When's the next night you're off duty?"

"Who is this?"

"When is the next night you are off duty?"

"Tonight. I'm not on duty tonight. What's this about?"

"I want you to go see a girl, and take the new surgeon. He's part of this."

"What girl? What are you talking about?"

"The woman you watched die a few hours ago, someone wants to talk to you about it. Go to Mona's Kitty Ranch, tonight at seven. The girl's hooker name is Ophelia. If she's not in the lineup when you walk in, wait for her at the bar. And make sure the new surgeon is there. He's part of this."

"Yeah, you said that."

- 19 -

Vince Strahan's hardtop Jeep Rubicon pulled into David's driveway, its headlights momentarily flooding the front room with light. David grabbed his jacket, locked up, and climbed in.

As Strahan drove them out of the neighborhood, David said, "Where are we going? You were rather cryptic on the phone."

"I had an interesting morning. Once we are out of town I'll give you a full briefing."

"Out of town?"

"We're going to see a girl."

"Look, I'm not really—"

"This is business, not pleasure."

Ten minutes later, the lights of Fallon were behind them and they were rumbling down US Route 50—two lanes, no shoulder, cracked pavement, a 55-mph speed limit. To the left of the highway, small clusters of light revealed the ranches and farms that followed the Carson River. To the right, nothing but undulating foothills seen only by the light of the moon. Even though David had been in the American West for just a few weeks, he'd gained an appreciation for the importance of water. Where there was water, there were humans, and where there was no water, only rocks, dirt, and sagebrush. Left side of the road, a river and ranches and farms. Right side, nothing except the coyotes, rattlesnakes, scorpions, and whatever else roamed the desert floor at night. After another mile or so, David turned toward Strahan. "Okay, we're out of town, way out, so maybe it's time to fill me in."

"Give me three minutes."

They crested a rise in the highway. Off to the left, two rows of perfectly spaced lights appeared—basketball-size orbs that started abruptly, traveled for a couple hundred yards, then ended abruptly, like Main Street in a small town but without the town.

"What are those lights over there?" David asked.

"The dam for the Lahontan Reservoir."

A few minutes later, Strahan turned in to the boat launch for the Lahontan State Recreation Area. Other than a gravel lot and a pair of restrooms, there was little else to the place. They parked at the top of the ramp. "Want a cold brew?" he asked. "Got a cooler in the back."

"You always travel with a supply of beer?"

"It's important to stay hydrated out here in the desert."

"Then why not," David said, presuming the flight surgeon understood the fallacy of his logic. Any self-respecting beer drinker knew alcohol acted as a diuretic and was, therefore, an instrument of dehydration.

Strahan joined David at the top of the boat ramp with two ice-cold bottles. David sipped his and studied the lake. It was a beautiful night, cool but calm, moonlight shimmering on the water, a light breeze ruffling the fall leaves clinging to the cottonwoods along the shore. He turned toward the flight surgeon. "Okay, nice place, but what are we doing here?"

"Around two thirty this morning, I got a call from the army biolab, requesting help with a medical emergency," Strahan said. He described the grisly scene at the fence and how a colonel in the United States Army had ordered everyone to stand down while the woman bled to death.

"She was inside the fence. Inside a secured area," David said, "which means she came from within the lab."

"Yes. They referred to her as a patient."

"And she was coughing up blood, just like Jimmy Miller."

"Yes."

David sipped his beer and pondered for a moment. "Doesn't make sense. Neither the state nor the CDC will commit a single investigator to study an undefined, uniformly fatal disease, so why would the army be interested?"

"I think we're about to find out." Strahan described the phone call he received after returning home, that someone wants to talk to them about the woman in the fence. "He told me to see a girl called Ophelia at Mona's Kitty Ranch."

"Mona's Kitty Ranch? A brothel?" David was glad he had familiarized himself with Nevada's long history of legalized prostitution. "That's where we're going?"

- 20 -

Twenty minutes later, Strahan pulled the Jeep into another gravel parking lot, only this one was well lit and full of dusty cars, muddy SUVs and four-by-four trucks, as well as two Mercedes, a BMW, and a Tesla. A chain-link fence topped with barbed wire ran the length of the lot and continued around the sides of the structure. Above a locked gate stood a sign bordered by blinking clear light bulbs. MONA'S KITTY RANCH filled the left half, while the right consisted of a pink neon cat, its back arched and rubbing against a pair of female legs in black fishnet stockings and stiletto heels. The cat had that jerky three-phase motion typical of neon signs. The building behind the fence was unremarkable—single story, dull-white clapboard, no windows. It looked more like a secret compound than a brothel, not that David had stood before many brothels in his lifetime.

Once they parked, Strahan leaned into the back of the Jeep and opened the cooler. "Ever been to one of these places?" he said as he handed David a beer.

"Never made my to do-list," David said as he twisted the cap off the bottle.

"No matter. This is how it works. When you walk in, all the available girls line up, and you can choose right then or hang at the bar. I found Ophelia's photo on the website. If she's not in the lineup, we'll go to the bar and wait."

"Then what?"

"She'll find us and ask if we want to party. We'll chat briefly, accept her offer, and go to her room."

David sipped his beer, then said, "When we were parked at the boat launch, I noticed a bumper sticker on your tailgate that said $C_9H_{13}NO_3$ Junkie."

"Yeah," Strahan replied. "It's the chemical formula for adrenaline. I had it custom made as an homage to an ex-girlfriend."

"We have a few minutes," David said, holding up his half-full bottle. "Let's hear it."

"All right," Strahan said. "Before TOPGUN, I was stationed in the Bay Area and dating a lawyer who lived on Nob Hill. A real beauty. Top-tier stuff. We'd been together a few months when I received transfer orders to NAS Fallon. I figured our relationship was doomed, but she invited me over whenever I had a free weekend. Now, from time to time I'd show up with a mud-covered Jeep, and in the past she had seen GoPro footage of me shooting beers and skiing off cliffs at Tahoe, shooting beers and riding dirt bikes through the pitch-dark Nevada desert with night vision goggles, shooting beers and bungee jumping and zip-lining."

"Flying and drinking, drinking and driving," David added, referencing the famous Chuck Yeager line from Thomas Wolfe's *The Right Stuff*.

"Exactly. Naval aviators are a fast-living, hard-drinking bunch. She'd been to the officer's club. She knew that. So one time I make the four-hour drive from Fallon to San Francisco, and she's all dressed up to go out, and when we come down to the street she sees the muddy Jeep and starts railing on me, calling me a reckless, immature adrenaline junkie and disrespectful for showing up in a dirty car. I apologized profusely, but after that I wasn't invited back."

"Sounds like a good one got away."

"Just as well. Until the navy is done with me, it's better to not be committed."

Strahan locked up the Jeep, and he and David walked over to the gate.

"When I hit the buzzer, look up at the camera and smile," Strahan said.

Both men did so. The gate clicked open.

As they approached the entrance a heavyset blonde stepped out, brandishing a handgun-style thermometer. "Sorry, but I gotta screen you gents." She aimed it at their foreheads, then said, "Either of you been sick recently? Fever? Cough? Aches, pains, runny nose? Problems with taste or smell?"

They answered no to all of the above.

"Welcome to Mona's," she said.

Strahan leaned in close to David. "Good enough for international air travel, good enough for admission to a brothel."

They entered a parlor where six smiling girls stood in a line. It was a varied group—some tall, some short, some covered by sheer lingerie, some wearing only bras and panties, two brunettes, three blondes, and one young woman with her hair dyed purple. Ophelia was not among them. "Thank you, ladies, but I think we'll have drinks first," Strahan said.

The lounge was right off a Hollywood soundstage—a small bar, pink LED ropes bordering both the mirror behind the bar and an archway leading to a corridor, the walls lined with red velvet couches and candlelit coffee tables, the latter cluttered with mixed drinks and bottles of beer. Several men and their "dates" sat in various degrees of entanglement on the couches and engaged in muffled conversation. The Eagles' "Hotel California" wafted from unseen speakers: "You can check out any time you like, but you can never leave."

David and Vince sat at the bar, and the flight surgeon ordered two Maker's rocks from the scantily clad and heavily tattooed brunette bartender.

"You gonna be able to drive us home?" David asked.

"Yeah," Strahan replied. "The bourbon is for sipping only. You can't sit at the bar in a butt hut without a drink."

"The butt hut?" David repeated with a grin.

Just then a small … woman? … girl? … came up to David and rubbed her body against his. She was young with short dark hair and dark eyes and stood no more than five feet tall—a brunette version of Ruby Parker, he supposed—and she wore a sheer white cover-up with a white-lace bra and panties underneath, and red four-inch heels.

"How are you gentlemen this evening?" she asked.

David glanced at Strahan.

Strahan gave him a slight confirmatory nod.

"We're doing well," David said. "And how are you?"

"Horny, actually. You gents here to party?"

"We are," Strahan said.

"Just the three of us, or should I get one of my girlfriends?"

"Only us."

"Okay. I'm Ophelia. Grab your drinks and follow me."

Halfway down a long corridor, Ophelia opened a door and entered the room. Once inside, she said, "How much cash do you guys have? I need to pay the cashier. Normally, the negotiated price for two men and a girl would be eight hundred dollars. I'll tell her we settled on six hundred because one of you is only going to watch."

The lieutenant said he had one-eighty in cash. David had one-fifty. "What about a credit card?" Strahan asked.

"No," David said. "No trail, paper or digital."

"Each of you give me a hundred," Ophelia said. "I'll make up the rest."

They handed her the cash. She told them to relax, she'd be right back.

David took the chair in the corner, Strahan the chair in the opposite corner, and they sat quietly, sipping their drinks.

The room was nicer than David had expected—a king-size bed, a couple of dressers, lamps draped with red scarves, which cast the place in a red haze. He was intrigued by the large Jacuzzi tub and open shower filling the far corner of the room, with natural stone tiles covering the walls, floor, and ceiling.

Ophelia came in and sat on the edge of the bed.

"Are you the person who wants to talk to us?" David asked.

"No," she said. "One of the girls will bring him over in a minute."

- 21 -

David and Vince sat quietly, while Ophelia, now shoeless and lean-ing back into the pillows on her bed, thumbed through a *People* magazine. David couldn't recall when he had last seen a millennial read a printed page. Then, two quiet knocks. Ophelia opened the door. Her friend Ryan shuffled an Asian man into the room and disappeared. He was midthirties, average height, thin with dark hair. The pallid look on his face was one of sleepless nights and high anxiety, his gaze darting from David to Vince and back to David as they rose from their chairs.

Strahan said, "You were at the lab last night. We spoke before the colonel arrived."

"Yes. I'm Philip Tang. Thanks for coming." He turned toward David. "Dr. Aaronson. It's good to meet you."

"Likewise," David said.

"The woman, did she die?" Strahan asked.

"Yes, unfortunately."

David handed Ophelia two twenties and asked if she would go to the bar for another round. Once she had gone, he said, "Is it okay to talk in front of her?"

"She wants to help," Tang said. "Her nine-year-old sister bled to death a few weeks ago."

"Yeah, I heard the story. Horrific," David said.

"That's why she's hosting us. Client confidentiality is crucial to these establishments, so the owners regularly sweep for cameras and listening devices, no cell phones allowed in the rooms. This is the safest place in the county to meet."

Ophelia returned with the drinks. David thanked her and said, "I'm sorry to hear about your sister. I hope you and your family are doing okay."

"It's just me and my mother now, and she's pretty much a basket case. But thanks."

Ophelia assumed her position at the head of the bed, shoeless, propped up by pillows, and wrapped in a fleece blanket. She resumed flipping through her *People* magazine.

David and Vince took their seats.

Philip Tang grabbed a chair and sat down in front of them. He sipped his bourbon, wincing slightly, then he said, "Eighteen months ago South Korean intelligence identified a new bioweapon—a virus—under development in China. Korean NIS agents stole a sample and shared it with us. Genome sequencing revealed it to be a member of the *coronaviridae* family."

"A coronavirus," Strahan said.

"Yes, what would later become CoVid19, but that was twelve months prior to the pandemic. We didn't know what we had or if it was transmissible to humans, but based on its similarity to MERS and SARS we started researching a vaccine. Before we made much progress, however, the project was stopped. The mission commander, Jonathan Neville—"

"The colonel from last night," David added.

"Yes. He was running the viral characterization group, and he tells us CoVid19 mutates into a much more contagious and deadly strain, so we shift our focus to what he designated CoVid23, and six months later we have a vaccine. But it's not a stick-a-needle-in-your-arm vaccination, it's an aerosol. It can be dropped from drones or pumped into the ventilation systems of schools, restaurants, and office buildings. Entire towns and cities, even sprawling urban areas, can be vaccinated without anyone realizing it. It's like a mass flu mist."

"And you tested it here in Fallon," David said. "Then you exposed the population to CoVid23, but twenty nonresponders died."

"Yes."

"But those patients did not present with flu symptoms and acute respiratory failure. They bled to death. Inflamed lymph nodes eroding the pulmonary artery."

"That's the pathophysiology of 23, a mutation of twenty-three genes that hyperstimulates intranodal immune cells."

"And why hasn't there been a single case of CoVid19 in Churchill County?"

"The vaccination for 23 is also effective against 19."

David glanced at Strahan, then back at Tang. "So, in summary," David said, "the army developed a vaccine that could end the current pandemic and prevent a future, more lethal variation, and to test their new drug they exposed unsuspecting US citizens to a virus that causes them to cough themselves to death." David looked over at Ophelia, hoping she had not heard his callous remark. She was thumbing through her magazine. Then, turning back to Philip Tang, he said, "I'm pretty sure the FDA did not sign off on this."

"No, but the president did."

David leaned back in his chair and folded his arms. "The president of the United States."

"You guys have seen what CoVid23 can do, and our animal studies demonstrated an eighty percent infectivity rate with one hundred percent mortality. In addition, it's very robust. Unlike Ebola and AIDS, it can live on nonbiologic surfaces for days."

"It has the potential to spread quickly and lay waste to large swaths of the world's population," David said.

"Yes, which is why the president approved our mission. Intelligence reports indicated that once CoVid19 had reached every continent, the Chinese were going to release 23 in the Middle East, Europe, and the United States and claim it was a natural mutation of 19. There was no time for FDA approval. This had to be done fast, even if it meant sacrificing innocent lives."

"How effective is your vaccine?" David asked.

"Our failure rate is less than one percent."

"Sounds like you accomplished your mission, albeit with some collateral damage, including a twenty-two-year-old farm boy and a nine-year-old girl." David again glanced at Ophelia, hoping she had not heard yet another callous remark. She was still reading her magazine. "So why are you telling us this? Why a clandestine meeting in a Nevada brothel?"

"What I just told you will be the president's account should the covert vaccination project become public knowledge. Now I'm going to tell you the real story, the story that will never see the light of day without your help."

David shared a look of confusion with Vince Strahan.

"CoVids 19 and 23 are not weaponized viruses bioengineered by China," Philip Tang explained. "They are of Chinese origin, but they're harmless. It was us, the USAMRIID laboratory thirty miles down the road. We added function to 19, then we created 23."

David shook his head. "What does that mean, to add function?"

"It's called 'gain of function' research. You take an existing bacterium or virus and engineer it to be more virulent than it is in nature."

"I'm still not sure what you're talking about," David said.

Tang gulped his bourbon, wincing as it went down, then he continued. "Following the SARS outbreak in 2003, the CDC formed a coronavirus task force. The SARS-CoV virus had a mortality rate of ten percent, but it was only moderately transmissible. Five months after it first appeared, it simply went away, killing only eight hundred people. However, the CDC believed that with the vast numbers of coronavirus species and the large number of animal reservoirs capable of hosting the virus, it was only a matter of time before a more virulent strain emerged. The Nevada USAMRIID lab was asked to collaborate, and soon after, a black operation was born."

"A black op, as in nobody outside the Fallon lab knew what was happening within the Fallon lab," Strahan added.

"Yes. Our goal was to weaponize a coronavirus species unique to a region of the world so, once deployed, the country of origin would be implicated as the source of the epidemic, and Neville wanted a vaccine should the epidemic turn into a pandemic. That program spawned the Middle East Respiratory Syndrome."

Philip Tang paused to sip his drink, then continued. "Neville led the gain-of-function research, and an army captain, Mark Wallace, led vaccine development. The goal was to upregulate the MERS-CoV virus found in the dromedary camels of Saudi Arabia, hoping it would jump to humans and decimate the Middle East. The virus did cross over, and it had a mortality rate of thirty percent, but like SARS it was not very transmissible, resulting in only eighty-six deaths. This was in 2012. When I joined—"

A burst of female laughter erupted outside Ophelia's door, followed by more laughing and giggling as the girls continued down the corridor.

Once the noise had subsided, Philip Tang said, "When I joined the lab a year later, interest in MERS had waned and the focus had shifted to a novel coronavirus found in Chinese bats. So same thing, different virus. Neville went to work adding function, Mark Wallace developed a revolutionary vaccine that could be administered covertly to large populations, and their work culminated in a highly contagious bioweapon and a means to control it. And by then, they had the right president in the White House to green light the deployment of the operation."

"CoVid19 has killed hundreds of thousands of Americans. What happened with the vaccine? Did it fail?" Strahan asked.

"No. Only Fallon and greater Churchill County were vaccinated, as a test of both the drug and the delivery system. That's why there has not been a single case here."

"If you have an effective vaccine," Strahan said, "why is it being withheld?"

"Based on our animal studies, Neville knew CoVid19 would spread easily, but it would not achieve the mortality rate he desired, so he added function to 19 and developed 23."

"You're losing me again," David said.

"The US released CoVid19 in Wuhan," Philip Tang replied, "and allowed it to spread around the world, even into the United States, to bolster the assertion that the pandemic originated in China. And while 19 has been spreading, the US population has been secretly vaccinated against 23. Very soon, drones will spread CoVid23 over Wuhan, and as it gains a foothold there, other Chinese cities will be infected. Then they'll do the same in the Middle East and Russia, and within weeks to months all enemies of the US will be crippled, if not decimated. Before 23 moves into nations allied with the West, the president will announce that his team of scientists have developed a revolutionary vaccine, and he'll share it with them."

"Let's see," David leaning back and rubbing his chin in a mocking fashion, "Canada's been a good neighbor, and we like India and South America. Now, Mexico—"

"Look," Tang said, "I don't know about the politics, but I do know the engineered RNA of both strains will be traceable to China, the world will blame them for a botched bioweapons experiment, and the United States will slow down, and eventually halt, both pandemics, making the president look like a hero."

"While creating a new world order," David added. He glanced at Ophelia, wondering if she was paying attention to the crazy talk going on near the foot of her bed.

"How do you know all this?" Vince Strahan asked. "You're a private contractor with—I presume—a low-level security clearance. It doesn't seem plausible that you'd be aware of a black ops conspiracy involving the highest levels of government and the military."

"Captain Wallace, Neville's next in command. He told me everything."

"Why would he tell you?" David asked.

"We also developed two lines of monoclonal antibodies to treat vaccine nonresponders that contract 19 or 23, and we've been testing them on human subjects in the lab."

"The woman in the fence," Strahan said.

"And you're okay with this?" David added.

"No, I'm not," Tang replied, voice rising, body tensing. "That's why I'm here, risking my life, and that's why Mark Wallace is likely buried in the desert. Once he witnessed the destructive power of what he helped create, he had a crisis of consciousness and wanted to blow the whistle. He didn't trust anyone in the military, so he made contact with an intelligence agent and was going to smuggle incriminating materials out of the lab, but then he disappeared. You"—Tang said directly to David—"were going to serve as the conduit."

"What?" David said. "How am I now involved in this?"

"Mark was waiting for you to arrive in Fallon. He was going to tell you everything and start passing off documents and files, whatever he could get his hands on."

"When did Wallace disappear?"

"Just over a month ago."

"I've only been here three weeks. How could he have known about me, let alone earmarked me as an accomplice?"

"I don't know, but he became increasingly paranoid and told me if anything happened to him, I was to find you, that you also had an intelligence contact who could be trusted."

"Look," David said, "I find the idea of testing a biowarfare agent on unsuspecting US citizens absurd, and if it really is happening, then I find it abhorrent, but I don't know anyone who could intervene in a conspiracy sanctioned by high-level members of the military and maybe even the president. It's up to the state board of health to investigate this cluster of unprecedented deaths, and if they find something other than an environmental agent—like drones flying around and spraying people with viruses—let them kick it up the ladder." David stood, picked up his glass, and finished the remainder of the bourbon. "And regarding the idea that the president of the United States is engaged in a scorched-earth conspiracy to take over the world"—he placed the empty glass on the table—"when you get some hard evidence, let me know. Now, if you'll excuse me, we're done here."

David went over to the bed, thanked Ophelia for the use of her room, and added, "If you or your mother need anything, come see me at the hospital."

"Okay," Ophelia said, "but if all this is true, promise me one thing: you will make somebody pay for killing my sister."

- 22 -

Strahan's Jeep rumbled down Highway 50 on the way back to Fallon. After ten miles of silence, the lieutenant turned toward David. "You don't believe Philip Tang, do you?"

"No, I don't," David replied.

"A lot of what he said made sense, don't you think?"

"A crucial component of any conspiracy theory. The greater the number of facts you can throw in, the more believable it sounds."

"But all those facts explain what's happening—the pandemic, the absence of cases here, the army and navy drawing blood from everyone in the county, twenty cases of a rare fatal hemoptysis—and I saw Philip Tang inside the highly secured area of a BSL-4 military lab. He'd have a front row seat to what's really going on in there."

"He's a private contractor. You think this badass colonel is going to share his plans to take over the world with a civilian?"

"Mark Wallace confided in Tang precisely because he is private and not military."

"Look," David said, "I just don't believe the US military would have the audacity to test a biowarfare agent and vaccine on its own citizens without their knowledge. And as far as the president of the United States signing off on the preemptive use of a bioweapon that could end the world, that's the stuff of Robert Ludlum novels and James Bond movies."

"Considering how Silas Bell wants to isolate this country and how he takes a daily shit on the rest of the world, I actually think the scenario is plausible."

Truth be told, the unexplained deaths of twenty people in a town of eight thousand had been nagging at David. Add to that the horrific death of a woman within a US Army installation, and Mr. White's relocation of David to within miles of that installation so he could act as a conduit for evidence exposing a conspiracy? On the surface it seemed preposterous, but upon closer examination it defied coincidence. David had no choice but to agree with Strahan and accept Philip Tang's conspiracy theory as plausible. But there was no way David could get involved. He was a fugitive, and he could not put himself in the spotlight by trying to blow the lid off a world-domination plot involving the president of the United States—not without hard evidence, anyway.

David turned toward Strahan. "Like I said before, I think we're dealing with an environmental agent of some sort. There are countless allergens and toxins, and even cancers that can enter the lymphoid system and induce an inflammatory response."

Strahan looked over at David. "Then why don't we see this all the time?"

David shrugged. "I don't know."

"And why would some random guy concoct an outrageous story and formulate an elaborate plan to meet secretly in a brothel with the new surgeon in town?"

"Who knows. Maybe he wanted to impress Ophelia. Maybe they're boyfriend and girlfriend."

David's phone rang. He lifted his head off the pillow and checked the time. Two in the morning. It had to be the hospital. Fortunately, the end of the drinking had coincided with the departure from the Kitty Ranch, and he had hydrated once he came home, so his head was clear.

"Dr. Aaronson," he said into the phone.

"Hi, Doctor." It was Gina from the surgical team. She was speaking quietly, and her voice was muffled as though she had her hand cupped over her mouth. "I'm so sorry to bother you, but we have an unstable patient on the table that we're prepping and draping for an emergency laparotomy, and I don't think Dr. Pennington should do this case."

"Why is the patient unstable?"

"Dr. Pennington thinks we're dealing with internal hemorrhaging."

"Did he get a CT scan?"

"No. We rushed her up here from the emergency department."

"And why don't you think Pennington should do the case?"

"He's drunk. I mean weaving-and-slurring-his-words drunk. He's never been this bad."

"Christ," David said.

"Look," Gina said, "I know we treat all of our patients the same, but if something happens to this girl—"

"Yeah, I know. Have six units of blood ready, set up the cell saver, and do whatever you can to get Pennington out of the way. I don't want to deal with the guy when I get there."

- 24 -

Nine minutes later David walked into OR 4. The anesthesiologist was inflating a pressure bag around a unit of blood. The respiratory tech was placing another pressure bag around a second unit—never a good sign. Nor were the alarms pinging and chirping. The patient was prepped and draped, but even from the doorway David could see the abdominal distension, which mimicked a five-month pregnancy.

The anesthesiologist: "Better hurry, David. She's crashing on us."

David: "She did have a negative beta-HCG, right?"

Gina: "Yes. She's not pregnant."

David: "Do you have a cell saver ready?"

Gina: "Yes."

David stepped out to the scrub sink and scrubbed his hands for about ten seconds, as opposed to the usual five minutes, then returned to the room and quickly gowned and gloved. As he moved up to the table: "Have a ton of laparotomy sponges ready."

Maria had scrubbed in and stood across from David in the first assistant position. "You operate the cell saver," he said to her.

The cell saver was a handheld suction device, but instead of suctioning the blood into a canister for disposal, the blood was collected in a sterile fashion in the presence of an anticoagulant. It was then bagged and transfused back into the patient, minimizing the amount of donor transfusion.

Maria grabbed the suction cannula.

Gina handed David a number ten scalpel.

David looked over the drape at Evan Mitchell, the anesthesiologist. "Are you ready? As soon as I open, her pressure is going to bottom out."

"I'm ready," Evan replied.

David made an incision from the sternum to the suprapubic region, cutting through skin, a thin layer of fat, and down to the midline fascia—the dense connective tissue that gives the abdominal wall its tensile strength. He traded the scalpel for the electrocautery device and quickly buzzed the larger bleeders in the skin and fat, then looked at Maria. "I'm going to make an opening just large enough for my finger and your suction tip. As soon as I do, blood's gonna pour out. Get as much of it as you can."

David used the cautery to open a hole in the midline fascia. Dark venous blood, most likely from the spleen or liver, gushed out as he slipped his finger inside the abdominal cavity.

Maria inserted her suction tip through the opening, the device gurgling and spitting as blood filled the tubing and emptied into the canister.

David lifted his finger, tenting up the fascia away from the internal organs, then opened the abdominal cavity the same length as the skin incision.

Blood poured onto the floor, the cell saver unable to keep up.

David to Maria: "Get a another suction in here."

David to Gina: "Lap sponges, two or three at a time."

David looking over the drape at Evan: "How's she doing?"

"Her pressure is down, but she's responding to fluid boluses."

"Okay. We'll have her packed off in a minute, and you'll be able to catch up."

When unfolded, laparotomy sponges were the size of small dish towels and very absorbent. The idea was to pack off each quadrant of the abdomen—right upper and left upper quadrants first, anticipating a splenic or liver injury—then the lower quadrants. Not only did the sponges soak up the blood, but when packed tightly, they also created pressure on whatever may be bleeding, thus slowing the blood loss and improving visualization.

Once the abdomen had been packed and the bleeding controlled, David placed the ring for a Bookwalter retractor around the incision and attached several retractor blades to the ring, exposing the abdominal cavity. With exposure maximized, David removed the sponges from the lower quadrants one at a time, examining the nearby organs as he did so. He found no bleeding or injuries in the lower half of the abdomen, so he turned his attention to the upper abdomen.

"I'm going to unpack the upper quadrants," David said to Evan. "Are you caught up with your blood replacement?"

"Yes. Her pressure is good."

"Okay. We'll start with the right side."

David carefully removed the blood-soaked sponges from around the liver and other organs in the right upper quadrant. No active bleeding was noted, which meant the injury was in the left upper quadrant, and judging by the amount of blood seen when they opened, the spleen was the likely culprit.

After adjusting the retractor blades, David started removing the laps. They were soaked with blood and caked with clot. He turned to Gina. "Have a curved Kelly clamp ready."

As David removed the last couple of laps, the bleeding started again. He slipped his hand around the back of the spleen and used his fingers to bluntly dissect the thin layers of connective tissue that held the organ in place. He then lifted it into the surgical field. Normally, the spleen would fill the palm of a hand, like a softball cut in half. This one was the size of a football—massive spleno-megaly—and it was mostly a gelatinous clump of clot with areas of active bleeding. The enlarged spleen had ruptured.

"Kelly clamp," David said to Gina.

She placed the clamp in his right hand while he used his left to retract the organ and put the splenic vessels under slight tension. Once he identified the splenic artery and vein, he clamped them. Now all he had to do was ligate several short gastric arteries, the spleen's secondary blood supply, and all blood flow to the organ would be cut off.

When David tied off the last of the short gastrics, the bleeding stopped. He divided the splenic vessels with a pair of Metzenbaum scissors, lifted the spleen from the surgical field, and placed it into a pan.

"How's she doing?" David asked the anesthesiologist.

"Holding her own."

"How many donor units has she had?"

"Four of packed red cells."

"Okay," David said. "Let's try not to give any more blood until we see what we're gonna get from the cell saver." He turned to Gina. "I'll need a Jackson-Pratt drain in a minute."

David tied off the splenic vessels with heavy silk ties, reinforced the ties with 0-silk sutures, then removed the Kelly clamp. He checked and rechecked for residual bleeding, found none, then irrigated the abdominal cavity with several liters of warm saline. And finally, he tried to identify the tail of the pancreas.

The splenic artery and vein travel very close to, and often within, the pancreas, and it was not unusual for the tail of the pancreas to extend to the hilum of the spleen. A common complication of emergency splenectomy was clamping, and then ligating, part of the pancreatic tail along with the vessels. As was usually the case with severe abdominal bleeding, all the tissues in the area were now swollen with edema fluid and discolored by blood, and it was hard to differentiate pancreatic tissue from other soft tissues. Thus, the reason for the Jackson-Pratt drain. If the tail of the pancreas had been injured, the digestive enzymes produced by the gland would drain through the Jackson-Pratt instead of accumulating in the abdominal cavity and wreaking havoc. David situated the perforated end of the drain near the ligated splenic vessels, then drove the spiked end out through the anterior abdominal wall. Using a small silk suture, he secured the drain tube to the skin a few inches from the incision, then cut the spike from the exterior tubing and attached a bulb that would provide gentle suction once the wound was closed.

After he cauterized any residual bleeders, Gina handed David an 0-Prolene stitch for the closure of the fascial layer and asked him if he wanted to close the skin with staples.

"How old is she?" he asked.

"Twenty-six."

For a young woman, most surgeons would close the incision with a running subcuticular stitch—a continuous suture that runs beneath the skin. The remaining scar is a single thin line as opposed to the railroad track that staples leave behind.

"I'll do a subcuticular closure," David replied.

After the skin was closed and the wound dressed, David started taking down the surgical drapes. As he uncovered the patient's face, he recoiled in shock. "Holy shit," he said.

"What's wrong?" Gina asked.

"This is Nova Featherstone."

"You know her?"

"I just met her Saturday night."

"Do you know who her father is?"

"Apparently he's some badass called Two Feathers."

"Badass is an understatement. I know you did your best here tonight, but we all better hope to God she comes through this okay."

David turned to Lori, the circulating nurse. Keeping family members updated as the case proceeded was her responsibility. "Is her father in the waiting room?"

"Yes," she replied.

"And her mother?" David asked.

"She doesn't have one," Gina said.

"Okay." David stripped out of his gown and gloves. "I'll go out and speak to him while you guys get her ready for transport."

"I should go with you," Gina said.

"Why?"

"I know the guy."

- 25 -

It was now 4:00 a.m. The surgery waiting room was empty except for three Native American men wearing faded jeans, cowboy boots, and sleeveless denim biker vests. They jumped up as David and Gina walked in. There was no question as to which man was Two Feathers. He towered over the others by six or seven inches, and he pretty much fit the description Vince Strahan had offered—powerfully built, dark skinned, long jet-black hair braided into a ponytail, a ten-inch Buck knife hanging from his belt.

David went over and held out his hand. "I'm Dr. David Aaronson, the surgeon who operated on your daughter."

"What happened to her?" Two Feathers said, making no effort to shake David's hand.

"Her spleen ruptured, and she bled into her abdominal cavity—a life-threatening amount of bleeding. I removed the spleen, which stopped the hemorrhage."

"What causes that?"

"Trauma is the leading cause, with motor vehicle accidents being the most—"

"What about hitting someone in the stomach?"

"Yes, but your daughter's spleen was massively enlarged. It most likely ruptured spontaneously."

Two Feathers' large biceps and forearms started tightening, his hands balling into fists. "Is she gonna be okay?"

"She's stable right now."

He nodded at the other two men. "Let's go."

"Where're you going, Billy?" Gina asked with an edge in her voice.

Two Feathers pushed David aside and started to leave.

Gina moved in front of him. "You can't do this. You don't know what happened to Nova. Dr. Aaronson said the spleen probably ruptured on its own."

"I don't care what the white doctor says. I know what happened." Two Feathers looked at one of the other men, "We're gonna need your truck," and then back at Gina, "now get the fuck out of my way."

David moved a chair next to Nova Featherstone's bed and sat down, then pulled a second chair in front of him and propped up his legs. Nova had been extubated, her vital signs were stable, she was making a lot of urine, and the output from the Jackson-Pratt drain was negligible. With the help of a morphine drip, she was sleeping quietly.

Jeannie, this week's night shift nurse, handed David a couple of blankets. "Fresh out of the blanket warmer," she said.

"Thank you," David replied. He wrapped one around his shoulders and draped the other over his legs.

"You haven't done this before," Jeannie said, "sleep at your patient's bedside. Do you have a special interest in this young lady?"

"She almost bled to death on the table and received multiple units of blood. You know the long list of potential complications she's facing—kidney failure, pulmonary edema, pneumonia. I just want to keep a close eye on her."

"Of course, Doctor."

- 27 -

At a tiny cracker-box house with a dirt front yard, the house indistinguishable from the other yardless cracker boxes on the reservation, Two Feathers kicked in the front door with his size-thirteen boot. The scrawny meth head passed out on the couch didn't even move until Two Feathers grabbed him by his hair and yanked him into a standing position.

The kid's eyes widened with terror.

Two Feathers drilled his giant fist into the tweaker's stomach, dropping him to the ground like dead weight. "The last time you hit Nova, I told you I'd kill you if you ever did it again."

"I didn't—"

Two Feathers kicked him in the ribs.

The kid clutched his side. "Please ... Billy," he said, grunting and trying to catch his breath, "we haven't ... seen each other ... for months."

"You know what to do," Two Feathers said to the other men.

One of them stuffed a dirty sock into the kid's mouth and duct-taped it. The other zip-tied his hands and feet together. Using the bound extremities as handles, they carried him out front and threw him into the back of a pickup truck.

- 28 -

On the back side of Table Mountain, deep inside a box canyon, the boy was taken from the bed of the pickup truck and thrown onto the ground. He writhed and moaned, kicking up a cloud of dust that wafted through the truck's headlights.

Two Feathers slipped his Buck knife from its sheath and walked over to the boy, ripped the duct tape off his face, and cut the zip ties binding his hands and feet.

The boy rose to his knees. "Please, Billy. I didn't—"

Two Feathers threw a shovel at the kid. "Start digging."

"C'mon, Billy. I swear I didn't hit her."

"Dig!"

"Please, Billy—"

Two Feathers reached inside his vest, pulled his Glock 31 from his shoulder harness, and shot the kid between the eyes.

Steve Nutomo, the owner of the truck, picked up the shovel. "Shit, Billy. When're you actually gonna make one of these assholes dig their own grave? You got no patience."

"Deeper this time," Two Feathers said. "I don't want the coyotes digging him up."

Jerry Wamblee, the other man, grabbed a second shovel from the back of the pickup.

Two Feathers leaned against the truck, then peered into the bed, something catching his eye. "What's the blood from? It's not the kid's. All we did back at the house was beat him."

"Dangerous Dan dropped a pronghorn from thirty yards last night with his bow," Jerry Wamblee said.

"Bullshit. Nobody gets within thirty yards of a pronghorn, not even Dangerous Dan. Those fuckers see, smell, and hear everything for miles. That's why they live out in the open. A mule deer? A bull elk? Maybe, but even Dan ain't gonna get that close to a pronghorn antelope."

"I seen it, Billy. A single arrow right through the pump. Dropped it right where it stood. No tracking it through the brush or nothing."

A large scorpion scampered through the light given off by the truck. Two Feathers walked over and stomped it with his boot and twisted his foot as if putting out a cigarette, driving the crushed arachnid deep into the parched soil.

David was awakened by the morning sun shining through the windows of the ICU. He climbed out of the chair, stretched, and glanced at his patient. Nova Featherstone was sleeping peacefully, bed raised to forty-five degrees, the blanket and top sheet folded back across her chest and tucked in tight at her sides. He picked up her hands one at a time and felt each of them between his. He then uncovered her feet and felt her toes. Her distal extremities were warm and well perfused—a reliable sign that her cardiac output was good. He walked over to the computer monitor that displayed her vital signs, urine output, drain output, blood gas results, and updated lab work. Everything was within normal range. Melissa, the day shift nurse walked up beside him.

"Has she been awake at all?" David asked.

"She stirred a couple of times, but not yet fully awake," Melissa said. "Why don't you go home and take a nap. We all know who this is. We'll take good care of her."

David did not have any cases scheduled, Nova was his only ICU patient, and the handful of ward patients on the surgery service were doing well. "I think I'll do that. Thanks."

- 30 -

By 11:00 a.m. David was back in the ICU, freshly showered, wearing a shirt and tie under his white coat, bolstered by a couple hours of sleep. Nova was sitting in a chair, clutching a pillow to her chest and abdomen. A face mask delivered 30 percent oxygen to her nose and mouth. The cardiac monitor silently traced her heart rhythm. Her eyes were at half-mast, the result of a long, difficult operation and a morphine drip. He approached, and when she recognized him her eyes widened a little and she smiled. She tried to speak, but her words were garbled by the face mask.

David removed the mask and let it hang around her neck. "Good morning, Nova," he said, taking one of her hands in his. "How are you feeling?"

"Okay, I guess." Her speech was soft and slow, morphine and exhaustion. "The nurse said I almost bled to death, and you saved me."

David moved a chair next to hers and sat down. "You were in pretty rough shape when you came in, but the surgical team did a fantastic job."

"What do you think happened?"

"Your spleen was enlarged, and I believe it spontaneously ruptured. We'll have to wait for the pathologist to determine why that happened. For now, all you have to worry about is keeping your lungs clear. That's why we have you up in a chair, and when the nurse asks you to cough and take deep breaths on your incentive spirometer I want you to do the best you can. Pneumonia is your biggest enemy right now."

"Okay, Dr. Aaronson," Nova said, sounding very much like a compliant ten-year-old.

"Good," David said. "I'm never far away. If you need anything, the nurse knows how to find me." David stood. "Will you lean forward? I'd like to listen to your lungs."

With the help of the nurse, Nova Featherstone leaned forward in the chair, grimacing as she did so. David opened the back of her gown, and after blowing on the diaphragm of his stethoscope to warm it, he placed it first on her lower back—left side, right side—then mid and upper back, asking her to take a deep breath at each position. He then had her sit back and listened to her heart. As he coiled his stethoscope and returned it to the pocket of his white coat, he said, "Your heart sounds fine, but there is congestion in your lungs, which is common after an extensive abdominal operation. It will be very important for you to cough and breathe deeply when the nurse asks you to."

"Okay," Nova said. She looked up and gave him a dreamy smile. "I'll do my best."

"Very good. I'll check on you later."

As David exited the ICU, he was startled by a hulking figure leaning against the wall across from the door.

Two Feathers.

He stepped toward David, looming over him. "I don't like the way you put your hands all over my daughter, and I don't like the way she looks at you like a long-lost puppy."

"First of all," David said, "I'm her physician and surgeon, and it's important for me to examine her, which means I have to touch her. Second, she's on a morphine drip for pain control, and that's why she has a dreamy puppy dog look on her face. And third, don't ever come into my hospital, put your hands on me in front of my nurses like you did last night, or tell me how to take care of my patients. Now," David said, "if you want to know how your daughter is doing, I'll be happy to update you. Otherwise, you can get the fuck out of *my* way."

- 31 -

David continued down the hall, leaving Two Feathers and the ICU behind him. After rounding the corner, he ducked into the surgeon's lounge and took a seat at the table, his body still trembling, but not with fear. He wasn't afraid. He had killed two men—injecting one with a lethal dose of potassium chloride and shooting the other in the head—and murder changes a person. So it wasn't fear. It was anger. How dare that ignorant fuck come in here and interfere in the care of his own daughter, who was less than twelve hours out from a complicated surgery and was by no means out of the woods.

David leaned back in the chair and glanced up at the always-on-and-tuned-to-CNN television hanging on the wall: *The Situation Room* with Wolf Blitzer.

The doorknob clicked. David turned. It was Pennington—shirt and tie, white coat, large Styrofoam cup of coffee in his hand, looking bright eyed for someone who could barely stand just hours ago. He sat down across from David.

"How's the girl?" Pennington asked.

"She'll be fine. She has youth on her side."

"I heard you found a massive spleen. Spontaneous rupture?"

"I think so. It was pretty friable, and nothing in her history indicates a traumatic event. The father thinks she was hit in the stomach, and as soon as I told him she was stable, he and his cronies blew out of here half-cocked. God knows what that was all about."

"Ah yes," Pennington said. "The father, one bad hombre. She have any risk factors for splenomegaly?"

"Not that I can determine."

Pennington offered no follow-up, staring into the rim of his coffee cup as he took a sip.

David watched him, an uncomfortable silence building.

Then, "About last night," Pennington said.

"Yeah. About last night," David countered.

"I'm sorry. Obviously unacceptable."

"Next time," David said, "call me before you're prepped and draped. In fact, call me before you leave your house. Better yet, call me when you are pouring your third drink."

Pennington stared into his cup for a moment, then looked up and said, "Fair enough."

- 32 -

That afternoon, David went down to the first floor to staff the surgery clinic. Two thirds of the scheduled patients were postops. The remaining one third were referrals for a variety of surgical problems like hernias, gallstones, skin lesions, and a young man with a mass on his right kidney.

With just a few patients remaining, David removed a chart from the plexiglass holder next to the door. Attached to the intake sheet was a yellow Post-it note that read, "Jimmy Miller's parents, would like to talk to Dr. Aaronson." David felt uneasy about this. Pennington had been the primary surgeon on the case, not David, so why had they come to see him?

When someone died in the operating room—particularly a young person—grieving parents, spouses, or other family members were often left with unanswered questions, and unanswered questions often festered into suspicion, which planted the seeds for a lawsuit. In this context, it was not unheard of for parents, spouses, or family to try to glean information from all possible sources: Did the surgeon do everything possible? Could anything have been done differently? Do you think the outcome could have been different? Believing that most lawsuits stemmed from a poor understanding of what happened, poor communication by the surgeon, and a perceived lack of compassion, David's plan going in was to offer some kind words, reassure Mr. and Mrs. Miller that everything possible had been done to save Jimmy, and explain anything they might not understand. Explain, reassure, empathize—these three simple acts usually satisfied a grieving family. David knocked and entered the room.

The Millers stood, each forcing thin smiles conveying both pain and humility. These were not grieving parents looking to punish the doctors who failed to save their son. These were two souls suffering from an immense mortal wound that would never heal, and as David studied their faces, his own wound tore open, taking him back to the side of that dark New Jersey highway eight months ago, watching his pregnant wife take her final breaths, a dreamy look on her face, tears glistening in her eyes, a steering wheel grotesquely deforming her sternum. And he heard her final words, punctuated by her gasping efforts to breath: "They're ... chasing me. Please ... David ... you have to go." David blinked hard, trying to stem the tears that wanted to form, then he said hello and introduced himself, the words not coming easily.

Mr. Miller reciprocated David's greeting. He was a weather-beaten man—his face a complex of deep wrinkles, the skin on the back of his neck thick and darkly pigmented—but add to that the grief and confusion surrounding the death of his son, and he looked like a bone-weary seventy-year-old trapped in the body of a forty-year-old.

The same could be said for Mrs. Miller. She had probably always been a thin woman, but *gaunt* was the word that came to mind. The fatigued posture, dark sunken eye sockets, and borderline emaciation were the same features seen in late-stage cancer patients.

David felt their pain as intensely as he was feeling his own. The three of them had lost something irreplaceable, and right now, for the Millers, the wound was deep and still bleeding. For David, his wounds remained raw, but at least the bleeding had slowed. He moved a chair close to theirs. They all sat down.

"We're sorry to take up your valuable time, Dr. Aaronson," Mr. Miller said, "but my wife and I ... well, we just don't know where to go from here. Jimmy has been buried, and we had a beautiful service, but now we're just kinda lost. I think we need some answers, because we don't understand what happened, and we're hoping you can help us."

"I'm happy to do what I can," David said, "but Dr. Pennington was the primary surgeon. Did he explain what we found during surgery and the cause of Jimmy's death?"

"He told us that something caused inflammation in Jimmy's chest, and this resulted in a connection between a big blood vessel and one of the main breathing tubes, but what caused the inflammation? What caused those two things to connect? He didn't tell us."

David explained how the surgical findings were unusual, that neither he nor Pennington, or the pathologist, had seen anything like this. "We're having a hard time figuring out the etiology—the root cause—of the inflammation. There are twenty patients in Fallon who have died from the same thing," David added.

"We know," Mr. Miller said, "which is why we're here. This has been going on for months, and there are other families in our position, but none of them knows any more than we do. Nobody has answers—not the coroner's office, not the state board of health, nobody."

"Dr. Pennington has spoken to the coroner on several occasions. She is aware that we're waiting for Jimmy's results, as well as the reports for the other cases."

"In the meantime," Mr. Miller said, "this town is being taken over by whispers and gossip. People think these deaths are related to the coronavirus, and the families who have lost loved ones are being treated like lepers. I can't even go to the feed store without being shunned by folks I've known all my life. And Mrs. Miller? She can't hardly leave the house to go shopping. None of her friends want anything to do with her. All this makes for pretty rough going in a small town."

"I'm not sure I can do anything," David said. "We have to wait for the coroner to determine the cause of death for these cases."

"Maybe you could make an announcement. Tell everyone this is not the coronavirus. You're not a Podunk surgeon from a Podunk town. You got your training in San Francisco. You have big-city experience. People will listen to you."

"I appreciate your faith in me," David replied, "but until we determine the cause of these unusual deaths, I can't make a public statement."

Mr. Miller leaned back in his chair and stared into his lap, disappointed, defeated, forlorn.

"I'm sorry," David said.

Once the Millers had gone, David did not jump up to go see the next patient. Instead, he sat for a moment, considering the Miller's request. For the second time in as many days, David had been asked to involve himself in something that seemed very big and very important, and for the second time in as many days, David refused the call to action. But what choice did he have? He had no facts, no evidence of a grand conspiracy. He didn't even have a pathology report. The dead townspeople were real. The young man whose pulmonary artery he'd ripped open was real. The bleeding woman in the fence was real. Were all these events connected? Seemed likely. Was Philip Tang's story plausible? Maybe. Was it David's job to unravel the mystery? No. He was a surgeon, not an epidemiologist. He worked for his patients, not the state medical board or the CDC. Was he in a position to kick the ant pile and, in the process, call attention to himself? Absolutely not. He was a fugitive, living under a rock, and he was not going to be the one to turn over that rock. Despite his convincing argument, as David stood and headed for the next room, he did not feel good about himself.

- 33 -

David's ward patients were doing well, so he concluded his evening rounds in the ICU. Nova Featherstone looked great for someone who'd been through major abdominal surgery no more than sixteen hours ago—the power of youth, indeed. She was sitting up in bed, a pillow clutched to her abdomen and chest. The face mask had been replaced with a nasal cannula, and the oxygen regulator bubbled softly in the background. The various monitors indicated all vital signs were normal, and her hair had been braided. The braids were intricate and adorned with a series of small feathers. She must have had a visitor.

Her face brightened as David approached. He went to her bedside and took her hand in his. Nice and warm and well perfused.

"Hi, Dr. Aaronson," she said with a smile.

David returned the smile. "Hi, Nova. How are you?"

"Okay, I guess, but really tired. And this tube in my nose, it's uncomfortable."

"I know. I wish I could remove it, but it will have to stay until your intestines wake up and start functioning. I'm afraid ice chips and sips of water are the only things we can give you until then. Your pain is under good control?"

Nova said yes and lifted her other hand, which held the button for the patient-controlled anesthesia machine.

"Good," David said. He took the stethoscope from the pocket of his white coat. With the help of the nurse, David leaned Nova forward and listened to her lungs. Then he lowered the bed flat, positioned the linens so she was covered from the waist down, and slid her gown up to just below her breasts. If Two Feathers were witnessing *this*, he'd probably take out his Buck knife and plant it between David's shoulder blades.

The abdominal-wound dressing, and the dressing around the pancreatic drain were both clean and dry. The suction bulb for the drain had a small amount of serous drainage, which was normal. David listened for bowel sounds but heard nothing, as expected. When the GI tract gets manhandled, it can take a day or two to start functioning again.

He put his stethoscope into his pocket and returned the bed to forty-five degrees. "Your lungs are still a little congested," he said, "so we'll keep you in the chair and upright in your bed as much as possible. I didn't hear any bowel sounds, but hopefully they'll return soon and we can start you on some liquids. Your urinary catheter can come out this evening, and tomorrow morning I'll remove the dressing from your wound. The drain will stay in for another few days, but it shouldn't cause you any pain. And also, we'll get you up and walking tomorrow. It will be good for your lungs, and it will help prevent blood clots from forming in your leg veins."

"Okay," Nova said in her compliant-patient voice.

"So you have a good night, and I'm never far away if you need anything."

"Thank you," Nova said. "You have a good night too, Dr. Aaronson."

David was about to turn and leave when something on the nightstand caught his eye—a large medallion and a maroon velvet pouch, both sitting near a vase of flowers. David went over and took a closer look. The medallion was circular, about the size of his palm, and divided into quadrants inlaid with gems of four colors—black, white, yellow, and red. Around the outer border a bear, wolf, buffalo, and eagle had been engraved, corresponding to each quadrant. From the bottom of the medallion hung two sterling silver feathers.

"May I?" David asked.

"Yes," Nova replied.

David picked up the medallion by its chain and examined it closely.

"It's a Shoshone medicine talisman," Nova said. "The different colors and animals represent spiritual, emotional, physical, and mental health."

"Beautiful," David said as he placed it back on the table. "And the pouch?"

"A medicine bag. It holds things sacred to me and the tribe. I can't tell you what's inside, or it will lose its power, but the idea of the talisman and pouch are to help me fight the disease or sickness that got me here. My tribal sisters brought those, and they've been praying for you and the staff."

"We appreciate it," David said. "We can use all the help we can get. Now, get some rest, and I'll see you in the morning."

"Okay," Nova said with a radiant smile.

- 34 -

The following morning—postop day one, David wrote in his progress notes—he transferred Nova to the ward. The congestion in her lungs had improved, the drain output was minimal, bowel sounds had returned, and she was able to walk with assistance. He wrote orders to discontinue her IV fluids and NG tube, and to start her on a liquid diet, then he headed for the operating room.

He was about two hours into a left hemicolectomy for a stage-one colon cancer when the OR phone rang. A few moments later, the circulating nurse came over to the operating table. "Dr. Aaronson," she said, "that was the head nurse on the second floor. Nova Featherstone's father just took Miss Featherstone from the hospital against medical advice. They tried to stop him, but there wasn't anything they could do."

David looked up at the nurse. "Are you kidding me?"

"No, Doctor. He put her in a wheelchair, rolled her out to the parking lot, and drove away with her."

David shook his head in disgust, then looked at Gina. "You know where the ignorant bastard lives?"

"Yes," Gina said, "but you really shouldn't go there. The reservation is Two Feathers' domain. You won't be safe."

"I don't care. That girl is my patient, and he's putting her at risk for serious complications." David peered into the open abdomen and shook his head again. "Stupid ignorant bastard." Then he looked up at Gina and held out his hand. "Long Metzenbaum scissors."

After the anesthesiologist and circulating nurse had taken the patient to the recovery room, Gina pulled David aside. "Let me go with you," she said.

"You have an afternoon case with Pennington. I can't wait that long."

"Then be careful what you do and say out there, and show Two Feathers at least a tiny bit of respect. He's killed for being called less than the things you said earlier."

An Indian reservation represents an area of land managed by a Native American tribe. Tribal laws do not fall under the state in which it is physically located but rather under the federal authority of the Bureau of Indian Affairs. This complex relationship grants limited sovereignty to the tribes, allowing them to enact their own laws. It was this limited sovereignty that allowed many tribes to legalize gambling and build casinos, which was formally recognized by Congress with the enactment of the Indian Gaming Regulatory Act of 1988. The revenues from these casinos did improve the rampant poverty found in many Native American communities, but the overall percentage of American Indians living below the federal poverty line has remained about 28 percent. In Nevada, where legalized gambling preceded tribal gaming by more than fifty years, there has been no incentive for the investment in and construction of casino resorts on tribal lands. For that reason, 60 percent of the Fallon Paiute-Shoshone tribe live below poverty level.

Indian reservations also struggle with public health issues. Substance abuse and violence occur in epidemic proportions, with Native American males facing a 4,000 percent greater chance of death related to drugs, alcohol, or violence than men in the general population. The incidence of diabetes is 800 percent higher than the national average, and other major illnesses such as kidney failure, cirrhosis of the liver, and vascular disease are also seen with much greater frequency, thus lowering the life expectancy for Native Americans to fifty-five years of age.

Living conditions on many reservations approach what is seen in third world countries. Government-supplied housing quickly falls into disrepair. Heating, cooling, and plumbing may be substandard. Water and power supplies can be unreliable, while streets and other infrastructure in need of repair are ignored. High school graduation rates for Native Americans averages 65 percent, 10 percent lower than the general population, and only 9 percent earn a college degree, compared with the national average of 20 percent. These poor living conditions—along with high unemployment, lack of opportunity, pervasive violence and substance abuse, and the systemic degradation of native languages and traditions—has led to the continued erosion of tribal life. As a result, younger generations of male tribal members often turn to gangs to establish identity and belonging. It was from this violent and depressed milieu on the Fallon Paiute-Shoshone reservation that a leader emerged—Billy Jack Featherstone, tribal name Two Feathers.

Two Feathers' upbringing was not uncommon for a male member of the tribe. Both his mother and father were alcoholics who later became meth addicts. He regularly witnessed the beatings his mother would receive on those nights when she made the mistake of standing up for herself. As the oldest child of four, Two Feathers assumed the responsibility of protecting his mother and siblings and often tried to pull his father off his mother during a violent attack even though he knew where his father would then direct his rage.

Although not the best student, the young Billy Featherstone sought refuge from his father's violence in the reservation library. The tribal name "Two Feathers" was given to the boy in recognition of his mixed ancestry—his mother a Shoshone and his father a Paiute—and at a young age Two Feathers became fascinated with the ancient Shoshone and Paiute tribes and their customs. He read books pertaining to his tribal history and developed a sense of pride for his people and what they had been before the scourge of the European settlers changed their society, and he would seek out the tribe's elders and ask questions. They recounted the long history of lies and abuse suffered by Native Americans at the hands of the US government and suggested he read *Trail of Tears* by John Ehle and *The Heartbeat of Wounded Knee* by David Treuer. He read and reread these books and developed a bitter resentment toward the authority of the federal government and the effect they had upon his culture. As the frequency of his library visits increased, he persuaded the librarian—his Aunt Andrea—to allow him late-night and predawn access. As a young man, and later as a gang member, to be seen using the library would have eroded Two Feathers' growing reputation as someone to be feared. In fact, during his early gang years, he went to great lengths to hide his advanced literacy and intelligence.

When Two Feathers was twelve years old, his mother and father were killed on the Pyramid Lake Highway north of Reno when the truck his father was driving crossed the centerline and ran head-on into a semi tractor trailer. After the accident, Two Feathers and his three sisters were taken in by his mother's brother. His uncle, Rob Lone Elk, and his aunt Andrea already had three children of their own, the five of them stuffed into a small two-bedroom house. Fortunately for Two Feathers and his sisters, Uncle Rob and Aunt Andrea did not drink or do drugs, and between his uncle's job at a tire store and federal subsistence, a basic living was provided. But, having no desire to live his uncle's life and seeing no utility of staying in school, Two Feathers dropped out of ninth grade and joined a gang.

By the time he was eighteen, Two Feathers had been blessed with a lean, muscular build and a tall stature, and even though he lacked a high school education, he was highly intelligent and had developed into a natural leader. At the age of twenty-five, he was ready to take over the "Branded Few" motorcycle gang. In a classic *coup d'état* he assassinated the gang leader White Fox, along with his top lieutenants, and assumed command. After merging with two rival gangs, he formed an "understanding" with the tribal police and built the gang into a lucrative methamphetamine enterprise spanning across northern Nevada and into parts of western Utah. Although the real prize was the Vegas meth trade, he and his gang were no match for the Mexican cartel that controlled most of the Desert Southwest and southern Nevada.

Although Two Feathers was a murderer and ruthless ruler of a drug empire, he was not a sociopath. He would, without hesitation, deliver violence unto those who challenged him, showed him disrespect, or became an impediment to his business. However, he did not kill wantonly or with enjoyment. And he had one inviolable rule that, if broken, carried a sentence of immediate execution: no drugs were to be sold on the reservation or to members of any tribe within his area of distribution. On the Fallon reservation, Two Feathers was the de facto absolute ruler, with his gang functioning as a shadow law enforcement agency. There was a tribal police force run by his cousin Dave, but Dave Humana had sworn complete loyalty to his younger cousin.

The Fallon Paiute-Shoshone Reservation was about ten minutes from the hospital. David felt conspicuous as he drove down the main access road in his black Chrysler 300. The car was appropriate for a physician and surgeon, but out here in the middle of the desert, the impression given off was government agent. Not that there were many eyes on him at the moment. The reservation was mostly wide-open space, acres of sagebrush patchworked with parcels of green farmland, punctuated with the occasional grouping of twenty or so houses—the Stillwater subdivision, the Spruce Trail subdivision.

A few minutes later, David turned into the Eagles Nest neighborhood. The houses were mirror images of each other—single story, one-car garage, probably two or three small bedrooms, single bathroom, family room, kitchen. Each house sat on a large piece of property, unlike back east, where everything was sandwiched together, but there was no landscaping—no lawns, shrubs, flowers, or trees—just dirt and weeds and a smattering of sun-bleached children's toys.

David turned into Bear Paw Court, drove to the end of the cul-de-sac, and parked in the driveway. As he climbed from the car, the ground-shaking *bap-bap-bap* of multiple Harley-Davidson motorcycles shattered the peace. The Harleys, four of them, rolled into the cul-de-sac and parked in a line at the end of the driveway. All four riders wore faded jeans, black leather boots, and denim vests that were frayed where the sleeves had been cut off. None of them wore helmets. Two Feathers leaned his Harley on its kickstand and approached David. The other three men remained seated on their bikes.

"White doctors are not welcome on the rez," Two Feathers said, getting so close to David he could smell booze on the guy's breath.

"I came to take Nova back to the hospital. Bringing her here was foolish."

Two Feathers said nothing, his eyes narrow and focused on David. Then, "The tribal doctor will take care of her."

"Really?" David said. "Does your tribal doctor have experience with pancreatic fistulas? Is he experienced with Jackson-Pratt drains and postop surgical-wound management? Does he know that fourteen days after surgery, Nova needs the Pneumovax vaccine to prevent post-splenectomy sepsis?"

"He's a smart man. He'll know what to do."

"No, he won't," David said, his voice rising. "She hasn't started eating solid food yet, and when she does her pancreas will start pumping out digestive enzymes, and if there's a pancreatic leak it could be disastrous. That's why she needs to be in the hospital where I can watch her, not here by herself while you're out drinking with your buddies."

Two Feathers' eyes blazed. He looked over at his crew and waved them off. They started their Harleys, pushed back from the mouth of the driveway and rumbled out of the cul-de-sac.

When the noise had subsided, Two Feathers turned back to David, eyes still blazing, jaw muscles tightened into knots, the palm of his hand resting on the handle of the Buck knife. "You disrespect me like that again and I will kill you."

"For fuck's sake, I'm just trying to take care of your daughter. Let me take her back to the hospital where she belongs."

An hour later, Nova Featherstone was back on the second floor of the Fallon-Churchill Community Hospital—same room, same bed, same nurses, all of whom were shocked David was able to bring her back. He listened to her lungs, examined her wound and checked the drain, then raised the bed to forty-five degrees. After folding the blanket and sheet across her chest and tucking them neatly at her sides, he moved a chair close to her bedside and sat down. "A dose of pain medication is on the way. I've ordered a clear liquid tray for you—juice, Jell-O, things like that—and maybe tomorrow we'll be able to feed you. Is there anything else I can do?"

Nova tried to smile, but it was more of a grimace. The ride home to the reservation, making her way into and then out of the house, followed by another ride back to the hospital had taken their toll. David instructed the nurses to be liberal with the pain meds.

"I'm okay," she said. "I'm sorry I put you through that, but please be careful around my father. I could tell he wasn't very happy with you."

"We had a good talk. We're cool," David said.

- 36 -

An isolated airstrip in an unnamed desert
Southeastern Kazakhstan, fifty miles from the Chinese border
0200 hours
The inaugural mission of the Night Fury

Despite the 2:00 a.m. hour, the secret airfield bustled with CIA agents, US Army bioweapons scientists, and high-ranking military officers, in addition to a multitude of support staff. The object of their attention—a single Unmanned Aerial Vehicle, commonly referred to as a drone, sitting in a flood of spotlights on the runway. But this was not a run-of-the-mill surveillance or armed tactical drone. This was DARPA's brand-new and most advanced UAV: the HoQA50 Night Fury.

The Night Fury's inaugural mission—the Wuhan flyover—would be straightforward. The Chinese city was three thousand kilometers from the airstrip, had a population of eleven million, and covered an area of nine thousand square kilometers. The Fury would reach its target in thirteen hours, drop its payload of silica-coated virions in a single pass from an altitude of one thousand meters, and return to the airstrip, all without being detected. Within seven days, the first symptoms of a previously unknown viral illness would appear. Within ten days, the city would be decimated.

The real genius of the mission, however, was the silica nano-powder coating each viral particle. Not only did the nanometer-size glass particles give the virus an ultrafine consistency that allowed it to readily dissipate into the air and behave more like a gas than a solid, silicon is the second most common element in the earth's crust. Its precursor, quartzite, can be found anywhere, including the Gobi Desert. The weaponized virus, whose RNA strands already bore signatures unique to its country of origin, was now coated with silica nanopowder also traceable to its base of production—China. And in the coming days and weeks as the Night Fury and dozens of its clones spread the Wuhan Supervirus around the world, the origin of the virus would be irrefutable, and as China, Russia, the Middle East, and any number of America's enemies fell to the viral plague, the world would blame the Wuhan Institute of Virology for a bioweapons experiment gone horribly wrong.

- 37 -

For the next nine days, Nova Featherstone was the ideal patient. She regained bowel function and was quickly advanced to a normal diet. She faithfully used the incentive spirometer, and the congestion in her lungs cleared. The more she walked, the stronger she became, and she was quickly weaned down to a small dose of narcotic analgesics. After several days of eating solid food with no signs of a pancreatic leak, the Jackson-Pratt drain was removed. On postoperative day seven, David removed the subcuticular Prolene suture he had used to close the skin on her abdomen. The scar left behind was minimal, and David predicted that within a year, it would be unnoticeable. A textbook recovery for a patient who had nearly bled to death.

But David's postop care hadn't been limited to checking vitals, labs, and wounds. At the completion of evening rounds, with the demands of the day behind him, he would move a chair next to her bed and spend time with her, talking about life on the reservation, life in a small desert town, life among disparate groups of people—cowboys and Indians, ranchers and farmers, prostitutes and working-class women, meth heads and TOPGUN pilots. Reservation life was not easy, but it was all she knew. Some of the elders, along with her father, looked down on her for having white friends in town, and small-town life was okay, but the opportunities were limited, thus the reason she was a receptionist in a dental office. The TOPGUN guys were too arrogant for her, but her white girlfriends were into them. She once dated a nice boy from the reservation, but he turned into a meth addict. She tried to help him, but he started hitting her, and her father put an end to that relationship.

The prostitutes? Most of them worked in the brothels and kept to themselves. She rarely crossed paths with the few who worked the bars in town.

The most fascinating topic of discussion, however, was the history of the Shoshone people, her mother's ancestral tribe. Nova loved talking about the tribe's origin and early way of life, the gods and spirits in which they believed, then and now, and how the tribe had spread north and east from Nevada and into Idaho, Utah, and over the Rocky Mountains into the western Great Plains. By the mid-1800s the Shoshone were a large, successful nation with many individual tribes, she said. And she was particularly proud that Sacagawea, the daughter of a northern Shoshone chief, had been instrumental in Lewis and Clark's success. But then she spoke with sadness about how the opening of the West to settlers resulted in stolen lands, widespread disease, and wars that all but decimated America's native peoples. "The population of the Fallon Paiute-Shoshone tribe is about six hundred and fifty, and I'm afraid one day we'll just disappear," she told David, the prospect of which he found both unfathomable and heartbreaking.

Every evening he would find that Nova's hair had been done by her tribal sisters during their daytime visits. Sometimes it was braided, sometimes it was pulled back and secured with a clip, and sometimes it cascaded unrestrained down to her waist, but it was always adorned with an assortment of feathers hanging from sterling silver clips. And every night, as David walked out of her room, the same powerful thought entered his mind: *My God, what an exquisite creature.*

On the morning of postop day number ten, it was time to send Nova home. As her physician and surgeon, David had nothing else to offer her. With the exception of a surgical wound that would not tolerate strenuous activity for a while and the ongoing need for small doses of opioid analgesics—to be alternated with nonnarcotic pain meds—Nova had returned to near-baseline health.

As he sat at the nurse's station writing her discharge orders, he summoned the highest levels of stoicism and professionalism he could muster. He had grown quite fond of her and was going to miss her, and it seemed she had grown quite fond of him. Even though their difference in age did not preclude dating, two things did. First, he was her doctor, and she was his patient, and for them to see each other socially would be wholly inappropriate. Second, and more importantly, he was a fugitive from multiple law enforcement agencies. He was settling into a life in Fallon, but by no means was he settled. He could be hauled away to face his past at any moment, so to date Nova Featherstone—and perhaps fall in love with her—only to be suddenly exposed for who and what he really was and then ripped from her life, would not be fair to her. He finished writing the orders, and for the final time he moved a chair next to her bed and sat down.

"You're all set to go," he said. "I know you've been doing very well these last couple of days, but when you get home and start moving around, you'll be easily fatigued. Don't regard this as a setback. It's entirely normal. At the same time, don't spend the next two weeks lying around on the couch. Stay physically active, within reason."

Jesus, he said to himself. After all the scintillating conversations they'd had, he now sounded like an officious old turd. But he could see the corners of her eyes start to glisten with tears, and he knew he had to make their goodbye efficient and to the point, just like any other patient, he reminded himself.

He stood and cupped her hand with both of his. "I'll see you in my clinic in a week, and I'm sure after that our paths will cross, so take care. You know how to find me, and I'm always here for you."

She looked up at him with the same dreamy puppy dog expression he'd seen the morning after surgery, except this time tears were building and would soon run down her cheeks. "Thank you for everything," she said. "The tribe will say a special prayer for you tonight."

"Thank you," David said, nearly choking on the words. Then he turned and walked out of her room, his heart weakening and his eyes watering.

- 38 -

With no cases scheduled and his rounds completed, David figured he would duck into the surgery lounge and use the computer to catch up on his medical records. As he walked in, the graphic across the bottom of the always-on-and-tuned-to-CNN television read, "Wuhan, China, Now Hit by Ebola-Like Disease." David grabbed the remote and turned up the volume, catching Wolf Blitzer in midsentence:

> … *getting reports out of Wuhan, China, that over half of this city of eleven million people have died suddenly over the past couple of days, apparently coughing up massive amounts of blood so violently and quickly that many of them did not even make it to a hospital. And it appears there is a subset of patients who developed massively enlarged spleens that ruptured and caused them to die from internal bleeding. We now go to Shanghai, China, where our Emily Chen is standing by.*

The studio shot cut away to a grainy, glitchy shot of a reporter sitting at a desk in a dimly lit apartment. In voiceover, Wolf Blitzer said:

> *That's pretty scary stuff, Emily. Even the Ebola outbreaks we've reported in the past have not moved as quickly or have been as lethal.*

> Emily Chen: *Scary indeed, Wolf. In fact, the doctors do not think this is related to Ebola or CoVid19, the latter of which has been waning here in China over the past few months with*

only occasional cases reported. The victims of this new outbreak are outwardly doing well and appear healthy until they start coughing up blood as opposed to Ebola patients who show flu-like symptoms for a number of days before the disease fully manifests itself, and even then, only a small percentage of those patients vomit or cough up blood. And this new outbreak is nothing like CoVid19, which is primarily a respiratory disease.

Wolf Blitzer: *If it isn't Ebola or CoVid19, do the doctors have any idea what it might be?*

Emily Chen: *The doctors and health officials I've spoken to have no idea what this new disease might be. They have never seen anything like it. But based on its rapid spread, high infectivity rate, and the apparent lack of physical contact required for transmission, they fear they are dealing with another airborne virus similar to CoVid19 or perhaps even a mutation of that organism. It's also important to note, Wolf, that Wuhan is home to China's only level-four biosafety laboratory, which is part of the Wuhan Institute of Virology, and government officials are already fending off rumors and accusations that this new organism is the result of a failed bioweapons experiment.*

Wolf Blitzer: *The proximity of both viral outbreaks to a government-run viral institute sounds very suspicious, indeed. Emily, you are in Shanghai. How much real-time information are you getting from Wuhan? If five or six million people have died in just a few days, the humanitarian crisis there must be staggering. Has law and order been maintained? Is there a system in place for dealing with that many bodies? Is the already-stressed health-care system still functioning?*

Emily Chen: *Wuhan and the entire Hubei Province are once again on lockdown, and I would add that they are in a media blackout. There are rumors of a massive military response within the province. There is virtually no information coming out. State-run media has acknowledged that a new viral threat exists and has told all citizens of China to resume CoVid19 precautionary measures, but beyond that, there have been few details.*

Wolf Blitzer: *This is a stunning turn of events, Emily. Please stay safe and keep us updated. And thank you for your excellent reporting. In an unrelated story, CIA Director Mike Kelly has abruptly resigned after allegations of an illicit—*

"Holy shit," David said loudly, blotting out the remainder of Wolf Blitzer's report. Then he picked up the phone, called the radiology department, and scheduled a CT scan of the chest for Nova Featherstone—to be performed STAT.

- 39 -

David hurried back to the surgery ward. Nova was still resting in bed, the discharge process usually not implemented until late morning. She smiled as he walked into the room. He forced an uneasy smile of his own and sat down next to her.

"Dr. Aaronson, you're back. You must have missed me," she said.

"I did, but unfortunately this is not a social visit." David explained that he'd been dictating her discharge summary when he came across a chest X-ray report he must have overlooked. The radiologist had noted a small abnormality in one of her lungs. "It's probably nothing," he said, "maybe an area of congestion that hasn't cleared yet, but I think it would be a good idea to get a CT scan of the chest just to make sure. You've done so well, I don't want to send you home with something that could blossom into a pneumonia."

As per the Hippocratic oath, the cardinal rule of medicine was "do no harm." Most physicians would agree that the second-most important rule was "tell no lies." Other than exposing Nova to a small dose of radiation, David was not harming her, but he was lying to her, and he hated himself for it. The alternative, however—telling a young woman she might be harboring an untreatable terminal condition—was far worse. Hippocrates had also mandated that physicians not become emotionally invested in their patients, but the thought that Nova would come into David's life only to be violently taken away—like Cassandra had been—was unbearable. "When I get the results, I'll come back and see you. I don't think this will delay your discharge."

"I'm sure everything is okay," Nova said.

40

With Nova on her way to radiology, David dropped down to the basement to see the hospital's pathologist, Dr. Susan Preston, who also served as the county coroner. The double doors leading to the morgue were unlocked. David let himself in.

The room was spacious, shiny, and new—two autopsy tables, lots of stainless steel cabinets, multiple sinks, and a plethora of counter space. Perhaps the county had dumped some money into the place, a kind of subsidy for a shared facility. In the far-left corner stood Preston's office, the door open. David knocked on the frame as he appeared in the doorway. She was seated behind her desk. She gave David a perfunctory smile as she stood and said hello.

Susan Preston was on the short side, maybe five feet five, and neatly dressed in navy-blue slacks and a cream-colored blouse. Her hair was dark and cut short. The organization of the office said meticulous. The photos on the wall said United States Navy. Among the various diplomas were a number of framed five by sevens of the doctor in military uniform—some in dress whites, some in dress blues. She was standing next to highly decorated officers, and judging by the medals and multicolored ribbons pinned to her left chest, she appeared to be highly ranked herself.

"What can I do for you, Dr. Aaronson?" Preston said as she gestured for David to sit.

"I performed a splenectomy on a twenty-six-year-old female ten days ago."

"Nova Featherstone."

"Yes. I've been waiting all week for the pathology report to show up in the hospital database, but it hasn't been uploaded. Also,

Jimmy Miller, the twenty-two-year-old male who died on the table about a week and a half ago."

"Hemoptysis."

"Yes," David said. "And Thomas Pennington tells me there have been seventeen other hemoptysis deaths in the county that didn't make it to the hospital."

"In addition to three ruptured spleens. It's quite an unusual cluster of cases, given the size of the local population. The pathology and histology were identical for each patient, including Miss Featherstone, but I have never seen anything like this, so I deferred completing the reports until I get some additional input. I've sent specimens to the AFIP in Washington, DC."

"AFIP?" David asked.

"Armed Forces Institute of Pathology."

"Do you have a working diagnosis?"

"This appears to be a highly aggressive variant of sarcoidosis, but there are no reports in the literature of any granulomatous diseases that approach the destructiveness of what I've seen."

"Do all these cases exhibit the same pathophysiology?"

"Yes. The pulmonary lymph nodes and spleens I examined were packed with granulomas structurally identical to what is seen with sarcoidosis."

"And you're certain this isn't an aggressive form of tuberculosis?"

"This is not TB. The lungs were not involved, and I did not find any *Mycobacterium* species in the tissue samples."

"Is it in any way related to CoVid19? Could it be a different strain or a mutation?"

"At the time of admission, Miss Featherstone was tested for the novel coronavirus by nasal swab and serum screening. Both were negative." Preston leaned forward and rested her arms on the desk. "I believe we are dealing with an airborne agent—a different virus, or toxin, or particle—something small enough to be inhaled and quickly passed into the bloodstream and the lymphatics of the lungs. The agent is then sequestered by the pulmonary nodes and the spleen, and it ramps up an overwhelming inflammatory response. This results in massively enlarged nodes in some patients and massively enlarged spleens in others, and these patients form bronchopulmonary artery fistulas or massive splenomegaly."

David leaned back in his chair, a feeling of despair taking root. He did not want this to be the bioengineered supervirus Philip Tang had warned him about. He did not want to hear that the same process that caused Nova's spleen to rupture might also be causing the lymph nodes in her chest to enlarge and inflame everything around them. Maybe they weren't. Maybe this was an either-or process. Either the virus ends up in the spleen or the nodes, but not both.

"The three splenic rupture cases," David said, "were the pulmonary nodes involved?"

Preston hesitated, and David knew why. If she answered yes, she was sentencing a young woman to death. But Susan Preston's hesitation had just given David the answer he did not want to hear.

"The pulmonary nodes were involved," she said. "They were not as massive as in the hemoptysis patients—only mildly to moderately enlarged—but they had already elicited a significant inflammatory response."

David tried to fend off the overwhelming pain bearing down on him. He had witnessed the deaths of many patients during his years of training—the very young and the very old, the chronically ill and those struck down in their prime—but Nova was different. She had entered him, her soul merging with his, her beauty, humility, and humanity filling the emptiness that had raged since Cassandra's death and the murders of his father and Richard Whitestone. He would not be able to survive another loss of such magnitude. He sat forward and cleared his throat. "If one were to find mildly to moderately enlarged nodes on a chest CT in a post-splenectomy patient," he said, allowing himself a small sliver of hope, "do you think it would be advisable to operate? To go in and excise as many nodes as possible?"

"No. It would be highly inadvisable. During my postmortem dissections, the tissues of the trachea, bronchi, pulmonary artery, and aorta were extremely friable. Everything I grasped with my forceps simply fell apart." She paused, then said, "I'm sorry."

41

Once David Aaronson left the autopsy room, Preston called Jonathan Neville on his secure line.

"Neville," he said, answering in his usual brusque manner.

"This is Preston. Our new surgeon was just here asking about the pathology results for patient twenty-four, the splenic rupture."

"What did you tell him?"

"That my preliminary findings were consistent with an aggressive form of a sarcoid-like granulomatous disease involving the spleen."

"You told him the truth."

"Yes."

"Why?"

"Because that's what I found. If he had asked to look at the histology slides or gross specimens, that's what he would have seen. Any first-year medical student is capable of recognizing granulomas when they see them."

"I know what first-year medical students are capable of. Has he tied this patient to the others?"

"Yes," Preston said. "He was there when Jimmy Miller died on the table, and he's aware of the other twenty-two cases. He also asked if this could be a new strain of the coronavirus. I told him no, that both screening tests were negative."

"Okay," Neville said.

"And there's one other thing. I think he has a special interest in this girl, beyond surgeon and patient."

"Why?"

"When I said she was not an operative candidate, effectively sentencing her to death, I could see the anguish in his eyes."

"Let me know if he keeps prying, and do a better job of withholding the truth. Until I say otherwise, the agent responsible for the death of these twenty-three patients—soon to be twenty-four—is the Hantavirus. Got it?"

"Loud and clear," Preston said, and she hung up the phone.

After he finished with the pathologist, Neville called the chief of his private security force.

"Get eyes on the new surgeon," he said.

"I suggest the in-town assets," the chief of security replied. "My men stand out too much."

"Fine, but tell those meth heads eyes only. No contact. Just see where he goes and who he talks to."

- 42 -

David went back to his office and made two calls, the first to radiology. "Is the chest CT for Nova Featherstone completed yet?"

"It is," the unit clerk answered.

"Is the radiologist there?"

"Yes," the clerk said.

David told her to tell him he would be down in ten minutes.

After googling the number for Mona's Kitty Ranch, he placed the second call. "Is Ophelia working today?" he asked, perhaps with too much desperation in his voice.

"Yes," he was told, "but the girls are not allowed to answer outside calls while they're on duty, and their cell phones are locked up."

David took the stairs down to the first floor. Dr. Jim Spielman had already pulled up the films. The two men sat down in front of the oversize monitor.

"I haven't done a formal reading yet," Spielman said. "What are you looking for?"

David scanned the images as he gave the radiologist the clinically relevant history. "This is a twenty-six-year-old female who is ten days post splenectomy for splenomegaly of unknown etiology. I'm looking for enlarged pulmonary and mediastinal lymph nodes."

As the words left his mouth, David spotted two enlarged nodes where the pulmonary artery passed over the left mainstem bronchus. He leaned back in his chair, his shoulders slumping, the last shred of hope dying. Any chance that Nova had been an outlier was gone.

Jim Spielman put on his glasses and, using the palm-size ball embedded in the keyboard tray, scrolled through the images. He then removed his glasses and turned toward David. "Remarkable," the radiologist said. "Just about every hilar and mediastinal node is enlarged to some degree, but these two, right here in station ten," Spielman pointing at the two nodes David had spotted, "they're the biggest. About four centimeters is my guess." He used the ball to draw lines at either end of the biggest nodes, then hit a key on the keyboard. Their lengths appeared between the lines—4.0 cm for one, 3.8 cm for the other.

Spielman listed the differential diagnosis of mediastinal lymphadenopathy, mentioning things like tuberculosis, histoplasmosis, sarcoidosis, lymphoma, metastatic cancer, "but the pattern we see here doesn't fit any of those, and none of these diseases presents with primary splenomegaly."

David thanked Jim Spielman, returned to the surgery floor, and sat down with Nova. She had changed from her hospital gown into street clothes—a pair of jeans and a white T-shirt under a maroon sweater—and she looked magnificent. On the way up from radiology, David had agonized over what to tell her, and now that he was sitting across from her, he still didn't know.

"Is everything okay with the scan?" she asked.

David looked into the depths of Nova's brown eyes—eyes that were conveying her trust in him. Whatever answer he gave her, she would accept it because he was her doctor, and he would never lie to her.

"Yes," he finally said, deciding a partial truth would have to suffice for this unprecedented set of circumstances. "You have a couple of enlarged lymph nodes in your chest near your heart. I don't think it's anything to worry about, but we'll want to keep an eye on you. I'll go ahead and discharge you home and bring you back for a repeat scan in a week or so."

Once again, David mentally flogged himself for lying to a patient, for lying to Nova, but there was no alternative.

After leaving her room he hurried down to the ground floor and stopped at the ATM in the lobby. Twenty-five minutes later he was buzzing the gate at Mona's Kitty Ranch.

- 43 -

Ophelia was not in the lineup, so David slipped out of his overcoat, took a seat at the bar, and ordered a Maker's Mark on the rocks. He spent thirty minutes sipping it slowly, then ordered another, and just as the drink arrived so did Ophelia. She nuzzled up to him and gave him a kiss on the cheek. "Hello, my king," she said. "Will you be joining me in my room today?"

"Yes, I will," David replied.

He grabbed his drink and his coat, and the two of them headed down the hallway.

Ophelia closed the door and turned toward David. He opened his wallet and removed seven hundred-dollar bills.

"Something tells me you're here for business instead of pleasure," she said. "Spy business, that is."

"Yes." David held out the bills. "Here's three hundred for this visit and four hundred for what you paid out of pocket last time, but I'm only going to stay for a few minutes."

Ophelia took the bills and tucked them into the side of her panties.

"The guy that was here the other night, the contractor from the lab—"

"Philip."

"Yes. Philip Tang. I need to talk to him, and it's urgent. Do you know how to contact him? Is he a regular client of yours?"

"No," Ophelia said. "The night you were all here was the first time I met him and the last time I saw him."

"How did he end up in your room?"

"One of the other girls, Ryan, she said Philip wanted to meet with you here at Mona's, in a room where he wouldn't be seen and nobody could listen in. He told her it had to do with my sister, and maybe he could use my room. She asked if I'd be okay with that."

"Is Philip a regular of Ryan's?"

"I don't know."

David softly grasped Ophelia's shoulders. "Can you find out? I really need to talk to him. It would help if I could talk to anyone from the lab. If Philip was a regular, maybe there are others. Will you ask around? Ask the other girls?"

"This is about the stories in the news, the people bleeding to death the same way as my sister. Philip was telling the truth, wasn't he?"

"Yes," David said.

"I'll see what I can find out."

"Thank you, but remember, Philip said this may involve people high up in the military and the government, so only talk to the girls you know well, the girls you can trust. Be very careful."

"I will," Ophelia said.

David finished his drink and started to leave but then stopped and turned around, a wave of guilt hitting him as he realized he was putting one girl at risk to save another. "If you are at all uncomfortable with this, I understand," he said. "I'm beginning to think we're dealing with some very dangerous people."

"Look," Ophelia said, "my dad was blown up in Iraq, the army killed my sister, and my mom has checked out, so I'm like Katniss Everdeen in *The Hunger Games*. I'll do whatever I can to help you take these fuckers down. What do I have to lose?"

"Okay," David said. "I appreciate it." He hugged her and kissed her on the cheek. "I'll come back here to see you. Don't try to contact me."

Halfway back to Fallon, David called Vince Strahan and asked if they could meet at the Stockman's.

"Uh, it's like one in the afternoon," the lieutenant replied, "but I could be there by seven."

At 6:55 David entered the casino, sat down at the round top table farthest from the bar and ordered a beer. It was a decent Friday-night crowd, the seats at the bar full, the round tops half-full, the casino buzzing with activity. A few minutes later Strahan walked in. The grievous look on his face said he already knew this was not a social outing. He sat down and ordered a beer. Once the cocktail waitress had walked away, he said, "I presume you've seen the news today."

David looked around, at the tables nearby, at the people sitting along the bar. Nobody was paying attention to anyone else, and the ubiquitous chimes, chirps, and bells emanating from the casino floor were enough to keep their conversation from carrying beyond the table. "I did see the news," he replied. "Man, did I fuck up."

"What do you mean?" Strahan said.

"Philip Tang. I blew him off."

"That was only a week ago. The plan had to be in place way before then."

"It's not that."

"Then what is it?"

David leaned in close to Strahan and lowered his voice. "What I'm about to say straddles the boundary of physician-patient confidentiality, but let's view this as a consultation between two doctors." The cocktail waitress returned with Strahan's beer. When she was out of earshot, David said, "This is in reference to the young woman on whom I performed a splenectomy ten days ago."

"Okay," Strahan said warily.

"I scanned her chest this morning, and it's full of enlarged lymph nodes, with the two biggest nodes sitting right where the pulmonary artery passes over the left mainstem bronchus. That's exactly what killed Jimmy Miller and Ophelia's nine-year-old sister."

"You're kidding me," Strahan said. "Can you do anything about it? Can you operate?"

"No. I spoke to the pathologist. Over the past several months she has autopsied three patients who died from ruptured spleens, and all of them had enlarged mediastinal nodes. She said surgical intervention would be a mistake, that all the nodes were matted together, and the tissues were inflamed and friable. During her dissection, everything fell apart."

The lieutenant leaned back in his chair, a pained expression overtaking his face.

David looked around, then back at Strahan. "We need to find Philip Tang. He said the lab had not only developed a vaccine but also a monoclonal antibody that could reverse the process."

Strahan leaned forward. "Let's go see Ophelia."

"I was over there earlier this afternoon. She had never met the guy before that night, and she doesn't know how to contact him."

"Somebody at Mona's knows him."

"Ophelia's gonna check with Ryan, the girl who brought him to the room, and she'll ask the other girls if any of them have regular clients from the lab." David sipped his beer, then rested his arms on the table. "What about you? Do you have any kind of affiliation with the lab? Can you walk in, show your military ID at the front desk, and ask for Philip Tang?"

"No," Strahan said. "The lab is army and totally off limits without special clearance to enter. And being navy, I wouldn't even be able to BS my way in."

"Can you ask around? See if anyone knows anything about the place? Find out if the private contractors live in the lab or in town?"

"I'll give it a shot, but from now on we're going to have to be careful. Philip Tang was scared, and Neville was clearly unhappy with my presence the other night."

"Of course," David said. "I'm already worried about Ophelia over at Mona's asking questions, but what else can we do?"

- 45 -

David was driving home from the Stockman's when an idea struck him. The lab was military, staffed by the military along with civilian contractors, many of whom had left wives and girlfriends behind when they deployed to the middle of nowhere. And what do young men do with their free time when far away from home? David turned his car around.

The Big Brown Beaver was moderate in size, booths along the walls, tables filling the middle of the floor, two pool tables in the back. The Primus song, "Wynona's Big Brown Beaver," blared from the jukebox: "Wynona loved her big brown beaver and she stroked him all the time." The bar's namesake? And if so, how many times a night did some knucklehead play it?

A haze of cigarette smoke clung to the ceiling, and nearly all the patrons sitting along the bar and at the tables had smoldering ashtrays in front of them. Smoking was still legal in Nevada's bars and casinos—a thoracic surgeon's paradise. And just like the Stockman's, no social distancing or masks—a coronavirus paradise. The bartender, a large, bearded man wearing a sleeveless leather vest with a biker-gang patch on the back—The Outcasts—came over. "What can I get you, Doc? It's on the house."

"How do you know who I am?" David asked.

"Everyone knows who you are, at least anyone who can read. You made the front page of the paper a week before you got here."

David ordered a beer and studied the room as he waited. The clientele was all white and predominantly male. Most of the men wore jeans and boots, sported varying degrees of facial hair, and more than a few had Buck knives hanging from their belts. David became acutely aware that he looked like a federal agent in his dark slacks, white dress shirt, and overcoat hanging off the back of his stool. At least he'd had the foresight to lose the tie.

The beer arrived. David placed a ten-dollar bill on the bar, thanked the bartender, and as he sipped the cold microbrew from Carson City, he studied the cross section of working-class white America. There was nobody in the place with the last name Tang, nor would there ever be.

David swiveled his stool back in line with the bar and took a hefty swig of his beer. The events of the day had left him exhausted and depressed, and he was ready to go home and clear his head. As he took another drink, someone sat down next to him. She had long blonde hair, was petite, quite attractive, and not at all shy. She swiveled her stool so she was facing him. "Hello, Dr. Aaronson. I've been wondering when I might finally run into you." She extended her diminutive hand. "I'm Miss Ruby Mae Parker, but you can call me Ruby."

David shook her hand. "Nice to meet you, Ruby," he said. "How did you know—"

"Please," she said as she finger-summoned the bartender. "Everyone knows we have a new surgeon in town, and you look like a surgeon. I mean, come on." She gestured toward the rest of the bar. "Any of this rabble look like they could take out a gallbladder?"

David shrugged. "I don't know. There's enough surgical-grade steel hanging from their belts to get the job done."

Ruby Mae smiled and laid her hand on David's knee. "You're cute. I was afraid you'd be a stick in the mud. Buy me a drink?" she said as the bartender arrived.

David looked up at the burly guy in the biker vest. "Sure."

"I'll have a glass of red wine."

The bartender's contorted expression said, *You? Red wine? Since when?* "I'll see if I can find some," he said.

"What brings you into a place like this?" Ruby asked.

She was wearing skinny jeans and a teal-green blouse. Her eyes were big, brown, and seductive. And she was expending little effort in keeping her legs from drifting apart.

"I'm looking for an old friend," David said, "a guy I went to medical school with. He's now a private contractor working at the army biolab outside of town. His name is Philip Tang."

"Tang?" Ruby said. "As in Asian?"

"Yes."

She smiled. "You won't find him here. No Asians. No doctors. No nonwhites."

The bartender delivered a glass of red wine in a white wine glass. Ruby held it up and said, "Cheers. I'm really happy to finally meet you."

"It's good to meet you," David clinking her glass with his.

As David sipped his beer, he glanced past Ruby. At the far end of the bar sat a heavyset man with hams for fists, head shaved down to stubble, and a plume of cigarette smoke spiraling up from the ashtray in front of him. When they made eye contact, the guy gave David a single nod, held up a tumbler of whisky, and gulped it down. David wondered if the knuckles on the guy's right fist would correlate with the four abrasions he'd seen on Hemingway's left temple a couple of weeks ago.

"May I ask," David returning his attention to Ruby, "where would an Asian guy go for a drink here in Fallon?"

"There's an Applebee's over by Dotty's Casino."

"Yeah, I've actually been there a few times," David said. "Anywhere else?"

"It's a small town, and everybody has their own turf. The cowboys hang out at the Comstock Casino south of town. The Indians stay on the rez. The tired old boozers prefer the Overland Hotel. The MAGAbillies are right here."

"Wouldn't those be fightin' words in a place like this?"

"More like a calling. All these guys and their skanky girlfriends," Ruby gesturing toward the room, "they believe they're the chosen ones. They think God has kept the coronavirus out of our county for a reason. They call themselves the Doomsday Virus Desert Preppers, and they've already formed four militias that will block access to Fallon when civilization collapses."

Ruby sipped her wine, grimacing as she did so. Then, "You know how Highway 50 runs east and west, and 95 runs north and south, and they meet in the middle of town?"

David said he did.

"Those highways are the only way in and out, and when the apocalypse hits and everyone wants to come here because we have water and crops and cattle and game to hunt and no coronaviruses, each militia will take a highway, set up roadblocks, and keep everyone out. And once the world is killed off by the plague, it will be up to us to repopulate the planet."

A slight grin creased David's lips as he peered out at the room—at the boots and hats and jeans and facial hair and Buck knives—and considered he might just be looking at the last island of humanity.

"What about you, Ruby? Are you a doomsday virus prepper?"

"No," Ruby Mae replied. "Those guys are retards. Personally, I think the secret army lab did something to keep us immune. Why else would they be checking our blood all the time?"

Ruby maintained a straight face as she said this.

David wasn't sure whether or not to take her seriously.

"Speaking of the army," David said, "what about the military personnel? There's a large navy presence here, plus the army biolab. Where do they hang out?"

"The TOPGUN guys pretty much stick to the base and the officer's club. Whenever they come into town there's usually trouble. You might find them at the Stockman's now and then."

"And the lab?"

"Couldn't tell you. The place is a black hole. Nobody knows anything about it, and you never see any of those guys around town, unless maybe they put on their civvies and lie about where they work."

Ruby sipped her wine, pursing her lips this time.

"Why don't I get you something you like," David said, waving down the bartender.

"Grey Goose straight up," she said when the burly biker approached. "You wanna do a shot with me?" Ruby Mae directing her question to David.

A shot? That was the last thing David wanted, but he was starting to regard Miss Ruby Mae Parker as a valuable resource, so he said yes.

Two shots of Grey Goose were placed on the bar in front of them. Ruby lifted hers and said, "To the new surgeon in town. I hope I only see you socially and never professionally."

"For sure," David said.

They downed the vodka and placed the empty glasses on the bar.

"Another?" Ruby said.

"No. Thank you. I have to work tomorrow and really should get going."

"You do surgeries on Saturday?"

"Only the occasional emergency, but I do have to go in and make rounds on my patients."

"How's that pretty little Indian girl doing? I heard her spleen ruptured."

"News really gets around, doesn't it?"

Ruby shrugged. "Small town."

"Well, I really can't say without violating patient-physician confidentiality."

"You'll want to take good care of her, you know, with her father and all."

"Yes. We've met." David finished his beer and stood. "It was really nice meeting you, Ruby, and thanks for the Fallon bar-scene orientation. I'm sure I'll be seeing you around."

Ruby Mae smiled. "Nice to meet you too, Dr. Aaronson. I hope you find your friend." She hooked a finger inside his shirt, pulled him toward her, and gave him a light kiss on the lips.

As David walked past the other end of the bar on his way out, the ham-fisted gorilla said, "Take care, Doc."

- 46 -

For the next week, while the media continued to report massive body counts and rapid spread of the virus across China and into Russia and North Korea, David spent his free lunchtimes, afternoons, evenings, and nights prowling the stores, markets, restaurants, and bars of Fallon, searching for Philip Tang, or any young Asian males. He did not find Philip, nor did he find anyone who had heard the name. In fact, the only Asians he encountered were just passing through.

Strahan struck out as well. Nobody associated with the naval air station knew anything about the USAMRIID lab, let alone how one might be granted access. It was almost as if it didn't exist, just like Area 51, which was only three hundred miles to the south—if *it* actually existed.

On Thursday night, David ran into Ruby Parker at the Beaver. She typically hit most of the bars in town but had not seen any Asians, not even at Applebee's. David wanted to cultivate their alliance, so he bought her a couple of beers and they did a shot of Grey Goose together.

On Friday night, David paid a visit to Mona's. Ophelia had checked with Ryan regarding Philp Tang, but Ryan hadn't seen nor heard from him.

"There's this one girl, Marina," Ophelia had said, "who has a regular that drinks too much and runs his mouth about the next-level shit they're doing at the lab in Fallon. He told Marina there was going to be some scary stuff in the news, but she didn't need to worry because he could take care of her if anything happened."

David asked Ophelia if she'd been able to talk to Marina.

"No. Someone in Marina's family is sick, and she went home to Ukraine. She's still on the payroll, but Mona doesn't know when she's coming back."

It was now Saturday morning, and despite his frustration, fatigue, raging gastritis and swollen liver, David needed to go to the hospital and make rounds. He opened the garage door to a beautiful fall day and was about to climb into his car when the neighborhood paperboy came sputtering up the street in his beat-up 1970-something Toyota Corolla. The driver—a white kid wearing an equally old, equally beat-up baseball cap—threw a rolled-up newspaper onto the driveway and hollered, "Your Saturday paper, Doc. Make sure and read all of it."

David held his hands palms up in a questioning manner as the guy drove past. David did not get the paper, and the kid knew this because he passed David's house every morning without delivering one. And why would a paperboy tell a customer to read the whole thing? Then David recalled Strahan's story, the woman in the fence, and a disposable cell phone hidden in a copy of the *Lahontan Valley News*.

David retrieved the paper and climbed into his car, where he removed the rubber band and started flipping through the pages. On page six, a note written in black Sharpie: *The Comstock. 8 p.m. tonight. IMPORTANT!*

47

David had never worn a pair of cowboy boots, but as he walked through the glass double doors of the Comstock Casino he found them to be surprisingly comfortable, even though they were brand new and far from broken in. The Comstock was older—meaning seedier—than the Stockman's and larger, maybe four basketball courts as opposed to the Stockman's two, but the bells, whistles, and chimes and the accompanying lights, strobes, and neon were identical. And like all of Nevada's casinos, the place was populated by zombielike gamblers hunched over slot machines and blackjack tables, sipping their complimentary cocktails while tendrils of cigarette smoke swirled around them. Noise, lights, free booze, and smoldering cigarettes, not to mention no windows to the outside world or clocks on the walls—a pillar of society's institutions. Now he just needed to figure out what he was doing here.

It didn't take long. Miss Ruby Mae Parker.

She was hanging off a muddy-booted blackjack player, fingering the brim of his cowboy hat while he was trying to play his hand. When she spotted David, she knocked the cowboy's hat off his head and made a beeline for the bar. As she approached, she looked David up and down.

"Well, look at you, handsome. New boots and jeans. Crispy white shirt. Not straight off the range, but cowboy chic nonetheless." She pulled him close and kissed him.

"Hi, Ruby. Nice to see you again."

David slipped out of his gray overcoat, which had serendipitously complemented his *nouveau*-cowboy ensemble, and took a seat at the bar. "Join me?" he said.

David ordered two beers and two shots of Grey Goose from the female bartender and placed a twenty on the bar. After she walked away, David said, "Is this a chance meeting, or were we destined to come together at this fine establishment?"

Ruby ignored the question for a moment, scanning the casino as if looking for someone, then returned her attention to him. "Fate," she said.

The bartender placed two longnecks on cocktail napkins and set the shots next to them. They clinked their glasses and downed the shots. David chased his with a sip of beer.

As Ruby again scanned the casino, David found himself becoming impatient.

"What are we doing here, Ruby?" he asked.

"Lean in close to me and smile, like we're on a date. And look at me with lust in your eyes. Shouldn't be too hard."

David complied, his face so close to hers he could smell her hair and perfume. Into her ear, he said, "What's going on?"

Something in the distance caught her eye. "Go to the men's room and find the lanky kid with a pheasant tail feather sticking out of his cowboy hat."

"What does a pheasant tail feather look like?"

"Long and skinny with black stripes."

David crossed the casino floor to the men's room. With the exception of the lanky kid, it was unoccupied. David stepped up to the urinal next to his. The boy was rail thin, with a beak of a nose and shoulder-length blond hair in need of a good wash, rinse, repeat. They exchanged glances. He reached over the partition and handed David a piece of paper folded to the size of a credit card, along with a flash drive. "Get this to your intelligence man," he said. "And beware of tweakers. They're the eyes and ears of this town."

Before David could respond, the kid had zipped up and was out the door.

David went into a stall, sat down on the toilet, and unfolded the page. It was an 8½ x 11 sheet of printer paper, without lines or text, just numbers. Each row started with four numerals, which were followed by two decimals separated by a comma. Some of the decimals had positive values, some were negative, and there was no apparent order or sequence:

1025	55.755825, 37.617298	1017	33.513805, 36.276527
1104	14.599512, 120.984222	1019	2.046934, 45.318161
1021	31.520370, 74.358749	1020	34.555347, 69.207489
1106	19.432608, -99.133209	1018	33.312805, 44.361488
1024	48.709591, 44.514172	1101	41.805698, 123.431473
1017	35.689198, 51.388973	1025	26.647661, 106.630150
1103	43.119808, 131.886917	1029	39.039219, 125.762527
1026	34.786072, 114.348152	1019	33.893791, 35.501778
1021	33.684422, 73.047882	1102	21.027763, 105.834160
1107	29.074499, -110.959442	1024	58.668800, 52.176470
1105	35.875439, -84.062248	1017	36.202106, 37.134.258
1023	52.346371, 71.880493	1014	30.991170, 49.447720
1102	12.120520, 13.174035	1103	1.352083, 103.819839
1017	24.713552, 46.675297	1027	30.592880, 114.305542
1023	59.007736, 61.931622	1110	28.639139, -106072807

With no idea of what he was looking at, David folded the sheet, slipped it into his pocket along with the flash drive, and exited the restroom.

He quickly walked the periphery of the casino floor, then moved within the rows of tables and slot machines, looking for a cowboy hat with a tail feather sticking out of the headband. There were a number of pheasant feathers but none associated with a lanky kid. He was gone.

Just as David returned to the bar, someone hit a large jackpot, triggering a burst of bells, chimes, lights, and cheers. "We need to talk," David said, leaning in close to Ruby, "but not here. Did you drive yourself?"

Ruby Mae explained how she had lost her license due to a bogus DUI charge but that it was easy enough to catch rides around town.

"Okay," he said. "Let's finish our beers and get out of here."

"Now we're talking," Ruby said, her face lighting up.

48

"Who was the kid at the Comstock?" David asked as he and Ruby drove north toward Fallon's central business district.

"Andy, a guy from around town," Ruby replied. "He drives a delivery truck."

"What does he deliver?"

"Meat, mostly."

"Does he go to the biolab?"

"I don't know. Probably. He works for a company out of Reno, and I think he's their only driver here in Fallon."

"Are you friends?" David asked.

"We went to school together, but we don't hang out."

"How did you know he wanted to meet with me?"

"I saw him earlier at the Tamarack. He gave me a hundred bucks to be at the Comstock by eight and make sure you spotted him and followed him into the restroom."

"Any idea what our meeting was about or who set it up?"

"No. I just did what I was supposed to do. If I'd a known it was going to turn into a date with you, I woulda done it for free."

"This isn't exactly a date."

"It could be," Ruby said, reaching over the console and dragging her finger up and down David's thigh. "So, what did Andy want?"

"He wanted to know if I could steal Percocets, Oxycontin, and fentanyl from the hospital. He said we could make a killing dealing the stuff. I told him to fuck off."

"Mmm. Hearing you talk dirty is totally hot. Sure we can't turn this into a date?"

David turned onto Main Street and parked near the Beaver. Most of the town's bars were within walking distance. "I'd like you to help me find Andy," David said. "Does he ever hang out at any of the places down here?"

"I see him mostly at the Tamarack, once in a while at the Beaver. But I thought you told him to fuck off?"

"Yeah, I did, but I want to know who put him up to it. What does he drive?"

David and Ruby covered a four-block area, looking for Andy's faded-orange pickup truck and stopping in at all the bars, but neither Andy nor his truck were anywhere to be seen. Ruby insisted on holding David's hand as the they walked the streets, and although David wasn't excited about it, he went along, not wanting to alienate a valuable resource. But as her grip tightened and she moved closer, guilt crept in. If he were not desperately trying to find someone, he would not be spending time with this young woman, leading her on, even if it was unintentional. He stopped and let go of her hand. "Look, Ruby," he said, "you're a lovely young lady, and I really appreciate your help, but I just moved here—"

"And you don't want to be associated with the town trollop. You'd rather save yourself for that pretty Indian girl."

"I'm not saving myself for anybody. I'd just like to get settled before I become involved with someone. I enjoy talking to you, and I look forward to seeing you around, but for now I'd like to keep things low key. And you're not a trollop. I find you quite attractive."

"Sure you do," Ruby said, staring down at the sidewalk, trying to hide her disappointment and embarrassment.

"Let's stop in at the Beaver for one more drink," David said, "a thanks-for-your-help nightcap."

- 49 -

The Brown Beaver was minutes from David's house, and by 9:25 he was sitting at his computer. With a combination of excitement and trepidation, he plugged Andy's flash drive into a USB port. David was hoping to see more documents, something that would explain the sheet of numbers, or even chemical formulas for the vaccine and antibody. Instead, a video player opened. Dread rippled through him. There would be no utility in recording biochemistry experiments or test tubes full of viral cultures. This had to do with the woman in the fence. David was sure of it. He clicked play.

The images were grainy and unstable, likely a hidden camera, three Native American women strapped to gurneys, screaming and fighting while people in white hazmat suits tried to draw blood from their veins and suction sputum from their nasal passages, a chamber of horrors that ran for ninety seconds. David went to the kitchen, filled a tumbler with Maker's Mark, then, as horrific as it was, he watched the video again, scrutinizing it for anything that might identify the place as the Fallon biolab, but he saw nothing—only screaming, frightened women.

David slipped the flash drive out of the USB port, leaned back in his chair, and picked up the page of numbers. After looking at them from top to bottom, bottom to top, right to left, and left to right, they made no more sense now than they had in the bathroom stall of the Comstock. Goddammit, he needed to find Philip Tang, or at least Andy. David took his drink, moved to the couch in the living room, and turned on the television. Following a string of commercials, the news returned. The banner across the bottom of the screen announced what he had feared: Deadly Virus Spreads through China and into Middle East and Russia.

This is Stephanie Kim reporting from Camp Humphreys in South Korea. During a meeting with US intelligence officials earlier today, Korean intelligence has confirmed that the resurgent virus first reported in Wuhan just over one week ago has spread across China and into North Korea in just a matter of days, resulting in millions of deaths. China's military bases have been hit particularly hard, decimating their army, navy, air force, and the strategic missile command, essentially leaving the country defenseless. The North Korean government appears to have totally collapsed. South Korean scientists have obtained samples of the virus from China's Hubei Province and other areas of the country and have confirmed it is a genetic variant, a mutation of CoVid19 that they're calling CoVid23. Chinese virologists are claiming this new strain is a natural mutation of CoVid19. American scientists say they have irrefutable evidence that the genome has been manipulated, meaning the existing virus was upregulated to be extremely contagious and highly lethal. South Korean and US intelligence have long believed that the Wuhan National Biosafety Laboratory, which is part of the Wuhan Institute of Virology, has been involved in bioweapons research and are blaming the outbreak on a breach of the facility's containment systems. And like China, information coming out of Russia has been scant and unreliable, but it is believed CoVid23 is racing across that country as well. In response to this new supervirus, every country in Europe and Asia has closed its borders and stopped all forms of international travel. Many borders had already been shut down in the wake of CoVid19, but we are now seeing all borders closed and troops amassing at key entry points. It has also been reported that many governments have issued shoot-to-kill orders to their troops.

This is Aaliyah Ahmadi reporting from Tel Aviv. CoVid23 has spread throughout the Middle East, killing tens of millions. Iran has reported the largest number of cases, with the highest concentration of deaths occurring in the capitol city of Tehran. Iran's military bases have also been decimated, wiping out the Iranian army and Revolutionary Guard. In fact, it's unclear who is in charge of Iran as the country faces tens of thousands of new cases each day. Makeshift morgues have been erected in parking lots, stadiums, and wedding venues to handle the dead, although, with the country's failing electrical grid, it's not known how these bodies can be kept cold. While this scene repeats itself throughout the Middle East, Israeli scientists have obtained samples of the virus from Tehran and other areas and have confirmed it is the same organism that first appeared in Wuhan, China, about eight days ago. Israel, like all European and Asian countries, has closed its borders and is reinforcing the closure with military force. Any Israeli citizens attempting to re-enter the country will have to submit to a period of quarantine.

The broadcast shifted from reporter to reporter, from Mideast capital to Mideast capital, and the story was the same everywhere. In Damascus, Syrian president Bashar al-Assad was rumored dead as his military forces crumbled and long-suppressed opposition rebels stormed the city. In Riyadh, the Saudi Royal Family was nowhere to be seen as the city erupted into death, chaos, and violence, and a ragtag coalition of the country's remaining military forces tried to guard the oil fields. Palestinians, Jordanians, Lebanese, and Iraqis were dropping dead in the streets. The death tolls in these countries had reached into the millions and were still climbing. There was virtually no part of the Middle East untouched by the virus, and early reports indicated the organism was spreading west into Arab North Africa and east into Afghanistan and Pakistan.

David slumped into the couch, unable to fathom that the scorched-earth conspiracy to vanquish any threat to the United States was really happening. He leaned forward, grabbed his glass of Maker's Mark, took a large sip, then fell back into the couch.

A knock on his front door startled him.

He went over and peered through the leaded-glass panels. A young woman was standing on his porch. Nova Featherstone. David opened the door.

"Nova," he said. "I didn't expect … is everything okay?"

"Hi, Dr. Aaronson," she said with the same alluring shyness he'd seen when they were introduced at the Stockman's.

"Come in," David said.

"I hope I'm not bothering you."

"Not at all. Let me take your coat."

Nova slipped out of a thigh-length salmon-pink down jacket that had a faux-fur collar and cuffs. Underneath, she was wearing tight-fitting jeans and a loose-fitting white sweater. Her hair was adorned with feathers, and around her neck she wore a gold chain necklace, from which hung a gold-lace dream catcher with a topaz stone in the center and three tiny golden feathers dangling from the bottom. She looked absolutely spectacular.

David invited her to join him on the sofa and asked if she needed anything.

She sat down and turned toward him, her posture erect, her hands folded in her lap. "No, thank you. I won't stay too long. I'm sure you have other things to do."

"Nova," David said, "it's ten o'clock on a Saturday night, and I'm watching the news. I can assure you I'm not busy."

"Okay," she said. She glanced down at her hands, then looked at him, her beautiful brown eyes deeply troubled. "There's talk around town that what's happening in China and Russia and the Middle East is the same thing that's happening here. People think it's related to the military lab, and they're confused and afraid. I just thought … do you know if there's a cure?"

David knew what she was asking. He moved closer and took her hands in his as he'd done so many times when she was in the hospital. Tears filled her eyes and ran down her cheeks. He wiped them away with gentle sweeps of his finger. She pressed her body into his and rested her head on his shoulder. He put his arms around her, held her tight, and quietly took a deep breath, drawing in the fragrance of her hair.

"There are people dying from ruptured spleens," she said, "and there are people dying from bleeding that starts in their chest. My spleen ruptured, and the scan of my chest showed something that had you worried when you came to see me afterwards. You tried to hide it, but I could tell."

"I don't know if there's a cure," David said, "but I'm trying very hard to find out."

Her body spasmed with quiet sobs. He tightened his hold as tears ran down his cheeks, and after a few moments Nova sat up, took David by the hand, and led him to his bedroom.

- 50 -

The lovemaking was slow and gentle, partly because Nova had undergone surgery two weeks prior, but mainly because that was what the chemistry between them dictated—two people who had deep feelings for each other, two bodies that simply needed a human touch, no gymnastics, no fireworks, just two souls yearning to make a connection beyond the merely physical.

Afterward, they lay quietly in each other's arms, no words spoken, the moment protected from the grim realities of the outside world, David experiencing an inner peace he hadn't felt in more than a year, and Nova—David hoped—feeling safe in his embrace and knowing he was going to do everything in his power to save her.

But then the grim realities of the outside world crept between them and established a foothold. "I better get home before my dad starts looking for me," Nova said.

David agreed, and after they had dressed, he led Nova into the kitchen and asked her to take a seat at the table. "There's something I need to tell you," he said. "With this being such a small town, I'm sure you've already heard that for the past week or so I've been running around with one of the local working girls."

A slight grin creased Nova's lips. "Ruby Mae Parker. But it's really not my business."

"Of course it's your business, Nova. We just made love, and I've only known you for a few weeks, but I have really strong feelings for you." David felt the flush of warm blood climbing his neck and spreading into his cheeks. "Fuck it. I'm just gonna say it. I love you."

Nova smiled, and with her ever-endearing shy embarrassment, she quietly said, "I love you too."

Only once before had David felt the all-consuming euphoria of admitting his love for another person and having it reciprocated. It was a feeling like none other, and after Cassandra's death on a dark highway in northern New Jersey, he was certain he would never experience the feeling again. Yet, here he was, sitting across from an exquisite woman who professed to love him. They stood and shared a deeply passionate kiss. Then came another grim reality: "I really do have to go," Nova said. "I'm sorry, it's just that—"

David shushed her by putting his finger to her lips. "I've met him. I understand."

"I promise—"

David shushed her again. "We'll figure out the logistics. What's important is that we know how we feel about each other. Nothing else matters."

David helped Nova into her coat, walked her out to her car, and leaned in through the driver's side window. "Ruby Parker is helping me find someone who may have access to a cure for the virus, so ignore anything you hear about the two of us running around together."

"Okay," she said, and as he watched her drive away, his heart splintered into a million tiny pieces.

Back inside he grabbed his tumbler of Maker's Mark, filled it to the brim, and took a large swig as panic and a barrage of contradictory thoughts flooded his brain. Did he really love Nova, or was he lonely? Did she really love him, or was this a case of the white coat syndrome, where patients fall in love with their doctors? Would Two Feathers welcome David into the family and the tribe, or would he haul him into the desert and shoot him in the head? Could he save Nova, or was he going to watch her die the same way he had watched Cassandra die? Was the world going to end, or could he do something about it? He took another huge swallow of Maker's Mark in an effort to mute the confusion, and as the warmth of the bourbon slid down his esophagus, settled into his stomach, and radiated throughout the rest of his body, one thing became clear: his love for Nova was real. The pain in his fractured, failing heart was telling him it was.

- 51 -

Shards of sunlight penetrated David's eyelids, slowly elevating his level of consciousness from basic brainstem function—heart beating, lungs breathing—to rudimentary wakefulness, then to fully awake, where he found himself lying supine on his living room couch, still dressed in his boots, jeans, and white shirt. He worked himself into a sitting position, but this only served to turn the dull thump in his head into a pounding headache. He planted his feet on the floor, and as his vision came into focus he was able to determine the agent responsible for his present state of malaise, increasing intracranial pressure, and eyes that felt like ashtrays. On the coffee table sat a depleted bottle of Maker's Mark, and next to the bottle, an empty tumbler sticky with bourbon residue. He leaned forward, planted his elbows on his knees, placed the palms of his hands on his temples and squeezed. Recalling it was Sunday morning, and Pennington was scheduled to make rounds and take call, David leaned back into the couch and closed his eyes.

Three hours later he awakened again, the pounding headache now reduced to a dull throb. He stood, gave his autonomic nervous system a few moments to equalize his blood pressure, then made his way to the bathroom. After brushing his teeth, washing his face, and swallowing eight hundred milligrams of Advil, he drove down the street to the Area 51 Deli and picked up two sausage-egg-and-cheese bagels. Armed with a bottle of orange juice and the bagels, he sat down at the coffee table and turned on CNN.

The top news stories revolved around the Wuhan Supervirus, how it was quickly spreading, and whether anything could be done to stop it. The Chinese were steadfastly denying the virus originated in their country. American intelligence claimed to have irrefutable evidence it had. The broadcast then returned to the studio, where Wolf Blitzer announced the president was about to make a statement from the White House. The studio shot switched to Silas Dixon Bell, standard blue blazer and red tie, sitting at his desk in the Oval Office:

> *Good morning. As you know, over the past nine days China, North Korea, and the Middle East have been wiped off the face of the earth by a deadly virus the Chinese unleashed on the world during a badly managed bioweapons experiment, or maybe they did it on purpose. Millions and millions of deaths have resulted. Diseases that thrive on sickness and death, like cholera and bubonic plague, are now running rampant across the continent. Governments are collapsing. Economies are collapsing. Societies are collapsing. And now, this Chinese abomination is projected to spread into Europe and the Americas in the coming days to weeks. It won't surprise me to learn soon that the virus has moved into Mexico as well, which has always been a dirty country with poor sanitation practices. So, after careful consideration, I have decided to follow the lead of our Israeli and European allies. Effective this morning all of our borders are closed. All commercial flights scheduled to land on US soil have either been grounded or told to return to their point of origin. All seagoing vessels, whether carrying cargo or passengers, will no longer be allowed to enter US ports. The ongoing collapse of nations and their militaries will allow redeployment of US troops, armaments, and military hardware back to this country to secure our borders. Thanks to the wall separating Mexico and the United States—the big, beautiful wall the Democrats did not want me to build—our southern border is secure, and nobody from Mexico, Central, or South America will be able to invade this country. I am less concerned about our northern border, in that our Canadian neighbors are fine people and will have no need to leave their country. I have already enlisted the finest and smartest and most talented group of scientists ever assembled by any president, and they*

will fast-track the development of a vaccine for this new strain of coronavirus, which will be shared with Canada and other nations in need. US citizens wishing to return to the United States will be required to submit to a fourteen-day period of quarantine at one of our European or Pacific military bases. Natural-born citizens will receive priority. Naturalized citizens will be considered on a case-by-case basis. Any naturalized citizen who immigrated from a Muslim-majority country or China will not be allowed to return. All other aliens, regardless of visa or green card status, will not be allowed to return. The last time I tried to institute similar measures, the courts struck down my executive order. This time I am declaring a national emergency, and I have determined that the entry of the aforementioned groups pose a direct threat to the United States. Therefore, Title 8 of the US Code of Laws grants me, as president of the United States, the power to enact these measures by executive order.

Bell paused and looked directly into the camera. David was convinced the man had a gleam in his eye and a smile on his lips. He then resumed:

Contained within the borders of this great country is the food we need to feed our people, the energy we need to power our cars, homes, businesses, and factories, and the raw materials we need to produce anything this great society requires. Therefore, we will no longer engage in trade with any foreign entity, nor will we serve as the dumping ground for the world's tired, the world's poor, the world's huddled masses yearning to breathe free, or the world's wretched refuse teeming on its shore. America will survive this horror that has been cast upon the world by the Chinese, and we will be greater than ever. Thank you, and God bless America.

The CNN talking heads quickly refuted the president's claim that he could deny entry to naturalized American citizens. Title 8 did give him the power to forbid aliens from entering if they posed a threat to the health or national security of the nation. It did not give him the right to keep American citizens—natural or naturalized—from entering. In light of the current circumstances, the panelists were okay with the quarantine period, but to politicize a public health apocalypse and use it against specific ethnic groups was viewed as a typical move from the playbook of a xenophobic president whose primary goal was making America white again. It appeared Silas Bell and his white nationalist supporters were finally going to get their way.

This was too much for David's hungover brain. He turned off the news and started thinking about the only thing that mattered to him—saving Nova. He picked up the page of numbers. Maybe a fresh, albeit impaired, perspective would allow him to see them in a different light. Maybe he'd been trying too hard. Maybe he just needed to put his hangover to use and blankly stare at the page, let the numbers tell him what they meant. He did so, and moments later he saw something he hadn't seen before. Many of the decimals had values that differed by only a few numerals, while others were quite disparate. Those close in value were preceded by four digits that were either the same or very close, and he was beginning to see them in sequence.

David went into his office, grabbed a yellow legal pad, and sat down at his desk with pencil in hand. He made a new list, ordering the decimals by their four-digit predecessors. The closer in value the four digits, the more similar the pairs of decimals, and as the four-digit numerals became more disparate, so did the decimals. The top half of the list was a group, somehow related, while the bottom half was more spread out. Then it hit him: Wuhan, China, was the first region affected by the virus, followed by neighboring provinces, the rest of the country, and North Korea and Russia, then the Middle East, Arab North Africa, and the Muslim countries of Afghanistan and Pakistan—America's enemies.

If the virus had originated in Wuhan and spread outward like ripples in a pond, this is the pattern that would emerge, a cluster of cases at ground zero, followed by enlarging circles of involvement. And as the circles enlarged, so would the disparity within the sets of numbers. David turned on his computer, opened his browser and googled, "What is the latitude and longitude of Wuhan, China?"

The answer: 30.581980, 114.268066.

The first number on David's list: 30.581980, 114.268066.

He googled a website where you could enter any latitude and longitude and get the location, or vice versa. He entered Pyongyang, North Korea.

The result: 39.039219, 125.762527.

The second number on the list: 39.039219, 125.762527.

"My god," David uttered as he leaned back in his chair and stared at the legal pad. He was looking at the master list of locations that had been, or will be, infected with the supervirus. He repeated the process for each set of numbers, writing down the cities and countries.

The entry 35.689198, 51.388973 resulted in Tehran, Iran. Followed by Beijing, Moscow, and a multitude of other locations throughout China, Russia, and the Middle East. Then Mexico and Colombia and Venezuela. Now the four digits preceding the latitudes and longitudes made sense. They were dates. The *1014* in front of *Wuhan* was 10/14—October 14—seven days before the first outbreak of CoVid23. Three days later, Tehran, Damascus, and Riyadh. Four days after that, Islamabad and Kabul. Each date preceded the outbreak by seven to ten days.

Then came the group at the bottom of the page: Los Angeles, San Francisco, Portland, Seattle. The Left Coast. Democratic bastions of liberalness. The president of the United States was going to attack his own country, his own citizens, simply because they did not support him, and it was going to happen in less than two weeks.

David jumped up and went to the bedroom. Bolted to the floor of the closet, a safe. Inside the safe, an untraceable TracFone and a business card with nothing more than a number printed on it. Mark Wallace had been correct. David did have a contact in one of the intelligence agencies. The card had been given to him by Jim Broderick, an NSA senior analyst, Richard Whitestone's former partner, and Heather Whitestone's godfather. But how did an army captain in Fallon, Nevada, know about Broderick? David would have to figure that out another day.

He entered Broderick's number into the TracFone and hit send. He heard nothing but a click, followed by dead air. There was no recording telling him the number had been disconnected or he had dialed incorrectly, please check it and try again. He reentered the number, making sure each numeral was correct. Again, a click, then nothing. He went to the NSA website, which conveniently provided a plethora of contact information. David entered the main number into the TracFone and hit send. He got the usual recording about entering the extension of your party if you already know it, otherwise stay on the line. He did, and a moment later an operator said, "National Security Agency, how may I direct your call?"

David was caught off guard. He didn't think phoning the nation's most secretive spy agency would be this straightforward. "Jim Broderick?" David said.

"One moment, please."

The line went silent.

The operator returned. "I'm sorry, but there is no record of anybody with that name currently or previously employed by the National Security Agency."

This time the line went dead.

David pondered this, wondering if he had misunderstood Jim Broderick the first, and only, time they had met. But he hadn't. Broderick had clearly said he and Richard Whitestone worked together at the NSA, both of them senior analysts in the same division—the Equation Group, the NSA's elite hackers—and that he and Richard had been recruited from Princeton together. If David could recall this level of detail, he was accurately remembering the conversation. He was not confused. He was not confabulating. Something had happened to Jim Broderick. He had been expunged by the NSA.

David leaned back in his chair and considered his next move. He had to get the master list and video to someone with the resources and credibility to expose a far-reaching conspiracy unprecedented in size, scope, and power. And it had to be somebody he could trust, not someone who said, "Thank you very much," then buried the evidence. That ruled out the federal government, the military, and—based on the encounter he just had with the NSA—the intelligence agencies. And David had no faith in his local law enforcement, and certainly not in the state medical board or the Churchill County Coroner's Office.

He called Strahan, but the lieutenant could not leave the base. "We're on lockdown," he said. "We've been elevated to DEFCON 3. The European theater is at DEFCON 2."

"Sounds ominous," David said.

"The last time we were three at home and two abroad was the Cuban Missile Crisis. And DEFCON 1 means nuclear war is imminent. So yeah, pretty serious."

"Can I come see you?" David asked. "This is really important—a matter of national security, actually."

"I'll set you up with a pass. I'm allowed to seek outside medical and surgical consultations under emergency circumstances, so bring your hospital ID and present it to the guard at the entrance. He'll direct you to the infirmary."

David hung up the phone, grabbed his keyboard, and used his remote access credentials to log in to the hospital's medical records system. He looked up the registration information for Jimmy Miller, wrote it down, and headed for the shower.

- 52 -

David drove south out of town and within minutes was passing through farmland. After two miles on the highway, he turned left onto a small two-lane road, and a mile and a half later he arrived at the security gate of Naval Air Station Fallon. David presented his hospital ID and driver's license. The guard directed him to the infirmary, where David parked next to Strahan's Jeep. The lieutenant emerged from a pair of glass doors and greeted him, but before they were able to get inside, a ground-shaking roar emanated from the runway. Unfortunately, a series of gigantic hangars stood between the infirmary and the flight line, and David was unable to see the planes take off.

Like the rest of the building, Strahan's office was neat and organized. Unlike Susan Preston's office, there were no photos or framed diplomas on the wall. Vince Strahan gestured toward one of two metal chairs facing the desk. David took a seat.

"Most of our squadrons will be deployed any day now, so the training schedule has been ramped up," Strahan said. Then he mournfully shook his head. "Some crazy shit happening over there. You think Philip Tang was right?"

"This office is a secure space? Nobody is watching or listening?" David asked.

"It's a physician's office, so yes. Not as secure as a brothel, but close."

"Then to answer your question, I know Philip Tang was right."

"How?"

David handed Strahan the page of numbers he'd been given the night before. "Some scruffy kid gave me this last night in the men's room of the Comstock Casino." Then David gave Strahan the revised list. "I worked this out an hour ago."

The lieutenant's eyes narrowed as he scanned the page. "This is a schedule showing where the virus has been and where it's going, proof this is not an accident." He looked up at David. "And it's heading for us."

"Any country that's a threat to our national security, any country that's been a thorn in our side, any country the president simply doesn't like, cities full of people the president simply doesn't like— they're all on the list."

"And," Strahan added, "if he hits a few American cities, it plays into the narrative that the virus originated in China."

"The scruffy kid gave me something else." David handed Strahan the flash drive. "There's a video on there I want you to see, but be forewarned, it's disturbing."

While Strahan was inserting the drive into a USB port on his computer, David's cell phone vibrated. He took it out of his pocket, looked at the screen, and smiled.

"What was that?" Strahan said. "The apocalypse is coming, we're committing treason, and you're smiling at a text message?"

"Uh, yeah," David said. "I have a date tonight."

Strahan leaned back in his chair, pondering, the gears turning. Then, "You dog. Don't tell me you're dating your patient, the one who is about two weeks status post removal of her spleen."

David nodded.

Another roar. Another pair of F-18s hurtling down the runway.

When the noise subsided, Strahan said, "All those fighter pilots on the sticks of those sixty-five-million-dollar planes taking off out there, how they would love to be in your place."

"Look," David said, "it just kinda happened. If the world wasn't falling apart and my judgment was intact, maybe I'd show a little restraint, but her days walking among us may be limited, and I just want to take care of her."

Strahan leaned his chair forward and rested his arms on his desk. "Of course. The CT scan. I'm sorry. I wasn't thinking about that."

"It's okay," David said.

After a moment, Strahan said, "Does her father know?"

"That we're dating, or about the lymph nodes?"

"The former? The latter? Both?"

"If he knew we were dating, I'd be taking a dirt nap in the desert. If he knew about the nodes and her prognosis, he'd blame me for it and put me down for a dirt nap anyway."

"Well, something tells me if anyone can handle Two Feathers, you can."

"We'll see," David said. "In the meantime, let's get back to our treasonous activities."

Strahan clicked his mouse, then sat back and watched. After thirty seconds he clicked again, pausing the video. "That's her," he said, "the woman in the fence. She's tied down, and they're experimenting on her, on all of them." He clicked the mouse and watched the remaining sixty seconds, then leaned back in his chair. "This is straight out of the Nazi Germany playbook. What are you going to do with this stuff?"

"That's why I'm here. I don't think we can trust anyone. If the navy allowed the personnel on this base to be part of the vaccination experiment, I don't think they can be trusted. If the highest levels of our government and military and intelligence agencies are flying drones over our enemies and spraying them with viruses, they can't be trusted. And if our own coroner, sheriff, and state medical board cannot be counted on to investigate twenty-three horrific deaths, they can't be trusted." David leaned forward. "Is there anybody—an officer here on the base, somebody from a previous deployment, a medical school professor—anyone you can trust that may have the clout to blow the whistle on something of this magnitude?"

"No," Strahan said, shaking his head. "Nobody."

"Then I have only one option left."

"Which is?"

David drove back the way he had come, and after a half mile turned onto a gravel driveway. A large metal-sided barn sat off to his right, a modest single-story home on the left. Several large, leafless cottonwood trees surrounded the house. Beyond the trees and structures were several acres of bare soil.

Mrs. Miller greeted David with a big hug. Mr. Miller gave David a vise-grip handshake and invited him inside. He was shown into the living room and took a seat on the couch, which faced a large picture window looking out over their fields. The Millers sat down across from David, their faces full of hope. A porcelain serving tray sat in the center of the coffee table.

"Can I offer you coffee or tea?" Mrs. Miller said.

"A cup of tea would be nice," David said.

"A little milk and sugar?" Mrs. Miller asked as she scooted forward in her chair and picked up a tea bag from the tray.

"Yes. Thank you," David replied.

"Helluva thing going on over there in China and the Middle East," Mr. Miller said. "A lot like what we're seeing around here."

"Exactly like what we're seeing here," David said. "That's why I've come to see you."

Mrs. Miller stirred the tea and handed the cup to David, her hands trembling. He thanked her, took a small sip, and set it down on the table. "I think Jimmy and the others in the area contracted the same virus, and it's related to the army bioweapons lab outside of town."

A roar interrupted the conversation, rattling the house and everything in it. When it subsided, Mr. Miller said, "F-18s taking off from the naval air station. The runway is less than a mile away. They use their afterburners during takeoff. Landing isn't near as bad." He paused for a moment as if anticipating something, and then came another roar. Once it had quieted down, he said, "Not unusual to get two pairs of two heading out together. And lately, there's been a lot of C-130s coming and going. That is unusual."

"The big cargo planes?" David said.

"Yes. In all the years we've lived here, we'd maybe see one a month. Now it's several a day. I think all of this is somehow related."

"Please, Doctor," Mrs. Miller placing her hand on her husband's, "can you tell us what you've found out about the virus and the lab?"

"Of course," David said. "I believe the army is working with the same virus that's spreading through Asia and the Middle East. I think they brought it here to study it and develop a vaccine, and maybe it escaped their containment system and spread through Fallon."

"But wouldn't we see a lot more deaths than the twenty-odd we've had here?" Mr. Miller asked. "The news is reporting a death rate as high as eighty percent. And the first case here in Fallon, we've come to find out, was six months ago."

"I'm not sure how to make sense of the disparities, but our cases here need to be investigated. I don't think the coroner and the state medical board are doing everything they can. Maybe the army is getting in their way."

"And you think we can do something?" Mrs. Miller said.

"Yes," David said, moving to the edge of the couch. "I would like you to contact CNN, tell them Jimmy's story, and talk about the others who have died in the same way. I'm hoping they'll come interview you in person, and you can invite other families. If this becomes national news, someone at the government level will have to investigate the lab, maybe the CDC or a congressional committee."

Mr. Miller leaned forward in his chair. "But you're the town surgeon, and you've seen this firsthand. Why can't you go to CNN or contact someone in the government?"

"I think if the rest of the country sees a room full of people who have lost their children and parents and loved ones to this hideous disease, it will have a greater impact than some surgeon speaking in clinical terms."

Mrs. Miller took a Kleenex from a box on the table and dabbed her eyes.

"And there's one other thing," David said. "Please don't mention my name. Don't say anything about the local surgeon urging you to come forward. Just tell them you've been watching the news, and what has been happening here looks a lot like what's been going on over there, and you think it has something to do with the bio-weapons lab. Please, nothing about me or my suspicions." David set a piece of paper—a phone number—on the table. "This is the CNN tip hotline. I'm sure they'll be interested."

- 54 -

The president's Sunday-morning speech was followed by a Sunday-afternoon meeting in the Situation Room. He had assembled the Joint Chiefs of Staff, top members of his cabinet, bioweapons expert Colonel Jonathan Neville, and private citizen Jack Prescott. The topic of discussion: the decontamination, occupation, and rebuilding of the Middle East.

After handing out a spiral-bound eighty-page booklet to each attendee, Neville—standing tall in his dress greens—moved to the head of the table. Holding up his copy, he said, "Everything regarding the decontamination of biological and nonbiological entities is in this manual, and it is structured in a step-by-step protocol fashion. In a nutshell, just like the AIDS virus, the Wuhan Supervirus is susceptible to simple household bleach. All clean-up personnel will have been vaccinated, hazmat suits with custom-fit N99 diffusion-type respirators will be worn as an additional safety measure, and frequent screening for viral infection will be instituted for all workers in the hot zone. Unclaimed bodies shall be cremated. Claimed bodies can be turned over to the claimant only after the body has been bathed with bleach, which is to include irrigation of the nasal pharynx and oral pharynx—the nose and mouth—with a bleach solution."

The presentation quickly devolved into a heated discussion of costs, logistics, hidden dangers, and all manner of political and humanitarian implications.

"With this manual," Neville said loudly to quiet the room, "I have provided the specifics for eradicating the virus. It's up to the rest of you to develop the supply lines, provide the manpower and training, rid the region of the roving bands of armed thugs and terrorists, and deal with the surviving population."

After Neville had finished, National Security Advisor Rex Masterson handed out a spiral-bound report compiled by the National Security Council addressing the securing and subsequent occupation of the now mostly ungoverned Middle East. His report was much thicker and included input from the Joint Chiefs of Staff, members of Congress, and current and former ambassadors, along with a multitude of regional experts from both government and academia. "The United States will secure and rebuild the region without the help of our European allies," Masterson said. "This is not a coalition or United Nations mission. We will establish a permanent military presence. We will establish regional governments. We will take control of all natural resources. In short, we are annexing the Middle East. All oil and gas currently allocated to China will be cut off. Any European nation currently dependent on Russian energy reserves will now be supplied by us. If there is anything left of China or Russia after the virus sweeps through, this move will further cripple their economies and drive the final nail into their coffins."

Another heated discussion ensued. Rex Masterson agreed that the plans were complex and incomplete and needed to be fluid as the geopolitical landscape changed in the coming weeks and months, but neither he nor the president backed down from declaring the Middle East now belonged to the United States.

The final presentation was made by President Silas Dixon Bell. After introducing Jack Prescott—whom many of the attendees already knew, at least by reputation if not personally—the president stated that all oil and gas fields, pipelines, and ports, "the entire energy infrastructure of the region," he said, "will fall under the management of Jack Prescott and his consortium of companies. There will be no competitive bids solicited. There will be no congressional hearings. The job is his. Period. And all other projects, including the restoration of public works, construction and reconstruction of private and public structures, even the building of our new military bases, will be performed by his companies."

There was no opposition to this declaration. Everyone in the room was familiar with the power Jack Prescott wielded—within the highest levels of government, international banking and finance, and the corporate world. And they were aware of his close ties to the president.

- 55 -

The Millers made the call Sunday after David left, and by midday Monday they were sitting on their couch in front of hot lights, a cameraman, and a correspondent from CNN's San Francisco affiliate. They had invited two other couples who had lost young-adult children, along with Ophelia's mother, but all declined to go on camera.

The scene outside the home was far different from the staid proceedings inside. About a hundred townspeople had shown up with signs and placards saying things like, Save Us, Help Us, This Is Not CoVid19, The Army Is Killing Us.

On the fringe of the crowd stood Ruby Parker. She was not holding a placard or sign. She was not there to make her voice heard or to advocate for the dead. Instead, she was waiting patiently, bundled up in a powder-blue hooded coat, her frosty breaths getting whipped around by a brisk wind.

The interview concluded, and as the CNN crew exited the Miller home, the cameraman paused to shoot some footage from the porch. This brought the frigid crowd to life, some of them shouting out the same slogans printed on their signs, others just shouting. The reporter made her way to the van parked over in the driveway. Ruby followed, pushing and elbowing her way through the mass of bodies in the front yard. The reporter turned around, startled to find her rapidly approaching.

Ruby removed the flash drive and David's lists from her coat pocket and put them into the hand of the reporter. "This stuff was smuggled out of the army germ lab."

"Who are you?" asked the reporter. "Who smuggled this out of the lab?"

Her questions went unanswered as Ruby turned and disappeared into the crowd.

A young man with rotting teeth and festering scabs on his face watched Ruby Mae Parker approach the reporter and hand something to the woman. After Ruby disappeared back into the crowd, he took a TracFone from the pocket of his coat and dialed a number. "You know the blonde hooker that the surgeon's been runnin' around with?" he said to the man on the other end. "She just gave something to a TV reporter out in front of the dead kid's house, and I think they got it from the truck driver I told you about at the Comstock Saturday night."

The man on the other end told the tweaker he had done good work, and his payment would be waiting in the usual place.

- 56 -

Monday morning had gone well enough. David performed three cases—two hernia repairs and a gallbladder removal—and, despite the distraction of the pending Miller interview, he'd been able to maintain his focus. The ability to maintain one's focus was the most important trait of a competent surgeon, not steady hands, as the lay public liked to believe. Manual dexterity was very important, of course, but when a surgeon was up to his or her ass in alligators during brain surgery, heart surgery, or a multiple-gunshot-wound trauma case, the ability to block out everything except each cut of the scalpel, each snip of the scissors, and the precise placement of each stitch was of paramount importance. Even though hernias and gallstones were not generally life-threatening, attention to detail during surgical intervention was essential for a good result.

By late afternoon the distraction was in full force. While he attended his surgery clinic, David learned that CNN had come and gone from the Miller home, and Ruby had delivered the flash drive and master lists.

Now David was home and in front of the television, still in his dark slacks and white dress shirt, the remote in one hand and a cold beer in the other. He didn't know how the network was going to handle such a big break in the most important story they've ever reported. Would they rush the processing and editing of the interview, both because of its importance and because prime time viewing hours were approaching? Would they take the time to vet the video of restrained Native American women serving as lab animals? Was there some far-reaching power that might quash the whole story? And what would they do with his master lists? Risk inciting full-scale panic in four of America's largest population centers based on obscure documents that had not been vetted and verified? David didn't know. All he could do was watch and wait.

Nova arrived with Chinese takeout. Their embrace was long and passionate with few words spoken. A quiet sense of urgency existed between them, and they were content simply being together. Nova served the food on real plates, poured two glasses of iced tea and added lemon slices, and as she brought everything over to the coffee table, David was hit by a intense jumble of pain and love and guilt. Cassandra had always taken the time to arrange takeout food on plates, and she often served glasses of ice water with lemon slices. As David watched Nova emerge from the kitchen, very much resembling Cassandra with her long dark hair and beautiful brown eyes, he acutely felt the pain of loss, the guilt of moving on, and the love he now had for two extraordinary women.

"Anything yet?" Nova asked as she sat down.

"No, but I have to believe they'll at least air the interview tonight. I mean, it's a pretty big story with huge implications." David took a bite of kung pao chicken, making sure to avoid the skinny black peppers, and as the news yielded to a series of commercials, he turned toward Nova. "I want to prepare you for something you might see." He described the video and told her he was certain the restrained women were Native American. "It's very difficult to watch, but I need to know if you recognize them, if they're from the reservation."

"It's been a year since one of our sisters went missing, but I won't be surprised if the women are Native. Angry, yes, but not surprised." Nova's voice took on an uncharacteristic edge as she described an epidemic of missing and murdered Native and Indigenous women across the United States and Canada.

Tribal police and investigators from the federal Bureau of Indian Affairs served as law enforcement on reservations, which were sovereign nations, Nova explained. The FBI had the authority to investigate certain offenses, and the Department of Justice would prosecute a major felony such as murder, kidnapping, or rape if they happened on tribal lands, but getting someone to investigate the initial crime was the hard part. Investigations were hampered by overlapping authority, like whether the crime occurred on the reservation or off, whether a tribal member was the victim or per-petrator, and missing person cases could be especially tricky. Did she disappear from the reservation, or did she disappear from town? Is the chief suspect a tribal member or a local? Is she a boozer or an addict or mentally ill? Maybe she just ran off with some man. "Native women have always been considered invisible and dispos-able," Nova said, "and when our boyfriends or husbands beat us to death, or when a predator drags us into the desert and rapes and murders us, the burden to prove that a crime was actually committed falls on the family, and this makes us vulnerable."

"I had no idea," David said.

"Of course you didn't. This problem, like so many other issues we face, gets no coverage in the mainstream press." Nova turned toward David. "The modern American Indian is an enigma to White America. There's a book you should read that will give you a great lesson in our history and how we changed from a nation of successful tribes occupying an entire continent to fragmented groups of refugees struggling to survive on government handouts. It's called *The Heartbeat of Wounded Knee* by David Treuer. My father read it and insisted I read it."

"Your father reads?" David blurted out incredulously. Then he quickly grabbed Nova's hand. "I'm sorry. I didn't mean to presuppose—"

Nova smiled. "Don't worry about it. If I didn't know the man, I wouldn't think he was a reader."

David wanted to ask how she reconciled her father the drug lord with her father the bookworm, but now was not the time. Until the current situation played out, family histories—his and hers—were irrelevant. "Did they find her?" David asked. "The missing woman?"

"Two months after she disappeared, a fisherman found her snagged in the exposed roots of a cottonwood tree on the banks of the Carson River. She was wrapped in plastic and duct tape."

"Did they make an arrest?"

"No."

The familiar sound of the CNN breaking news intro drew their attention to the television. It was primetime—5:00 p.m. in the West, 8:00 p.m. in the East—and if the story was going to air, it was going to air right now. It did.

> *This is Anderson Cooper, and we have a bombshell of a story tonight that only CNN is reporting, but let me warn you ahead of time, don't panic. It is a frightening story, but listen to the full report. We have learned that there have been more than twenty deaths in a small western Nevada town that are identical to what has been spreading through Asia and the Middle East. So why not panic? Is this not the first indication that the new viral pandemic has reached American soil? Not necessarily. Fallon, Nevada, is a farming community with a population of eighty-five hundred that, over the past six months, has experienced twenty-three deaths related to uncontrollable hemorrhaging from the trachea and internal bleeding caused by ruptured spleens. Yes, these are the same symptoms the rest of the world is experiencing, but recall what I said earlier. This has been going on for six months. The Fallon cases precede the initial outbreak in Wuhan, China, by more than five months, and it has not spread beyond the town, nor has it had a mortality rate in the eighty to ninety percent range that has been reported elsewhere. So what's going on here? It's unclear for now, but earlier today Larissa McClure from our San Francisco bureau spoke with one of the families who lost a loved one to this heinous affliction.*

The studio shot cut away to the prerecorded Miller interview, and the couple had done exactly as David had asked—called attention to the similarities of the events overseas and the horrific deaths of their son and others in the area. They voiced their concern that the deaths had something to do with the US Army biosafety lab, which was only a few miles outside of town. And, they noted, they'd been unable to get any information from local or state authorities regarding the official cause of death of their son, nor had any government or military officials addressed their concerns regarding the lab. Even to the casual observer, the parallels between Fallon and Wuhan, China, were unmistakable. If this report and the damning video recorded inside the lab didn't blow up the ant pile, nothing would, David told himself.

Anderson Cooper reappeared and introduced Larissa McClure. A head-and-shoulders shot of the young reporter appeared with the San Francisco skyline filling the screen behind her. "Larissa," Cooper began, "if these deaths are indeed related to the army's biowarfare lab on the edge of town and they occurred months before the first outbreak in China, this is a shocking revelation with untold implications."

"Yes, Anderson. 'Shocking' is the operative word here, and it further applies to events that occurred as we were wrapping up the interview with the Millers. An unidentified person approached me and passed off a flash drive that was allegedly smuggled out of the lab."

The list, David thought. *What about the list?*

"As you know, Anderson, CNN has tried to determine the source of the flash drive and to validate the authenticity of the video it contains but has been unable to do so. Normally we would not air something from an unknown source that has not been vetted or authenticated, but in this case, its relevance to the Miller claims—I believe—mandates that we show it."

"Our producers agree," the in-studio shot returning to Anderson Cooper. "I would like to warn the viewers that the video portrays extremely disturbing scenes of what appears to be human experimentation."

The video played unedited for the entire ninety seconds. Tears quickly filled Nova's eyes and streamed down her cheeks as she watched the women, all three of them strapped to their beds, all three of them screaming and fighting to get loose while ghostly figures in hazmat suits did things to them. David held her tight as Anderson Cooper returned to the screen, also visibly shaken. He asked Larissa McClure if she had been able to reach local, state, military, or federal officials for comment.

"Nobody is willing to speak to us," she said.

Nova looked up, tears still running down her face, her eyes pleading. "What's going to happen now, David?"

"The American people will see this, and their fear will rise even higher, and they'll demand answers. Somebody has to investigate the lab, and inside the lab is a vaccine to stop the virus and a drug to treat those who already have it. That's our only hope."

Nova lay her head against David's chest. "You're the unidentified source of the video."

"Yes," he said.

"And that puts you in danger."

"Yes, it does."

- 57 -

David was right. The Miller interview and the human-experimentation video blew up the ant pile. Every press organization from around the country sent their reporters to Fallon to dig deeper, to get the facts, to assess the risk to the rest of the country. *Find the lab and see if you can get in. Find the families of the victims and get the scoop. Nag the authorities—local, state, federal, military—until you get someone to talk. Find the county coroner, and get someone from the state medical board. They must know what's going on. And what about the navy? They're right next door. Surely they know something.*

Every hotel and motel in Fallon filled up. Vans with large antennae and obnoxious signage filled the lots. Many members of the press, along with their support staff and crewmembers, wore surgical masks and latex gloves, garnering looks of both humor and fear from the townspeople. *Maybe we should be wearing masks and gloves,* some of the locals must have been thinking, while others figured if they weren't dead yet, they were probably immune.

David had no cases scheduled for that Tuesday morning, so he sat in the surgeon's lounge and watched the spectacle unfold on CNN. The White House quickly denounced the Miller interview as fake news staged by the Democrats and attributed the human-experimentation video to Democratic operatives who had hired actors to stage the scene. Colonel Anthony Foster, Commander, United States Army Medical Research Institute of Infectious Disease, stated emphatically that human experimentation was not currently, nor had it ever been performed at any USAMRIID facility. The Fallon deaths, the White House stated, were purely coincidence. The Armed Forces Institute of Pathology had reviewed the cases and determined them to be similar, but unrelated, to the new viral pandemic sweeping the globe. David sat forward and leaned on the table, a sickening feeling building in his gut. He had expected lies and denials from the president, but if the AFIP and the commander of USAMRIID were on his side—if they were co-conspirators—there was no way David would be able to take down the Goliath of a far-reaching government conspiracy. He smirked at his own David and Goliath reference, then let his head fall onto his forearms and closed his eyes. What the hell was he going to do now? The answer came a moment later. CNN announced that Dr. Susan Preston, Churchill County coroner and chief of pathology at Fallon-Churchill Community Hospital, was going to hold a press conference at noon.

- 58 -

The cafeteria was the only room in the hospital sizable enough to accommodate a crowd. The tables and chairs had been pushed against the walls and a lectern placed at the far end, upon which technicians were mounting a variety of microphones, each sporting the logo of the home network or affiliate. The front half of the room had already filled with reporters, the back half quickly filling. An excited buzz emanated from the crowd as everyone jostled for position. David entered through the doors at the far end of the room and leaned against the back wall.

Once everyone had settled in and the cameras and microphones had been checked, Dr. Susan Preston took her place behind the lectern. She cleared her throat, took a sip of water, shuffled through a number of printed pages, then began to speak:

> Good afternoon. The Churchill County Coroner's Office and the Nevada State Health Division thought it would be a good idea to explain what has been going on in the town of Fallon with regards to a cluster of unusual deaths that closely mimic the viral pandemic now responsible for millions of deaths worldwide. To date, this office has performed postmortem examinations on twenty patients who died from hemoptysis—the coughing up of blood—and three patients who died from massive splenomegaly and rupture of the spleen.

Preston went on to state the epidemiological data for each patient, including age and sex, where they lived—in town, outside of town, on farmland or ranchland, near the naval base, near the old nuclear test site—preexisting health conditions, and any known exposures to environmental toxins or infectious agents. In summary, she said, this was a healthy group of individuals with no known acute or chronic illnesses that would predispose them to hemoptysis or splenomegaly, nor were there any known exposures to environmental toxins or previously diagnosed infections. She then followed with a discussion of the autopsy results:

> *All twenty hemoptysis patients demonstrated the same mode of death—rapid onset pulmonary edema, followed by bleeding into the lungs from ruptured pulmonary arterioles and venules, resulting in hemoptysis and fatal hemorrhaging. All three splenomegaly patients died from intraabdominal hemorrhage secondary to splenic rupture. The underlying cause of both pathologies was determined to be the Hantavirus.*

The room erupted with questions: *What is the Hantavirus? Is it contagious? Is it the same virus that's infecting the rest of the world? Is it one hundred percent fatal? How do you treat it?* Preston quieted the group, promising to answer all their questions. The Hantavirus, she explained, was common to the Desert Southwest but had been reported in all regions of the country. It was carried by rodents, specifically mice:

> *To contract this disease, you must come into contact with the urine, saliva, or feces of infected mice. Most commonly, the viral particles are inhaled as the victim sweeps out a garage, cabin, barn, or any structure or space where the mice are endemic and leave their droppings. The fecal particles dry, and the viruses become airborne by the sweeping motion. The primary symptoms of the disease include fatigue, fever, and muscle aches, and is often mistaken for the flu. There is no cure or treatment, but most patients recover after days to weeks, and human-to-human transmission does not occur. Let me repeat that: The virus is not transmitted from human to human. There is a subset of patients, however, that develops what is known as HPS, or Hantavirus Pulmonary Syndrome.*

In these patients, the lungs quickly fill with edema fluid, and the resulting pulmonary congestion results in the rupture of the small blood vessels of the air sacs. These patients begin to cough up massive amounts of bloody edema fluid, and without immediate treatment—which means endotracheal intubation and placement on a ventilator—the patient essentially bleeds to death while suffocating on his or her own secretions.

The room erupted again, the reporters yelling out: *Can the virus be diagnosed before it progresses to bleeding and suffocation? Why couldn't these patients be saved? How come outbreaks like this aren't reported more often if the virus is so widespread? How does the virus affect the spleen?* Preston answered all these questions in turn, but never once mentioned enlarged mediastinal lymph nodes or bronchopulmonary artery fistulas.

After the death of Jimmy Miller, David researched the Hantavirus and the pulmonary syndrome associated with it. There were no documented cases of any patients presenting with, or dying from, hemoptysis or splenic rupture anywhere in the United States or around the world. Preston was lying. But, to a community and a country in a state of fear, she had said all the right things. Her description of Hantavirus Pulmonary Syndrome satisfactorily explained what had been seen in Fallon. Scientists at the Armed Forces Institute of Pathology had isolated the Hantavirus from tissue samples sent to them by Preston, and they had sequenced RNA from those specimens and compared it to the RNA of the coronavirus sweeping the globe and determined they were two separate organisms. The state health division had not detected the spread of any cases beyond Fallon and were continuing a surveillance program to ensure it didn't. All lies, and the government had deftly used them to wrap everything in a nice package. This press conference, combined with the president's lies discrediting the video, would quell the fear of a local community and the nation at large, and it would deflect any suspicion that the United States government had any role in unleashing a killer supervirus on the world.

"Fuck," David muttered under his breath.

- 59 -

The plan David formulated as he rode the elevator to the basement was simple. He would ask Susan Preston about the press conference, point out her inconsistencies with his own understanding of the Hantavirus Pulmonary Syndrome, and press her on the discrepancies between what she'd told him the first time they spoke and what she had reported upstairs. He wanted to make her uncomfortable, maybe get her to reveal something important, but at the same time he did not want to alienate her as a possible ally. He had no doubt she was part of the conspiracy and an instrument of the coverup, and as such, she was a potential connection to the lab. But as soon as he walked into her office, his plan left the rails.

"What the fuck were you talking about up there?" he blurted out. "The twenty-three patients that died in this county were not victims of the Hantavirus. There are no reported cases of hemoptysis associated with the Hantavirus anywhere in the world, and there are no reported cases of the virus having any effects on the spleen or other lymphoid organs."

"Severe pulmonary edema is often associated with hemoptysis," Preston said. "I shouldn't have to tell you that."

"Yes, it is, but you get frothy, blood-tinged secretions. I watched Jimmy Miller bleed to death, and what was pouring out of his trachea was pure blood, not bloody edema fluid. And you told me he had enlarged lymph nodes in his mediastinum and a bronchopulmonary artery fistula, the same findings you saw in all of the patients. There was no mention of that upstairs."

Preston looked down at her hands, which were folded on her desk. "Based on the AFIP's review of the cases, I've amended my conclusions."

"You mean someone amended them for you." David stepped closer to Preston's desk and grabbed a picture frame. He looked at it, then showed it to her. "Your kids? Your husband? You allow them to live here despite the risk?"

"We don't live in a barn, and they're not sweeping mouse feces into clouds of dust, so yes, they live here."

David placed the photo back on her desk. "They were immunized before everybody else, weren't they? That's the deal. Do your part to help cover up a government program that's testing a vaccine on human subjects, and your family is first in line."

Preston stood and crossed her arms, trying to look defiant but looking shaky and unsure instead. "I'm not sure what you're referring to, so, unless you're here to discuss a specific case related to your surgical practice, I have work to do."

"Look," David said, softening his tone, "there's a twenty-six-year-old woman with enlarged lymph nodes eroding into her left mainstem bronchus and pulmonary artery. I know they're real. I've seen the CT scan. What I don't know is whether or not I should go in and remove them. Based on your recommendation, which you based on your autopsy findings, I've decided not to operate. I've put my complete trust, and her life, in your hands, and now you're telling me those findings are no longer valid?"

Preston sat down and folded her hands on her desk, glanced at them, and then looked up at David. Very quietly, she said, "Do not operate on her. It would be a mistake."

David sat down. "Then help me. I know the biolab engineered CoVid19 and 23, and they tested 23 right here before releasing it in China. I also know they developed a monoclonal antibody therapy and tested it on the women in the video." David sat forward and planted his forearms on Preston's desk. "I need access to the antibody. I need it to treat Nova Featherstone. I don't care what's going on in the rest of the world. I don't need to be a hero. I just want Nova to live."

Preston leaned back in her chair, trying again to look defiant, and failing again. "I don't know what you're talking about. The cluster of deaths we've experienced here in Churchill County were caused by the Hantavirus."

Pressure exploded into David's head. He wanted to flip the desk on top of the lying bitch, but instead he folded his arms across his chest and leaned back in *his* chair. "Then get ready for a media shitstorm like you've never seen."

- 60 -

After David Aaronson stormed out of her office, Susan Preston called Colonel Jonathan Neville on a secure line.

"Neville," he said.

"This is Preston. The surgeon was just here. He knows everything."

"What do you mean he knows everything?"

"He ran through the list of things that can never go public—that we isolated the Wuhan virus, we engineered 19 and 23 and released them in China, our human experimentation—and he's threatening to go to the press."

"Christ," Neville said. "What does he want?"

"He wants access to the monoclonal antibodies. He's trying to save the dying girl. He implied he'll stay quiet."

"Implied? What the fuck does that mean?"

"He said he doesn't care about going public. He just wants to save the girl."

"How did he learn all of this? Did he say?"

"No, he didn't say."

"Did you ask him?"

"No."

"Why not?"

"He was very agitated. When I told him I didn't know what he was talking about, he stormed out. If I had asked him how he got his information, that would have confirmed his suspicions."

A pause, then, "All right. I'll take care of it."

Using the same secure line he had just used to speak to Susan Preston, Jonathan Neville called a number in Washington, DC.

- 61 -

Just down the hall from the Oval Office in the White House is a small, almost forgotten office. It's not much bigger than the desk that sits within it. There's no reception area, nor is there a secretary who greets visitors or answers the phone. It's just a space with a desk and a secure line linking directly to the president of the United States. During the Nixon presidency, this space was occupied by E. Howard Hunt, a former CIA operative who became one of Nixon's "Plumbers" and helped organize the break-in of the Democratic National Committee at the Watergate complex in 1972. Now the office belonged to Robert "Bob" Dietrich. Much like E. Howard Hunt, Bob Dietrich's primary job entailed stopping leaks and dispensing with any other issues that might harm or embarrass the president. In other words, he was the president's fixer.

At 4:22 p.m. Dietrich's phone rang. He answered, was told to report to the Oval Office immediately, and did so. He left five minutes later with explicit instructions: take out the surgeon, make it look like an accident, and get the blonde hooker and truck driver while you are there. Two hours later, Dietrich and an associate were boarding a private jet at Andrews Airforce Base that would deliver them to NAS Fallon.

- 62 -

Following the completion of evening rounds, David went to the Stockman's, sat at his usual table, and ordered a Maker's Mark. As the cocktail waitress walked away, he rested his elbows on the table and let his face fall into his hands. He had failed. His efforts to draw the Fallon biolab into the spotlight and prompt an investigation, his hopes of sending someone into the black hole of the lab to emerge with a cure for Nova, had all been thwarted. The government was winning. The president was winning. David was no match for them.

His drink arrived.

He took a huge gulp and ordered another before the waitress could get away. He had discharged the last of his patients that evening and had no cases scheduled for tomorrow. No cases, no patients to round on—he was taking tomorrow off.

He texted Nova: "I need to talk to you. Call me when you can."

He finished his first drink as the second arrived, and as he took a sip from number two his phone rang. He and Nova exchanged hellos. David quickly looked around to see if anyone was eavesdropping, then he said, "I let you down. I thought I could get someone to investigate the lab, but I failed."

"David—"

"And I did something really stupid. I showed them my hand. They know I know everything, and that I leaked the video to the press."

"What is it you know, David? You're scaring me."

"I can't tell you. It will put you in danger."

"David—"

"Look," he said as three ounces of ninety-proof bourbon crossed the blood-brain barrier and intensified his emotions, "I love you, more than anything, but I don't think we should see each other until this plays out. I'm in a dangerous spot, and I don't want you—dammit!" David said as the bells and chimes and hooting and hollering of a large jackpot interrupted him.

When the noise subsided, Nova said, "Where are you?"

"The Stockman's."

"Stay there. I'm coming to see you."

David started to protest, but Nova ended the call.

He tried calling her back. No answer.

He tried texting her. No response.

Fifteen minutes later she walked through the door, a look of panic on her face.

"This is a bad idea," David said as Nova sat down.

She reached across the table and took his hands in hers. Tears filled the corners of her eyes. "Is there some way out of this, David? I'm really scared."

"I know you are. I'll figure something out. I'm not ready to give up. But for now we can't be together. I want you to stay close to your father. He'll keep you safe. Now let me walk you to your car."

Nova gripped David's hands tighter. "Don't let this be the last time I see you."

"It won't be. I promise."

David walked Nova out to the parking lot.

Two men—one sitting at a nearby blackjack table, the other in front of a bank of slot machines—watched them go. The slot player followed David and Nova out to the lot, where he watched them from a distance. The other man, the blackjack player, walked away from the table, took out his phone, and made a call.

David watched Nova drive away, then hopped in his car and drove to the Beaver. He had to find Andy, his only connection to the lab.

David sat at the end of the bar, waved a finger at the bartender, and pointed at the Maker's Mark bottle on a nearby shelf. Despite the unmistakable similarity between the world-ending CoVid23 pandemic and Fallon's "Hantavirus" epidemic, all the usual suspects were here. Why let a deadly supervirus get in the way of weeknight drinking and pool?

"Hey, Doc," yelled out a guy wearing a "King Ropes" baseball cap. "If you're here tonight, must be safe. I mean, you ain't wearin' a mask and gloves, right?"

David gave the guy a nod and a half smile.

The bartender set David's glass of bourbon in front of him. "Yeah, Doc," he said, "what about that? Coronaviruses killing people around the world. Rat viruses spreading through Fallon. I got a wife and a couple little girls at home. Should I send them away from this place?"

"Sorry, but I don't have a good answer for you. Whatever's going around has been here for at least six months, so by now you either have it or you don't."

The bartender poured himself a shot of Jack Daniel's and held it up. "Fair enough," he said, and he downed his shot.

"Hey," David said before the bartender wandered off, "have you seen Andy the truck driver around recently?"

"Nah," the bartender said. "He got in a nasty fight with that fucker over at the pool table who was just talking to you. Hasn't been around since."

"Thanks," David said, and as he tipped his head back and took a big swallow of his drink, a petite blonde hopped onto the stool next to his.

"Hello, handsome," Ruby Parker said as she hooked a finger in his shirt and pulled him in for a kiss. "Lookin' hot in your dress slacks and shirt. Just finish up at the hospital?"

"Yes. All done for the day. How're you, Ruby? You been out and about this evening?"

"Yeah. The usual."

"I don't suppose you ran into Andy."

"No. Haven't seen him," Ruby said, "but ever since I first met you, you've been looking for someone. I have a feeling the stuff you had me give to the reporter is what Andy gave to you at the Comstock, and I think he got it from the Asian guy who works in the army lab."

"You're right. You've connected the dots, but that also puts you in danger, so be careful."

The bartender placed two shots of Grey Goose in front of David and Ruby Mae. "Courtesy of Miss Parker's friend," he said.

David glanced at the far end of the bar. Hams-for-Fists held up a shot glass of something brown. They gave each other a nod and downed their shots.

- 64 -

Submerged in the depths of an alcohol-fueled blackout, David was unaware of the sound of his front door getting kicked in, and before his depressed state of consciousness could process what was happening, two men jerked him off the couch, slipped a black bag over his head, and zip-tied his ankles and wrists together. By the time his cortex was fully functional, he'd been dragged out the door and thrown into the trunk of a car.

David was now wide awake, his wrists and ankles stinging where the zip ties were cutting into him, something sharp stabbing him in the ribs, but he could do little about it. He was wedged between car body and spare tire, and his restrained limbs were of no use. He tried to calm himself with deep breaths but gagged on the smell of gasoline, grease, and rubber.

The car made a series of turns, knocking David around, the sharp object digging deeper, his wrists and ankles lighting up with pain, but then the ride leveled out and the speed increased. On the highway now, he thought, and heading to the middle of nowhere. He had stepped on the wrong nerve, and now he was going meet his end—a down-on-your-knees-bullet-to-the-back-the-head execution deep in the desert. The thought of never seeing Nova again brought tears to his eyes. But worse than that, the thought of her dying alone, the thought of her bleeding to death with nobody to help her—that made him sick to his stomach.

Twenty minutes later, the car slowed and turned onto a dirt road, and the farther from the highway they traveled, the rougher the road became. It tossed him around, filled the trunk with dust, the stinging and stabbing getting worse. Gravel crunched under the tires. Large rocks scraped the undercarriage. The dust was relentless, making it hard to breathe. Whoever was driving did not want his body to be found.

The car stopped. Both the driver and passenger doors opened and closed. Two sets of footsteps came around to the back. Rusty springs groaned and popped as the trunk opened. David was hoisted out, carried by his ankles and wrists, and thrown onto the ground. The *sha-shink* of a shell being chambered in a semi-automatic handgun filled the frigid desert air as a single set of footsteps moved behind him.

The zip tie binding his ankles was cut.

He rose to his knees.

Then nothing but silence.

He closed his eyes tight as he imagined his executioner standing over him, aiming the muzzle of a pistol at the back of his head.

Still nothing but silence.

What the hell is he waiting for? David wondered. *Is he taking pleasure in the moment? Is he savoring the adrenaline rush of ending a human life?*

Then the wrist zip tie was cut.

David tentatively reached for the black bag on his head. His captives said nothing as he removed it. He was blinded by the headlights of the car, then a long-handled shovel emerged from the light and hit him in the face and chest.

"Start digging," a voice commanded.

David knew the voice, and as he shielded his eyes from the glaring light, he recognized its source. Two Feathers, backlit by the headlights and looming over David like a mythical giant. A second man stood off to the side, pointing a gun at David.

"Dig!" Two Feathers repeated.

"For fuck's sake, man. Are you kidding me?" David said.

In one swift move, Two Feathers ripped his pistol out of its shoulder harness, chambered a round with another loud *sha-shink*, covered the three feet between them and jammed the barrel of the gun into David's forehead.

"You think I'm fucking around?"

David squeezed his eyes shut and raised his hands. "She's dying!"

Two Feathers jammed the muzzle of the gun even harder into David's skull bone. "What did you just say?"

"Nova's dying. She has the same thing that killed the twenty-three people they're talking about in the news."

"That's how Gary Kinghorn died," the other man said.

Two Feathers looked over at him, then back at David.

"Is that true?" Two Feathers said.

"Yes. The virus that's killing millions of people? The new virus? The army biolab created it here, then tested it on the town before they released it in China. Most people die from coughing up blood, but some get enlarged spleens that rupture." Two Feathers backed away. David rubbed his forehead and wrists. "I did a CT scan before she left the hospital. She has enlarged lymph nodes in her chest that will eventually kill her."

"Can't you do something about it?"

"No. Surgery is not an option. The lab developed a cure, but they're keeping it a secret, so I've been trying to get someone to investigate, to expose what they've done. The Miller interview? I set that up. The video of the women in the lab? I passed that off to the press. I'm doing everything I can to save Nova."

Two Feathers slipped his gun back into its harness. "Well you better fuckin' save her, or you're dead."

- 65 -

Andy drove his delivery truck up the dirt road leading to the lab, shielding his eyes from the morning sun. The order to be delivered was typical—a variety of frozen meats from the company in Reno, as well as fresh fruits and vegetables, and desserts like you might find in a school cafeteria. In addition, there were pallets of water, soda, and iced tea. The food and beverages were carried in from the loading dock by lab employees, who then returned with a stack of empty pallets. Andy waited until he was back in town to pull over and check for an envelope. It was there, stapled to the underside of the top pallet. He opened it to find two one-hundred-dollar bills and a note: *The Brown Beaver, tonight at 7 p.m. Make sure the surgeon is there.*

- 66 -

David climbed off the couch and shielded his eyes from the midday sun as he staggered into the bathroom. He needed ibuprofen for a pulsating headache, and he needed to change the dressings around the zip-tie cuts on his wrists and ankles, which he'd applied in the early-morning hours after being returned home by his would-be assassins. The quarter-size bruise in the middle of his forehead and his black-and-blue ribs—well, there was nothing to be done there.

To say the ride home from the desert had been a long strange trip would be a gross mischaracterization. David had ridden in the back seat of a 1970s four-door Pontiac Grand Am. His possible future father-in-law—David wanted to laugh at this—sat up front on the passenger side while a guy named Dan drove. The ride had been slow at first, the car rocking right and left, up and down, forward and back due to the deep ruts in the road, but then they came to a stretch that was more evenly graded, allowing for higher speeds. Dan picked up the pace, gravel pelting the car as they sped down the straights and fishtailed around the turns. Every few minutes Two Feathers would turn and glare at David, his jaw muscles knotted up like golf balls as the glow from the dashboard lights cast him as a hulking mass murderer from a horror movie. Finally, Dan spoke up. "Look, man," he had said to Two Feathers. "Yeah, he's white, but there ain't no good options on the rez, and he's better than those cocky-ass flyboys. Face it, Billy, Nova's choices are limited. The town surgeon? Not so bad." Two Feathers turned around and stared straight ahead.

And that's how it went—every few minutes Two Feathers glaring at David, Dan telling him to lighten up, there were bigger things to worry about, apocalyptic things that might make Nova's choice of who she dated a moot point.

Two Feathers' parting words as they dropped David off in front of his house: "Fuckin' save her, or you're dead."

David finished dressing his wounds, grabbed a beer from the refrigerator, and sat down on the couch. The ibuprofen hadn't touched his headache. Maybe a couple of beers would, the old hair-of-the-dog thing. He turned on the news. Russia was history. The military had surrounded the Kremlin, but the rest of the country had been reduced to collections of violent gangs and tribal factions vying for power, but power over what? Food production, energy production, retail, communications, banking, everything had ground to a halt. Images of pickup trucks stuffed with machine-gun-wielding thugs flashed across the screen, along with burning piles of dead bodies and people scurrying about in surgical masks. Who had the keys to the nuclear arsenal now?

David's phone rang. An unknown caller told him his paper was on the porch. David rushed out the door and looked up and down the street, hoping to catch the paperboy in his oxidized black Toyota Corolla, but he saw nothing. He picked up the paper and went inside. Like before, there was a message at the top of page six: *The Big Brown Beaver, seven o'clock.*

The crowd at the Beaver was much like the night before—the obstinate ones—the jukebox playing "Gimme Three Steps" by Lynyrd Skynyrd. David grabbed his usual seat at the end of the bar and ordered an IPA. His first look around the room revealed nothing—no Andy the truck driver, no Ruby Mae Parker.

"Excuse me for sayin' so, Doc," the bartender said as he brought David his beer, "but after last night, I thought you'd be layin' low for a couple days."

David felt the heat of embarrassment rising in his cheeks. He remembered little from the night before, aside from being bound and gagged, hauled into the desert, and told to dig his own grave. "Yeah, well, with the end of days coming, might as well live a little. Hope I didn't cause any trouble."

"Not at all. Ruby Mae took you home."

"Uh, yeah, that was nice of her."

"Thing is, Doc? Didn't seem like you drank too much, not enough to get sloppy, anyway. I've seen you put away quite a bit with no problem, but last night Ruby could barely keep you upright as she helped you outta here."

David tried to recall at least a scrap of what had happened—in the bar, during the ride home, at the house—but came up with nothing. "Guess things just got away from me. Hey," David said, impatient to change the subject, "you haven't seen Andy, have you?"

"No," the bartender replied.

"And Ruby? Has she been around tonight?"

"She was here a few minutes ago. Her *manager*"—the bartender adding air quotes—"is back there playing pool."

David took another look around the room as he sipped his beer. Hams-for-Fists was, in fact, in the back corner, lurking in the shadows. A moment later, a petite blonde in tight jeans and a yellow blouse emerged from the hallway that led to the rear of the building and the restrooms.

Andy pulled his pickup into a parking space on Main Street near the Brown Beaver and lit a joint. Only a couple of hits, he told himself. Maybe three or four. Just enough to take the edge off. He didn't really want to go into the Beaver. He didn't really want to see that asshole Mitch Wallingford. Son of a bitch had been bullying him since middle school, and if he kept it up, Andy was gonna kill the bastard, drive him way out into the desert, gut him like a mule deer, leave his entrails in the dirt for the coyotes, and then bury his gutless carcass in a hole full of quicklime.

Bob Dietrich sat in his rented sedan across the street from the Big Brown Beaver. He had backed into the parking spot so he could watch the place. The doctor and the whore were already inside, but the truck driver was hesitating, sitting in his pickup for some reason. Did something spook him? Doubtful. There were only two people in this shit stain of a town who knew what was about to happen—himself and his operative, who was in the basement below the Beaver. Dietrich texted him: "The truck driver is hesitating. Do not put plan into motion."

The operative texted back: "Too late. Old pipes. Setting the timer and getting out."

"Dammit," Dietrich said. He screwed a silencer onto his Glock 19, walked across the street, and after he checked that the sidewalks were clear of pedestrians, he shot the kid through the left temple. The driver's side and passenger-side windows exploded. The kid fell over in a lifeless slump onto the bench seat and lay there in a pool of glass, blood, and brain. Dietrich dropped several bags of meth and some fifty-dollar bills on the floorboard of the truck, went back to the car, and pulled around to the alley behind the bar.

His associate threw his duffel bag in the trunk and climbed in the front. They drove two blocks over and parked.

"What happened?" Dietrich asked as he turned off the engine.

"The pipes were really old. As soon as I put my wrench on a coupler, they broke apart, and gas started leaking fast. Good news, the basement is concrete, but the floor above and the rest of the building is wood framing—old wood, like the pipes. When the gas blows, the blast will be directed up into the bar. Should thoroughly destroy the place."

Ruby Parker crossed the room, coming toward David. She seemed dejected or distracted or maybe tired. Her gait was not as confidant, her posture not as erect. As she approached, she barely looked up. She just sat down and stared straight ahead.

"Thanks for driving me home last night," David said. "I hope I behaved like a gentleman."

"You did. You're always a gentleman."

"Can I get you a drink? A thank-you shot of Grey Goose?"

"No thanks. Not tonight."

"Is everything all right?" David asked. "You're not your usual … spirited self. You sure I didn't do or say anything stupid last night?"

David spotted a tear running down Ruby's right cheek. Then she turned toward him, exposing the left side of her face.

"Jesus," David said. "What happened?" Her left cheek was bruised purple, and her eye blackened. Tears streamed down both cheeks. "What happened to you?" David repeated.

"When I got you home, I was supposed to use my phone to take pictures of me sucking your … of me giving you oral, then you giving me oral. We were gonna use them to blackmail you, but I couldn't do it, so I took a beating."

"Let me guess, Fuckhead sitting back there in the corner?"

Ruby said nothing.

"Did he hit you anywhere else?"

"No," Ruby replied, staring down at the bar.

"Did you go to the ER? Make sure you don't have any broken bones?"

She shook her head.

"Did you call the police?"

Ruby looked up at David. "I don't want to talk about it. It comes with the territory."

"Okay, but one last question. Did that asshole drug me last night?"

A giant hand grabbed Ruby Parker's arm and jerked her off the barstool.

David jumped up. "Listen, shithead, don't hit her again."

"Or what?" Hams said, getting in David's face, the smell of cheap bourbon and cigarettes turning his stomach.

David inched closer. "I'll bring her to the hospital, and I'll x-ray her, and if she has any fractures, old or new, I'll call the sheriff myself, and if she doesn't, I'll find X-rays from other patients that do show broken bones, and I'll put her name on them, then I'll call the sheriff. In fact, I'll produce X-rays of old fractures in places where you've never hit her. I'll make you look like the second coming of the Marquis de Sade. You really want to go down that road? Your word against mine?"

Hams moved his face even closer to David's, their noses almost touching. "I don't know who the Markee duh shod is, but you best watch yourself, Doc. You ain't been here long enough to learn the lay of the land. This town will fuck you up."

Hams dragged Ruby Parker down the sidewalk by her arm, jerking her hard, head snapping, hair flying. "You stupid bitch," he said. "You better not have told him about last night."

Ruby pulled free, said, "Fuck you, asshole," and started walking quickly ahead of him.

Then she came to Andy's truck and stopped.

Shards of glass littered the street on both sides.

She slowly walked over and looked inside the cab, then recoiled in horror at the sight of Andy's lifeless body and the giant bloodstain on the front seat.

Hams came up behind her. "What the—"

Ruby turned and ran, up the sidewalk, back into the bar, down to the end where David had been sitting. He wasn't there. She frantically waved at the bartender. "You know where he went?"

"Bathroom," the bartender replied.

Ruby moved quickly across the room and down the long hall toward the restrooms. Just as she reached the men's room, David exited.

"They killed Andy," she blurted out, tears streaming down her face. "Shot him through the head right out there on Main Street."

"What?" David said.

A blinding flash and concussive force pushed Ruby into David's arms and sent both of them hurtling backward as the sound of the explosion caught up to the force of the blast.

Bob Dietrich heard the blast, felt the ground shake, saw the flash of the fireball and the billowing cloud of smoke, followed by the glow of flames and the smell of burning wood. "As soon as the coroner IDs the bodies, we'll get out of this shithole of a town," Dietrich said to his operative.

- 68 -

Ruby and David landed at the base of a wall, half-buried by splintered wood, and chunks of brick, and drywall and glass and a barstool. David sat up, not knowing where he was or what had happened, his ears ringing, his eyes watering. His lungs struggled to move dust-laden and smoke-filled air. He wiped his eyes and coughed repeatedly while looking around, left and then right. They were in the alley behind the Big Brown Beaver, which was now a smoldering, gaping hole. The alley itself was hardly recognizable, clogged with debris and detritus.

Movement to David's left.

Ruby. She was balled up under splintered wood and drywall. He carefully removed the debris and helped her sit up. She groaned in pain, pushed his hands away, clutched her left side as her head fell back against the wall, eyes closed tight. David cleared more debris, then gently tried to move closer and get a better look.

"Don't touch me!" she said. "It hurts too much."

"I need to see what's causing the pain. Take some deep breaths and try to relax."

She did, and David was able to lean over her and look at her left side.

Oh shit, he said to himself.

Her hands were clasped around a shard of wood, a splintered two-by-four about one-inch thick in one dimension and a half inch in the other. It narrowed to a sharp point and protruded from her left flank about four inches. Blood was seeping onto her yellow blouse from both the entrance and exit wounds. "You have a piece of wood piercing your left side," he said.

Her grip relaxed, and she used her fingertips to feel the object. "Feels like a stake you'd drive through a vampire's heart."

"Exactly, and it passed from back to front, so I'd like to reach around behind you and see how long it is."

"Please," she pleaded, her face grimaced with pain, her eyes still closed tight. "Don't move me, even a little bit. It really hurts."

From off in the distance came the sound of multiple sirens. "I'll be careful," David said.

He gently laid his hand on her side near the stake and carefully moved his fingers toward her back. If he bumped the protruding end, the pain would be severe. He found it and estimated that about four inches of the wood extended beyond the skin, same as the front.

She looked up at him, tears running down her cheeks. "Am I gonna die?"

"No."

"Can you just pull it out? Like a big splinter? It'll really hurt, but we'd be done with it."

"No. If it pierced your colon and I removed it, that would allow fecal matter to enter your abdominal cavity, and you'd get very sick very fast. If it pierced your kidney or spleen and I pulled it out, you'd bleed into your abdomen."

"Sorry I asked," Ruby said with a pained smile. Then she started coughing, one hand gripping the stake, the other on her chest, her dusty cheeks streaked by tears.

The sirens were rapidly approaching.

"We have to get out of here," David said. "I need your phone."

"Back pocket."

David reached behind Ruby and felt for the phone. It was still there, thanks to the tight fit of the skinny jeans. He dialed Vince Strahan.

Thank Christ, David thought when the lieutenant answered.

"I need your help," David said. "The Brown Beaver was blown up, and Ruby Parker has a significant injury."

"We were just put on alert," Strahan said. "The base is launching a mass-casualty response. Choppers are gearing up to evac patients to Reno and Carson City. Ambulances are on the way."

"We can't use an ambulance or go to a hospital."

"Why not?"

"I think the explosion was meant for us, for Ruby and me, so I need you to come get us, and we're gonna need some medical supplies. Do you have a portable ultrasound machine?"

"Yeah. I do a lot of GYN stuff on the female staff and the wives of the pilots."

"Good, bring it, along with a basic surgical tray, local anesthetic and syringes, gauze pads and rolls of dressings, bottles of saline and antibiotics for wound irrigation, several liters of IV fluid—D5 lactated ringers or D5 normal saline. Make it six liters. And some IV morphine, if you have it." David thought for a minute. Was there anything else? "Oh yeah," he said, "a variety of sutures and a blood pressure cuff. And a blanket. Can you get all that?"

"I can, but what're we dealing with?"

"An impalement injury—a shard of wood about fourteen inches long impaled through the left flank."

"Is she stable?"

"For now."

"Where are you?"

"In the alley behind the Beaver, but we need to get out of here before someone finds us. Nobody can know we survived the blast." David again looked left and right, orienting his sense of direction. "We'll follow the alley two blocks north to the backside of the old Golden Nugget. There's a small park nearby that's part of City Hall. Come up Carson Street and you'll see it. We'll be waiting there."

David turned off Ruby's phone, pulled his from his pocket and turned it off, then threw both of them into the burning crater.

- 69 -

Traveling two city blocks on level ground sounded easy enough, but it was cold, David had no coat, and he had a ninety-five pound woman cradled in his arms. And as he carried her through the smoldering debris field, every step he took nearly toppled him while jostling her and the wooden stake impaling her side. Ruby also had no coat and was now shivering and had become less responsive. Worst-case scenario? She was bleeding internally and going into hemorrhagic shock. Best-case scenario? The shivering and depressed mental status were the result of the cold, the pain, and the stress of a significant traumatic injury. Either way, he needed to warm her up, and he needed to do a proper examination. If he detected any signs of internal bleeding, he would take her to a hospital, regardless of the risk.

The wreckage from the bar tapered off after thirty yards, making for easier travel, but the cold and the pain of his own injuries were setting in, and he was starting to shiver. His arms were covered with cuts and scrapes, and, judging by the sting, he presumed his face was cut up as well. The back of his head, neck, and shoulders ached from the impact with the wall. At least his cough had subsided and the ringing in his ears had abated—and he didn't have a spear piercing his side.

The emergency vehicles were coming in waves now. The first wave of sirens had arrived and gone silent, but more could be heard in the distance. He needed to get across West First Street before the entire area was buzzing with ambulances, fire trucks, cop cars, and military choppers. He looked left, then right, saw nothing up or down the street and quickly crossed, and twenty yards later David found the park. It was small, more of a courtyard attached to City Hall, but there were picnic tables and benches nestled among the landscaping that would offer a place to wait while hiding them from the street. David's back was beginning to tighten, but he kept Ruby cradled in his arms as he sat on a bench. She needed any body heat he could give her. Ten minutes later, Vince Strahan's Jeep pulled up to the curb.

The lieutenant held Ruby as David climbed into the front seat, then he carefully placed her in David's lap, left side facing forward so the wooden stake wouldn't bump up against anything. She grimaced and moaned with the movement but otherwise tolerated it well. David did his best to feel Ruby's abdomen. It was soft and not distended. The blood stains on the blouse had spread, but for now he was satisfied she was not bleeding internally. Strahan grabbed a blanket out of the back and covered Ruby, then hurried around to the driver's side.

"Thanks for coming," David said, "but before you get in, I need you to do something."

"Sure," the lieutenant replied.

"My car is parked one block over on Main, halfway between the Nugget and the Beaver. There's a duffel bag in the trunk. We're gonna need it." David took his car key from his pants pocket, trying not to move Ruby. "Do your best to not be seen. Quick in and out. Remember, everyone needs to think we're dead."

"Shouldn't be a problem. All attention will be on the smoking crater where the bar and the buildings on either side used to stand. How did you guys survive such a huge blast, anyway?"

"We were way in the back, near the restrooms."

Five minutes later, Vince Strahan returned to the Jeep and threw a medium-size nylon duffel into the back. "Where to?" he asked as he climbed into the driver's seat.

"Highway 50 West," David said, "and I'd like you to call Mona's and see if Ophelia is working tonight."

- 70 -

Thirty minutes later, Strahan steered the Jeep into the gravel parking lot of Mona's Kitty Ranch. The ride had gone well enough. As she warmed up, Ruby became more responsive. She could state her name, that she was in Fallon, and she knew the day of the week—in medical terms, she was oriented to person, place, and time—but unclear about what had happened, disoriented to circumstance. This was typical among trauma patients, so David was not overly concerned about a head injury. And he had periodically checked her radial pulse, which remained strong.

"Okay," David said as Strahan parked. "There's two hundred and fifty thousand dollars in that duffel bag back there. We need—"

"There's what?" Strahan said.

"It's a go bag—cash, passports, disposable cell phones. If I live long enough I'll explain everything, but for now we need a room, and privacy. Tell Ophelia I will pay whatever it takes to have her and her room for an undetermined number of days, like the NBA player who shacked up in one of these places a few years ago, hanging with the girls and doing drugs for a couple of weeks until they found him comatose. And we need to park around back in the employee lot, and to come and go through the same entrance the girls use. We have to be assured there are no cameras in the lot, at the door, or in the hallway. Complete privacy at any cost."

"They'll do it," Ruby said in a dreamy voice. "I used to work here."

"Okay," David replied, relieved to hear his patient speak coherently. "So grab several stacks of that cash back there and make it happen," he said to Strahan.

Vince returned twenty minutes later. "It's a go," he said as he started the Jeep. "Fifteen grand a day. Complete privacy."

Strahan drove around to the side of the building, aimed a garage door opener at a chain-link gate topped with razor wire, and passed through once it had opened. Ryan was waiting for them at the back entrance.

Once inside, they moved quickly down the hall to Ophelia's room. She had already covered her bed with extra sheets and towels. David carefully laid Ruby down and used a pillow to prop her up on her side so she wasn't lying on the wooden stake. At this point, her blouse was more crimson than yellow.

"Oh my God," Ryan said, recoiling in disgust.

Ophelia took one look and assumed a resting bitch stance—arms crossed, hips cocked to the side, one leg angled out beyond the other. "What's she doing here?"

"Uh, she's been impaled by a shard of lumber. Sounds like you know her," David said.

"From high school, and we used to work together."

"Not the best of friends?"

"You could say that."

"Well, she has been helping me expose the people responsible for your sister's death, and now she's paid a heavy price, so with your assistance we're going to take care of her."

With Ryan's help, Strahan retrieved the ultrasound machine and surgical supplies from the Jeep, and as the lieutenant checked her blood pressure, David asked Ruby her name, month, day of the week, and if she remembered what had happened. She half opened her eyes, answered the first three questions correctly, and then followed with, "There was an explosion, and a sharp pain in my side since then."

"Do you remember me telling you there's a piece of wood penetrating your left side?"

"Yeah, and something about my colon and kidney and spleen."

David looked up at the lieutenant. "Awake, alert, and appropriate," he said. "Blood pressure is good?"

"Yes," Strahan said.

"Okay. Let's get the ultrasound machine set up."

While Strahan grabbed what looked like a medium-size suitcase, placed it on the bed and opened it, David checked the supplies. They had everything they would need unless major organs were involved.

"Ready," Strahan said.

David went around the side of the bed and dropped to one knee, lowering himself to Ruby's level. "First thing I'm gonna do," he said, "is cut off your blouse and examine your wounds more closely. Then I'm going to place an ultrasound probe on your abdominal wall and move it around. At times I may have to push hard to get a good look, and it might hurt, but try to bear with it. I need to determine if any of your organs have been injured. If everything is good internally, we'll numb the entrance and exit wounds and remove the piece of wood."

"Okay," Ruby said in the same compliant-patient tone Nova had used after her surgery.

David used shears to cut off the bloody blouse. Ophelia covered Ruby with a fleece blanket while David examined the impalement injury. As he had noted in the alley, the shard of wood was an inch thick at the distal end and tapered to a sharp point at the proximal end. Blood continued to ooze from the skin edges of the entrance and exit wounds, but it was not life-threatening. Most encouraging was the path of the projectile. David could see and feel the piece of wood under the skin. It appeared too superficial to have entered the abdominal cavity. He would confirm this with the ultrasound, but he was confident he'd be able to remove it without serious complications.

David finished his exam, picked up the ultrasound probe, and coated it with gel.

Ryan asked if they needed her, then excused herself and left the room.

David peered into the screen of the ultrasound unit as he moved the gel-covered probe, first around the upper abdomen, then the lower abdomen, and finally along the path of the stake, changing the angles of the probe as he pushed lightly, then deeper. Ruby grimaced and moaned, but overall she tolerated the procedure well.

"It looks like the colon, spleen, and kidney are not involved. I did not see any blood pooling anywhere. I think this is basically a through-and-through soft tissue injury."

"And if it's not?" Strahan said.

"At the first sign of bleeding or fecal contamination of the abdominal cavity, we'll take her to the hospital."

David asked Vince Strahan to start an IV in Ruby's right arm and hang a liter of D5 lactated ringers. While the lieutenant and Ophelia took care of that, David filled two 10cc syringes with 1 percent lidocaine, mixed two liters of saline irrigation with betadine antibiotic solution, and set up the instrument tray and dressing supplies on the bed next to Ruby. Again, he went around to the other side, got down on a knee, and took her hand in his.

"Okay," he said, "it's time to get this vampire stake out of you. First, I'm going to numb the skin along the path of the wood. You'll feel multiple needle sticks and burning as I inject the local anesthetic, but it will quickly become numb, and you shouldn't have much pain after that. Now, when I start to remove the stake, you're gonna feel tugging and pulling, and this will be uncomfortable and maybe a little painful, but the pain should not be severe. Just try to bear with it. After it's out, I'll irrigate the wound and dress it. Are you ready?"

Ruby opened her eyes and said, "You talk too much. Just get the fucking thing out."

David smiled. She had plenty of fight left. A very good sign.

Strahan said, "Now that we have an IV, you want to give her some morphine?"

"A small dose, one milligram. We don't want to snow her and mask any signs of abdominal bleeding or contamination."

Strahan drew up the morphine and slowly injected it into a port on the IV tubing.

David asked Ophelia to remove the shade from one of her table lamps and move it closer.

Now they were ready.

David donned a pair of surgical gloves, painted the skin around the entrance and exit wounds with betadine, infiltrated the wounds and the skin overlying the projectile with lidocaine, and had Ophelia and Strahan roll Ruby farther onto her side so the shard of wood was parallel to the bed. He then gripped the fat end of the stake and gave it a gentle tug. It did not slip right out as he had hoped, so he pulled again, harder this time.

Ruby moaned and said what sounded like "Is it out?" But her words were slurred. The morphine had done its job.

David pulled firmly, maintaining steady traction as one would do when trying to open a lid stuck on a pickle jar, and after a few moments the shard broke free and slipped out.

"Fuck!" Ruby Mae Parker said as clear as day.

"Holy Christ," Vince Strahan said as he sized up the sixteen-inch piece of bloody wood David was holding in his hand.

"My God," Ophelia added.

"You okay?" David asked as he leaned over Ruby and softly stroked the top of her head.

She didn't reply. She was sleeping.

David dropped the wooden shard on the bed, grabbed stacks of four-by-four gauze pads in both hands, and compressed the entrance and exit wounds, which were now bleeding briskly.

71

After holding pressure for five minutes, David was able to reduce the bleeding to a slow ooze. He then irrigated the wound with antibiotic solution, and since it had been exposed to a dirty foreign body for a couple of hours, he packed the length of the wound with betadine-soaked gauze instead of suturing it closed. Strahan asked David if he needed any further assistance, then excused himself. He should be helping with triage at the blast site, he said. Ophelia helped David remove bits of debris from Ruby's hair, clean the dust from her face and arms with warm washcloths, and slip her into a pair of silk pajamas. And now she was tucked into Ophelia's bed, resting quietly, her IV fluids infusing at a steady rate for ongoing hydration, her vital signs normal. Her extremities were warm and well perfused, and her color was good—reliable indicators that she had not lost a significant amount of blood. David's plan going forward: check the dressings for continued bleeding and change them as necessary, perform a basic neurologic exam every couple of hours to watch for delayed signs of a head injury, monitor vital signs, and palpate her abdomen periodically to rule out intraabdominal hemorrhage.

Ophelia came up beside David as he checked the rate of the IV fluids. "That was hella cool," she said, "but I think it's time you take care of yourself."

David knew what she was getting at. He was covered with dust and had a number of small cuts and abrasions on his arms and probably his face. He glanced at the shower and bathtub filling the corner of the room, which had been designed more for recreation than personal hygiene.

"I'll go get us some drinks and give you some privacy," Ophelia said, "and I'll see if I can borrow a robe from Ryan. She's not quite as tall as you, but she's taller than me. Tomorrow I can do your laundry. Maker's Mark?"

"Can you make it a double?"

"How about a full bottle, two glasses, and a bucket of ice?"

"By all means."

"There's towels in the real bathroom, and shampoo and soap."

After Ophelia stepped out, David stripped off his dirty clothes and checked his face in the bathroom mirror. His suspicions were correct. He had numerous small cuts and scrapes on his face and scalp. The real pain, however, was coming from the back of his head. He did his best to visualize that area of his scalp, searching for a laceration, but he couldn't get a good look. His hair was not matted with dried blood, so this was unlikely. He did have large bruises across his shoulders, and his neck was tender to palpation, but these injuries, along with the scalp contusion, were all treatable with ibuprofen—and a couple of bourbons. Ironically, he'd been in much worse shape after his seventy two-hour stay in the Tombs.

Ophelia returned with a bottle of Maker's Mark, glasses and ice, and a red silk robe she'd borrowed from Ryan. David put on the robe, poured two drinks, and sat down in the corner chair. Ophelia took a seat in the other chair.

"Thank you for your help, with Ruby and the room," David said. "Without you, we'd be in serious trouble right now."

"Is she gonna be okay?"

"We'll know for sure in the next few hours, but I think so."

"The news was on in the bar. Were you there? Is that what happened to you guys?"

"Yes," David said. "What are they saying about survivors?"

"They haven't found any and don't expect to."

"Shit," David said quietly.

Ophelia and David sipped their drinks in silence, and when Ophelia had finished hers, she slipped out of her shoes and climbed on the bed. "You're welcome to join me," she said, wrapping herself in a fleece blanket. "There's room for all three of us."

"I'm good," David replied. "I think I should take some time to gather my thoughts."

"You can do that over here while you share some of your body heat with me."

David was exhausted and stressed beyond measure, and he was building a nice buzz from the bourbon. Feeling the body of an attractive young woman against his would be a sublime pleasure, but he loved Nova, and he wasn't sure he could trust his impulse control at the moment. On the other hand, Ophelia had been a great help, and David owed her at least a few moments of warmth and human connection and the feeling that someone truly cared about her. He climbed onto the bed and leaned back against the headboard. She balled up next to him and rested her head on his chest. He put his arms around her and held her, and as she relaxed, and her breathing slowed and deepened, she felt real to David, a young woman with an inner life and profound struggles, lonely and vulnerable and facing a difficult future with little help, and he wondered what was going to happen when she finally grew tired of selling her body.

72

Ophelia was now sleeping, tucked in opposite Ruby. The bed was large, so she'd been okay with this arrangement and noted there was room for David as well. He had declined, opting for a blanket and pillow on the floor when the time came. For now, he just wanted to relax and regroup, so there he sat, sipping his drink and observing two young women of similar age and circumstance, sleeping in the soft light of a single table lamp, a little blonde head on the far side, a little brunette head on the near side. This reminded him of the black-and-white yin and yang symbol—two young women who seemed to be opposites, contrary to each other, Ruby who wore her bravado on her sleeve and exuded confidence, and Ophelia who put on a cloak of eroticism when called for but harbored an unseen loneliness and vulnerability. But what did David really know about these girls. He'd never been alone with Ruby Mae, seen her in her natural state. Perhaps she was every bit as lonely and vulnerable as Ophelia. And he hadn't seen Ophelia outside the brothel. Perhaps when at her real home, with her grieving mother, she was the strong one, a Katniss Everdeen of sorts. Regardless of whomever and whatever was hidden below the surface of these two souls, David wanted to make sure each of them had a chance to expand their inner selves and thrive. He didn't know what his future held, but at least he could see to it that these girls were able to retire from their present positions and leave this shadow world for the brightness of stability, security, and safety—yin and yang, darkness and light in harmony.

David sipped his drink, set it on the table next to his chair, and retrieved his duffel bag from across the room. Back in the chair, the duffel at his feet, he zipped it open, dug through the bundles of banded hundred-dollar bills, and grabbed a TracFone. As soon as he had regained his senses following the explosion, he had agonized over whether to call Nova. She now knew the full extent of the danger he faced, and when she heard about the Beaver, she would put two and two together and call or text to see if he was okay. He had thrown his phone into the crater so he couldn't be tracked, but he was holding an untraceable TracFone in his hand. He hit the power button and considered sending Nova a quick text. "I'm okay," is all it would need to say. But what if this supremely organized, far-reaching conspiracy was monitoring her phone? The origin of the text would be untraceable, but they would know it was him. They would know he was still alive, which would put her in even more danger. As much as he ached to communicate with her, he couldn't.

David set the phone on the table and sipped his drink, overcome with regret for never asking the bartender at the Beaver the ages and names of his daughters, regret for dragging Ruby and Ophelia into a dangerous situation, and regret for failing to save Nova. What was he going to do now? What was his next move? Was there any way forward? The impossibility of the situation was crushing. David took another large sip of his drink, leaned back in the chair, closed his eyes, and drifted into a dark void.

- 73 -

A ping startled David out of a deep sleep and into a realm of momentary confusion—of dim light, a bag of IV fluids hanging from a coat stand, a bed with two silhouettes under the covers—but his surroundings quickly became familiar, the events of the last several hours recalled. He had fallen asleep in the chair with his neck hyperextended over the back, and his effort to sit forward was met with a bolt of pain shooting down his contused cervical spine. He slowly sat up and was massaging his neck when he noticed a blue light blinking on the TracFone. New text from 667-747-2119, it said on the screen. David didn't recognize the number or the area code, and who had this anonymous number, anyway? Richard Whitestone had given David the phone. He was the only person who knew it existed, and he was dead. David unlocked the screen and read the message: "Are you alive? Jim Broderick."

David slumped into the chair, hope and possibility flooding through him. He texted back, his trembling fingers barely able to type the simple word: "Yes."

"In Reno. Where can we meet? Must be isolated. A place where a tail would be easily spotted during the drive in."

David knew the perfect location. "Boat launch. Lahontan State Recreation Area."

Moments passed without a reply. Then, "Google maps shows two launches. One off US 50. One off US 95."

"Highway 50."

"I'll be there in one hour. Do not get there before me. Give me fifteen minutes to check out the place. Any problems, I will tell you to abort. If you think you are being followed, abort."

David struggled to get out of the chair—his back and neck really tight now—then went over to Ruby's side of the bed. He pulled down the comforter and examined her, taking care not to wake her. Her hands and feet remained warm and well perfused, her radial pulse strong, her heart rate sixty-two. No reason to wake her with the blood pressure cuff. After blowing into his cupped hands to warm them, he unbuttoned the bottom three buttons on her pajama top and examined her abdomen. It was soft, with no signs of distension, and the dressing showed some blood-tinged drainage but no active bleeding. She was doing well. He went around to Ophelia's side, shook her gently, and asked if he could use her car. "And I'll need a coat," he added.

74

At 4:06 a.m. David turned off Highway 50 into the boat launch. There was a single car in the parking lot, tucked behind the restrooms out of sight of the highway. David parked next to it, climbed out, and slipped into the overcoat and leather gloves Ophelia had taken from the lost and found at Mona's. Near the top of the boat ramp stood a man—a silhouette of trench coat and fedora backlit by a three-quarter moon. A light breeze rippled the surface of the lake. Moonlight shimmered off the water. David's breaths condensed into frosty puffs as he approached, gravel crunching with each step. The man extended his gloved hand. It was indeed Jim Broderick, Richard Whitestone's partner from the NSA's elite hacking unit the Equation Group.

"Dr. McBride," Broderick said. "Or should I call you Dr. Aaronson?"

"Jim Broderick," David said as the two men shook hands. "Am I happy to see you."

"Are you okay?" Broderick asked, studying the cuts and abrasions on David's face.

"Nothing serious."

"How did you survive the blast? The news is reporting no survivors."

"I was blown through the back wall of the building into an alley. But how did you hear about the explosion, and what made you think I might be involved? How'd you know I was living in Fallon, Nevada?"

"Your relocation here was not random," Broderick said. "Richard needed to hide you, and Fallon seemed like the perfect place, but he had a higher purpose in mind."

"To save the world?" David said with a hint of sarcasm.

"We didn't know it at the time, but yes, that might turn out to be the case."

A distant burst of high-pitched yips and cries interrupted the conversation. "A pack of coyotes," David said.

"Can't say I've heard that before," Broderick replied. "Richard really wanted you off the beaten path."

"I *am* wanted by every law enforcement agency in the Northeast United States."

"And the FBI and NSA, but that's only part of the reason why you're here. Eighteen months ago, right before Heather got sick, Richard and I intercepted chatter regarding a Chinese bat virus the South Koreans had procured for US Army scientists. Then, about a year ago, I received an encrypted message from a trusted source in military intelligence. He wanted to meet with me." Broderick described a meeting in Rock Creek Park, just outside of Chevy Chase, Maryland. "Real spy stuff," he said. "The park is huge and has been used for dead drops and clandestine meetings for as long as there have been spies, and there we were, in a deserted picnic area in the middle of the night."

"Sounds like he had a bomb to drop," David said.

"A real bunker buster. He tells me about an army captain who works at a bioweapons lab in Nevada."

"Mark Wallace," David added.

"Yes, but he disappeared before you got here. How do you know that name?"

"Three weeks ago I met with a civilian contractor who works in the lab. He told me about the captain and the colonel who commands the facility."

"What did he say?" Broderick asked.

"That the biolab created CoVid19 and CoVid23, and they released 19 in China to set the stage for the release of 23 after the US had been vaccinated. The contractor said Wallace thought the conspiracy went all the way to the president. I blew him off, told him I didn't believe it."

"Wallace was right. Bell is involved, as are high-ranking military and intelligence officials, so he didn't know who to turn to. By then you were growing a kidney for Heather, and Richard was constructing your new identity, so he set you up here as a conduit. Wallace was going to smuggle documents and files out of the lab, get them to you, you'd get them to me."

"Two birds, one stone—hide a fugitive, recruit a spy."

"You were the perfect person. The new surgeon in a town that needed a new surgeon. Not the slightest hint of government agent or law enforcement. You were mobile—could go anywhere and talk to anyone without raising suspicion. Can you imagine if I had pulled into town, taken a room at the Comfort Inn, and started asking questions?"

"But then Mark Wallace disappears."

"Yes, and the NSA—my own people—have been surveilling me since then. I found your number on my phone two weeks ago and had to delete it, but I concluded you made a new contact within the lab. And when I saw the stories on CNN, I was certain you had. Then I learn one of the president's fixers—a hatchet man named Dietrich—is taking a hastily arranged military flight to Fallon, and I figure you've been exposed and he's coming out here to eliminate the leak. I followed him, but I was six hours behind. There was nothing I could do about the bar."

"But why rely on Wallace or me or any human to smuggle physical evidence? Why not hack into the lab's computers? Richard hacked the American Board of Surgery and two major universities and sent me here as a fully credentialed surgeon."

"BSL Fallon is what we call a dark site. It has no connection to the internet."

David shook his head. "How's that even possible? Who isn't connected to the internet?"

"People engaged in black ops. They use an intranet for analyzing, sharing, and storing data, and for communicating within the lab. There are no outside communications—no phones, no email, nothing that can be hacked, traced, or eavesdropped."

"I would think that's hugely inconvenient for a government installation located three thousand miles from the home base."

"We had the same thought, so to verify there wasn't a backchannel we could exploit, we ran a program called Bonesaw." Broderick explained that Bonesaw was a software application used to track computers, servers, and routers around the world and provided the geolocation and IP address of every piece of hardware connected to the internet. The program determined what software was running, what entry points existed, then compiled a list of exploits.

"So that's how Richard hacked bank accounts, medical centers, universities, and private individuals," David said.

The sound of a vehicle hurtling down the highway interrupted the conversation. Both men glanced up at the highway. The car sped past.

"When you pair Bonesaw with our library of zero-day vulnerabilities," Broderick continued, "there aren't too many computers or servers around the globe the NSA can't hack."

"Yet here you are, in the Nevada desert on a cold October night, looking to enlist the help of a human."

"We need everything on every hard drive in the lab, and we need a human asset to go in there and get it."

"Why can't the FBI or SEAL Team Six storm the place, grab all the computers and servers, and carry them out the front door?"

"First, they'd literally see us coming from miles away, and they'll have software in place to wipe all their drives. Second, Washington is now controlled by a deep state of government officials, military leaders, the intelligence community, and even leaders of finance and industry. There's a man named Jack Prescott who controls the president and the colonel—his son-in-law, by the way—and Prescott is associated with a shadow elite of very powerful men with unparalleled influence and access to intelligence that stretches around the world. Even I have no idea whom to trust, so calling in the FBI or the SEALs is not an option."

"But you think I can get inside the lab and topple a conspiracy that extends all the way to the Oval Office?"

"You or somebody you know. Is there anyone? The private contractor?"

"When I learned Philip Tang wasn't blowing smoke I scoured this town looking for him, but he disappeared. And last night the truck driver who smuggled the materials I passed to CNN, he was shot in the head right before they blew up the bar. Someone has connected the dots."

"But now they think you're dead. That gives you an advantage."

"Yeah, but for how long, twenty-four hours?"

"At most, so now's the time to move."

"Okay, let's say I'm able to walk into a US Army level-four biosafety laboratory and sit down at one of their computers. What would I be able to do?"

Broderick reached into the pocket of his coat and retrieved a thumb-size hard drive.

"Really? An Office Depot flash drive?" David said.

"This is not from Office Depot. This is DARPA technology. You plug it into any USB port of any computer in the lab, and it will copy every file on every drive from all computers and servers in the facility, provided they're all connected."

"And all that data—what, terabytes worth—will fit on that little thing?"

"It uses quantum technology to zip and rezip, then archive and zip the archives until everything fits into one folder, up to one hundred terabytes."

"Then what, I email it to you? That would take about a week."

"No. Once you insert it into any network-connected USB port, the single file is sent directly from that IP address to a second IP address only I can access, and it happens almost instantaneously. No extraneous routers, servers, or email clients." Broderick handed the flash drive to David. "Now we just have to figure out how to get you in there."

David stared at the drive, then out across the lake—at the silhouettes of the hills forming the far shore, the moonlight flickering on the water, the tiny waves lapping against the rocks—and as he did so the name Marina came to mind. Ophelia's coworker Marina. From Ukraine. And she had a regular who worked at the lab, drank too much, and ran his mouth.

"There is one possibility." David explained the situation to Broderick—the use of the brothel as a safe house, the alliances he'd formed, Marina and her loose-lipped regular. "But there's a problem. Marina's been in Ukraine. I don't know if she's back, and even if she is, we'd have to get the guy to come see her tonight. Then what? Ask him to stick a flash drive into his lab computer for twenty minutes and return it to the brothel?"

"No," Broderick said. "He can't be involved. We don't know where his loyalties lay. You have to go in his place. You have to impersonate him and get inside."

"That's preposterous," David said, shaking his head. "I don't know what he looks like, if we're similar in height, if we even have the same skin or hair color."

"Hair and skin can be covered. The spine can be lengthened or shortened by simply changing posture."

"I'm sure there's an ID badge and biometrics involved."

"Have the girl get him drunk and steal his ID. You figure out how to make yourself look like him. I can handle the biometrics." Broderick removed an iPhone from his coat and handed it to David. The home screen displayed three icons for three apps—an eye, an ear, a thumb. "Tell Marina to open the eye app and take a close-up photo of one of the subject's eyes."

"How close?"

"About an inch. Then have her use the ear app to record him saying, 'My name is,' and follow with, 'I am a private contractor employed by the United States Army.' And with the thumb app, take a photo of his right thumbprint. Again, about one inch."

"How're we gonna get him to do all that?"

"Once he's liquored up, make the eye pic a clumsy attempt at a selfie. Make a game out of the voice recording and fingerprints. She'll need to be creative. And when he's ready to run his mouth, have Marina question him about what it's like to live in the lab. How many floors are there? Which floor do they sleep on? Does he have his own room, his own office? Where are the offices, computer workstations?"

The coyotes burst into another flurry of yips and cries, closer and louder this time.

"As for you," Broderick continued, "approach the security gate in the subject's car and flash his ID badge. Figure out a way to hide your face. Spill hot coffee in your lap. Piss your pants. Whatever you can think of. Go early in the morning when the guard is tired. He's probably seen you come in after a night out, so act sloppy and he might wave you through. Entry into the building may require one, two, or all three of the biometrics. If the system wants the retina scan or thumbprint, open the appropriate app, and you'll see a QR code. Hold it an inch from the scanner. And if it asks you to speak—"

Broderick paused as a jacked-up four-by-four rumbled past.

"Play the recording," David added as the taillights of the truck disappeared into the dark.

"Once you're in," Broderick said, "you might encounter other people, and there will be CCTV cameras watching, so stagger a bit and act drunk and stupid, rant about the hot coffee burning your crotch or the piss running down your leg. Nobody wants to deal with that."

"Jesus," David said. "I can think of fifty ways this could go off the rails."

"It's not a perfect plan, but it's our only plan. You have to be ready to improvise."

"You're the spy. Why aren't you doing this?"

"I sit behind a desk all day. Besides, I can't procure the files. I need to be in DC on the receiving end. They'll be protected by DoD level-five encryption, which I can decrypt but not on a laptop at the Holiday Inn in Reno. I have to get back to Washington, where I have the computing power to get the decryption done quickly and send the files to the appropriate people."

David slipped the flash drive into his coat pocket. "Okay, so if by some miracle I'm successful, there's something you need to do for me."

"Of course," Broderick said.

David told him about Nova and the lymph nodes growing in her chest. "She must be your highest priority. Find someone to synthesize the antibodies and get a dose to me as fast as possible. If I don't survive, get it to the other surgeon in town, Thomas Pennington. Do not let them take time to study its safety or test it on animals or any of that FDA stuff. Please give me your word. Get it synthesized and get it back here."

"You have my word."

"Okay. Wish me luck. I'm gonna need it."

"You can do this. I have complete faith, as did Richard."

David turned to go, then stopped. "By the way," he said, "how did the agency handle Richard's death?"

"A quiet funeral attended by me, his wife, and Heather, and he was expunged from the NSA data base."

"The Russian?"

"His body was handed over to their consulate."

"And Heather?"

"Thriving. The kidney is functioning perfectly, she's returned to her baseline health, and she has resumed her studies at Georgetown."

75

Jim Broderick left the boat launch parking lot, heading west toward Silver Springs, then Fernley, and on to Reno and a flight that would take him back to Washington. As David watched Broderick's taillights disappear into the darkness, he felt alone and overwhelmed and full of despair as he considered the inevitable "what ifs" and "hows" of what lay before him. What if Marina was not back in town? What if she was but couldn't contact her client, or what if she did but he couldn't see her tonight? And if she was back, and he came to see her, would she be able to extract the information they needed and scan his eye and thumb and record his voice? And if she were successful and David actually made it into the lab, how was he going to walk the halls, find a computer, plug in the flash drive, and steal every bit—every byte—of information from a system belonging to the Department of Defense? And if he succeeded, he still had to get out. And if he did get in and get out, and he actually procured the chemical formula for the monoclonal antibody, would it be in time to save Nova? He had no answers to these questions and none were forthcoming. He would just have to treat this like a multiple-injury trauma case in an unstable patient. Prioritize each injury, get in and fix it, then move on to the next. Follow established norms whenever possible, improvise when you had to. So he would do what he'd always been good at, compartmentalize and prioritize, don't think too far ahead, don't allow himself to become overwhelmed. Take one step at a time.

David arrived back in Ophelia's room to find the two girls still sleeping, as one would expect at five-thirty in the morning. Like he had done earlier, he blew into his cupped hands to warm them, then gently lowered the comforter and linens on Ruby's side of the bed and examined her. She stirred slightly as he felt her hands and feet. Still warm and well perfused. He unbuttoned the bottom of her pajama top and examined her abdomen. It remained soft, with no signs of distension. The blood-tinged drainage on the dressing had not advanced since his earlier exam. She continued to do better than expected.

David went around to Ophelia's side and gently shook her. She lifted her head off the pillow, bleary eyed and confused. "It's David, Dr. Aaronson," he said.

"Oh yeah," she said as her eyes closed and her head fell back to the pillow.

"Remember the girl from Ukraine you told me about?"

"Yeah," Ophelia replied in a sleepy voice.

"Is she back? Has she returned to Mona's?"

"She came back yesterday." Ophelia opened her eyes and yawned. "Or maybe the day before, I think. What day is it?"

"It's okay. As long as she's here."

David sat down in the corner chair and took a moment to gather his thoughts. He had one more task to complete before he'd be able to sleep. Using the throwaway TracFone, he googled "bus station Carson City." There was indeed a Greyhound bus station thirty minutes away and only a couple of blocks off Highway 50 in downtown Carson City. He grabbed his duffel bag from behind the chair and went into the bathroom where Ophelia kept her clean linens. He counted out ten banded stacks of one-hundred-dollar bills—a total of one hundred thousand dollars—and dropped them into a pillowcase. He counted ten more stacks and dropped them into a second pillowcase, placed both pillowcases and the TracFone back in the duffel, grabbed Ophelia's keys, and headed for Carson City.

76

David never believed in luck or fate or the hand of God, but he was starting to. Since the Broderick meeting, everything had gone David's way. After returning from the bus station in Carson City, he'd slept for six uninterrupted hours. Ruby was back to her spirited self, and he'd successfully repacked her wound without stirring up new bleeding or inciting a flurry of F-bombs. Ophelia had introduced David to Marina Orlov, who'd been able to contact her biolab client and entice him to pay her a visit. And he'd found a pharmacist in Carson City who allowed David to prescribe himself a 30ml bottle of ipecac syrup and four 1mg Ativan tablets. But it was Marina Orlov who seemed heaven-sent, and not in the sense that she was an angel. She appeared to be anything but.

Marina blew into Ophelia's room and immediately took over, as she likely did anytime she walked through a door. Her full-length white negligee flowed behind her like a cape, and the gauzy material, untied and gaping open, did nothing to conceal her black-lace D-cup bra and G-string panties. At six feet plus—which was all legs, augmented by six inches of black stiletto heels—she stood eye to eye with David. Her short blonde hair framed a stern but beautiful face. Her eyes were a dark shade of brown, almost black, and her lipstick was a bright shade of red that reminded David of well-oxygenated blood. Her mascara, or eye liner—David didn't know the difference—tapered away from the corners of her eyes, giving them the cat's eye appearance that was popular among Mona's girls.

"Yes, I have a regular client working in the secret lab," she had said after being introduced to David. "He likes to drink and then shoot his mouth. Always bragging about some high-level shit they work on over there. Something he says will change the world. A very dangerous virus."

"Did he give you any details?" David had asked. "Did he mention a vaccine or a cure for the virus?"

"No. He just tells me things in the news will get scary, and if I become frightened, I can call him. He will take care of me."

"You said he likes to drink when he's here."

"Yes, and sometimes too much. I intimidate him, so he drinks to build up his nerve. One time he got very sick and paid me five hundred dollars extra to drive him to the lab and tell the guard he ate bad shrimp. I drop him off there, and one of the girls gave me a ride home."

And that's when David's plan crystallized, prompting the return trip to Carson City for Ativan and ipecac, and a stop on the way back at a greasy roadside diner for a jumbo plate of spaghetti and meatballs.

77

David and Marina sat in Marina's red Honda Accord, watching the parking lot. The lot was a long rectangle, but for fire safety reasons, parking was prohibited along the fence paralleling the front of the brothel. The far end was all entrance and exit, leaving a single row of spaces along the outer border of the lot and a shorter row at a right angle to that. Marina had parked on the short arm of the L, backed up against a fence, which gave her and David an unobstructed view. There were ten or twelve cars in the lot—a Porsche, a Tesla, trucks and SUVs, and next to the Accord sat a black Dodge Challenger, also backed up against the fence. The pink neon light from the frisky cat danced across the hood of the Dodge.

David checked his watch. "It's ten after eight. Any chance he showed up early and he's waiting at the bar?"

"No," Marina said. "I do not see his vehicle."

"That's not his Tesla or Porsche over there?"

"No. He spends too much money on me to afford those cars."

Marina said this while staring straight ahead, all business, not a hint of a smile. David would love to know more about these girls, but this was not the time for small talk. Besides, they were probably tired of answering the same old questions: How did you end up working in a brothel? Do you actually enjoy the sex? How often does some John offer to "white knight" you and take you away from all this?

A pair of headlights shone straight at them as a white Audi pulled into the dirt lot and parked on the long part of the L.

"That is maybe him," Marina said.

An Asian guy of average height climbed out of the car and started across the lot, then turned back. He slipped out of his coat—a hooded parka—and removed an ID badge and lanyard from his neck. He threw both onto the front seat, locked the car, and headed for the gate.

"Yes. For sure it is him," Marina said. "I now go to employee entrance and take my time to come in so he has a drink at the bar. I make sure he takes another to the room. He can have that one while I dance for him, then I will tell him to have another while I finish dancing. Probably he will be getting good and buzzed in forty-five minutes."

The guy had a slight stagger as he crossed the lot, and halfway across he caught a toe and almost fell. "I'd say he's already sporting a pretty good buzz," David said.

"Maybe I should not get him to drink so much."

David reached into his pocket and came out with the four Ativan tablets, then turned toward Marina. "I think one drink at the bar, then once you're in your room go out and get him a second, but before you return crush one of these and mix it in the second drink." He handed the pills to Marina.

"What is this?" she asked, scrutinizing the small white pills in the palm of her hand.

"Ativan. It's a weaker cousin of the roofie, but we still need to be careful."

"Okay, so just two drinks."

"Yes. We want him to sleep for a few hours. We don't want him to stop breathing. If after thirty minutes he still seems coherent, give him a second pill. And that reminds me." David removed a roll of hundred-dollar bills from another pocket and peeled off twenty of them. "When you go out to see the manager, pay for the whole night."

Marina unbuttoned the leopard-print faux-fur coat she was wearing over her white negligee and black lingerie and tucked the bills into her bra.

"And there's something else," he said, reaching into his back pocket. He came out with two banded stacks of hundred-dollar bills and handed them to her.

She thumbed the bills as if they were a deck of cards, then looked up at him. "This is many thousands of dollars."

"Twenty thousand."

"For what?"

"For helping me. You're taking a big risk tonight. It's my way of saying thanks."

Marina stared at the bills, then looked up at David, her stern face softening a little. "This helps my family very much. Thank you."

"My pleasure," David said.

"Okay, so now we go. I will have Ophelia meet you in the bar."

As David and Marina crossed the parking lot, David questioned the wisdom of having a drink in the bar. Perhaps the president's operatives had eyes on the place. If they did, they would have seen him coming and going by now. On the flip side, David needed every scrap of information he could gather about the man he was about to impersonate.

The lounge was quiet—two men at the bar and two on the couches, one of whom was the target. The other three already had their dates glommed on to them, leaving the Asian guy to sit alone and ponder his drink. David took a seat at the bar, ordered a Maker's Mark, then Marina came through the doorway, her long white negligee billowing behind her, her gait mimicking that of a runway model. She plopped onto the couch next to her date and draped one of her legs over his, giving David, the bartender, and anyone else who might be interested a full view of her black G-string. She picked up his drink from the table, helped herself to a sizable swig, then said, "Hello, my king." Before he could respond, she kissed him on the cheek and said, "How are you tonight, my lovely man?"

The target spoke in quieter tones with only the occasional slur. His level of intoxication seemed perfect, as long as Marina proceeded with caution and did not suppress the respiratory center in his brainstem with too much Ativan.

Moments later, Ophelia nuzzled up against David. She was wearing a sheer, thigh-length pink negligee, red bra and panties, and glossy black stilettos. "Hello my love," she said. "I'm so happy you're back. You must have missed me."

"I always do," David said.

"You want to finish your drink out here or in my room?"

"Let's hang out here for a few minutes, if you don't mind."

They did, and when Marina led her date down the hallway, David and Ophelia followed. David did not glean much useful information, but he did get a good feel for the guy's height, about two inches shorter than David. Once inside the lab, he would need to stoop a bit and stagger a little.

Since David had prepaid for the room, there was no need for Ophelia to step out to the manager's office. Instead, she kicked off her shoes, climbed onto her side of the bed, and draped a fleece blanket over her shoulders. Ruby occupied the far side. She was propped up against the headboard, surrounded by pillows and covered with blankets, thumbing through one of Ophelia's *People* magazines. She looked comfortable, though she winced with any small movement. David took his usual spot—the chair in the corner—but instead of settling in he leaned forward and faced the girls.

"I'm not sure how this is gonna go tonight," he said, "but I think there's a good chance I may not see you again. So, just in case, I have something for each of you." David removed the Greyhound locker keys from his pocket and gave one to Ophelia, then walked around the bed and gave the other to Ruby. "You've both been a great help to me, and you've assumed extraordinary risk in doing so. These keys belong to lockers at the bus station in Carson City. Inside, you'll find ... let's call it a cash stipend. It's my way of saying thanks, and it's also enough to open the door to a brighter future. Personally, I'd like to see you spend it on college tuition, but you may have more pressing matters to take care of. Either way, the money is yours."

The girls exchanged looks of confusion, then thanked David. And in an unexpected reversal, tears formed in the corners of Ruby's eyes, while Ophelia assumed a more stoic posture.

David poured himself a drink—possibly the last he'd ever pour— and settled back into the chair. It felt odd, leaving a considerable amount of money to these two young women and nothing for

Nova, but they needed it more than she did. If he lived through the night—assuming his mission was a success—she wouldn't need to worry about money. If he didn't live, neither would she, not long enough to spend a couple hundred grand. He sipped his drink and let his head fall to the back of the chair. The thought of failure—the thought of never seeing Nova again—was bearing down on him, but he forced those thoughts from his mind. *Worry about the next move*, he told himself, *not the end game.*

David finished his second drink and poured a third, but he didn't need to worry about dulling his senses. It would all be coming back up before long. He wondered how it was going with Marina, if he should send Ophelia down there to check, and, as if on cue, there was a knock on the door and Marina Orlov blew into the room.

"Here they are," she said, holding up a key fob and the DARPA iPhone in one hand and a pair of dark slacks and a white dress shirt in the other.

"He's already passed out?" David asked.

"He sleeps like baby," Marina replied.

"And his breathing is steady?"

"Slow, but strong and deep."

"You were able to get a retina scan and all that? And he gave you the layout of the place?"

"When men get drunk and horny, they do whatever you tell them and say whatever you want to hear."

"How many of the pills did you use?"

"I give him two to make sure he sleeps for at least five hours."

David considered the wisdom of giving—

"What is the guy's name?" David asked Marina.

"Peter Shen, P-H-D," she replied.

David considered the wisdom of giving Peter Shen, PhD, two milligrams of Ativan. The idea was to titrate the dose, give him one, see how he reacted, then give him two or even three if he needed them and do this over time, not just suddenly flood his cortex with Ativan on top of the alcohol already circulating. But there was no going back now.

"Okay then," David said, looking at the three women. "I guess this is it."

Marina left the room to get her coat. Ophelia stepped into the bathroom to change into street clothes. In the corner near the shower, David changed into Peter Shen's black slacks and white dress shirt, then went over to Ruby's side of the bed. "If I'm not back by tomorrow morning, go see Dr. Pennington at the hospital. He'll make sure you're doing okay, and he'll check your wound and change your dressings." He bent over and kissed her on the forehead. "Thanks again for your help. I've enjoyed your company."

"You'll be back," Ruby said as a new set of tears rolled down her cheeks.

David turned to leave, then stopped and turned around. "Last night it occurred to me that we've spent a lot of time together, but I don't know anything about you."

"Like what?" Ruby said, wiping tears off her face.

"Uh, I don't know. What are your parent's names?"

"Wally and Linda."

"Did you have a favorite pet growing up?"

"I had a barnyard full of favorite pets, but why does this matter now?"

"I'm not sure," David said. "I just wanted to know something about you."

Ophelia came out of the bathroom in jeans and a sweater.

Marina returned wearing the same leopard-print coat she'd had on earlier, her white negligee billowing from below the hemline.

"Sure you don't want to change those?" David nodding toward her black six-inch heels.

"They will be fine," she said with a seductive smile.

- 79 -

David climbed behind the wheel of Peter Shen's Audi and started it as Marina slipped into the passenger seat, but before pulling out, he took a small bottle from his pocket and swallowed the contents.

"What is that you are doing?" Marina asked.

He held up the bottle. "Ipecac, thirty milliliters."

"Why do you take it?"

"In about fifteen minutes you'll find out."

As David turned to look out the rear window, he noticed a basketball and a pair of Air Jordans on the back seat of the Audi. He pictured an Asian man of average height running up and down a basketball court, perhaps trying to hold his own against a bunch of guys who were taller than him, and now that man not only had a name and an advanced degree, he also had another dimension to his personality. He was Peter Shen, PhD, virologist and basketball player, and David hoped to God he was still breathing.

David and Marina drove out of the lot, Ophelia following in her car, and the two vehicles turned onto Highway 50 and headed east. Twelve minutes later they pulled into the Lahontan State Recreation Area boat launch.

"Now what? You are okay?" Marina asked.

"For now," David said as he opened the driver's side door.

Marina shook her head. "I do not understand."

David climbed out of the car, went around to the passenger's side, and leaned against the front quarter panel. Marina jumped out as well, carefully negotiating the gravel lot in her six-inch heels, the cold wind whipping the bottom of her negligee.

Ophelia pulled up behind them, her headlights illuminating David and Marina. "What's wrong?" she asked as she joined them.

"Something is going to happen, but he does not say what," Marina replied.

And she was right.

The first thing to hit were the stomach cramps, and they hit hard.

David clutched his abdomen and doubled over, his heart racing, his mouth salivating, his eyes watering.

The girls frantically asked if he was okay.

He waved them off and turned to face the car.

And then he blew.

He covered the passenger-side window and door with a gruesome amalgam of spaghetti, meatballs, Maker's Mark, grease, and stomach acid.

The second wave came on the heels of the first.

He aimed this one at the left sleeve and front of his parka—Peter Shen's parka—which was now coated in the same gruel covering the side of the car.

David bent over with his hands on his knees, hyperventilating, tears streaming from his eyes, his nasal sinuses clogged. He cleared his throat and spit onto the ground.

The third wave was half the volume and intensity of the first two. David let it fly into the dirt at his feet, then straightened up.

Both girls just stood there, staring.

"Part of the plan," he said, wiping the tears from his face with the back of his hand. "Let's get out of here. Marina, you drive."

- 80 -

They drove down Highway 50, all windows open except for the front passenger's side. David had his head resting on his clean right arm, which was propped up on the door against the closed window. He kept the vomit-covered left arm in his vomit-covered lap. The cold desert air did little to abate the horrid smell, nor was it helping with the nausea and pounding headache.

Twenty minutes later they were passing through downtown Fallon. They caught the red light where Main Street intersected the highway, and David lifted his head just enough to get a quick look. Several blocks down, night had turned into day. Telescoping light standards illuminated fire trucks, ambulances, smoldering debris, and first responders searching through the rubble of the Big Brown Beaver. He wondered what the final body count would be, who all was there last night, how many families had been affected, but he quickly pushed those thoughts out of his mind. *You are at war,* he told himself, *and there is always collateral damage.* He would mourn the losses at a more convenient time.

The turnoff for the lab was fifteen miles east of town. There was no sign, no guard station, no brightly lit compound off in the distance, just a dirt road leading up a hill. Marina knew where to turn. She'd made the trip before.

The road was well maintained, so it was neither rocky nor full of potholes, but it did have a washboard surface that shimmied the car and bounced the rear tires into a slide more than once. Fortunately for Ophelia, who was following about twenty yards back, a powerful crosswind was blowing the dust sideways off the road and out of her way.

About fifty yards from the gate Marina unzipped her coat, untied her negligee, and made sure both were gaping open. While she was exposing her wares, David pulled the hood of the parka over his head, lowered the window, and let his vomit-covered left arm dangle outside the car while resting his head on his right arm. Marina slowed to a stop.

Even though David was portraying a passed-out drunk, he was able to assess his surroundings from under the hood of the parka. The lab proper—a single-story red-brick building circa 1950s or '60s—was another fifty yards up the road. A few of the external windows were backlit, but for the most part it was shrouded in darkness. It seemed impossible that such a nondescript structure served as the portal to five subterranean levels of an advanced bioweapons research facility, but according to Peter Shen, it did. A twelve-foot hurricane fence encased in coils of razor wire enclosed the grounds. The entrance to the compound was blocked by an iron gate, which was backed up by a row of antiram bollards, the guard shack also protected by steel bollards. Floodlights illuminated the area.

The guard exited the shack and walked toward them. He was young, early twenties, wearing sand-colored camos, and he had a large pistol holstered at his waist. And the guy was bright eyed and sharp with his movements, indicating he had not been asleep, even though it was well after midnight. "Can I help you … ma'am? … miss?" his voice trailing off with confusion.

"I have one of your men here," Marina said. "He takes me out on date, eats bad shrimp and gets sick, and now I would like to be done with him."

The guard stooped a bit and peered into the car. "This is highly unusual," he said.

"Not really," Marina replied, handing the lanyard and ID to the guard. "Not so long ago I have to do same thing. I think I will not go out with him anymore."

"Is she with you?" the guard pointing back at Ophelia.

"Yes," Marina said. "Since *this* car belongs to *this* man, she will need to take me home."

The guard studied the ID badge. "A contract worker," he said.

"I don't know what that means," Marina replied.

The guard came around to David's side of the car, then stopped abruptly. "Fuck's sake," he blurted out.

"Now you see what I mean?" Marina said. "I would like to take him to the front door and be finished with this. It does not smell like flower in here."

The guard came back around to Marina's side and handed her the ID. "This man is a disgrace to our mission and our country, and he does not deserve to walk the same halls as the uniformed men and women in this facility protecting the United States of America. Get him out of here. After he cleans himself up in the morning, he can come back."

Marina planted her right stiletto on the console and spread her legs, exposing her G-sting panties. "I think this is not a good idea," she said. "With stories about this town and this lab and what is going on outside in the world, if CNN knows one of your men visits a hooker at the kitty ranch and drinks too much and talks about the 'next-level shit' going on here, I think this looks real bad for you. In my country, you get one-way trip to labor camp."

There was a long silence. Then, "Okay. Drive him up to the lab and see if you can roust him enough to get him inside. If not, leave him in the car. I'll call for assistance."

"What about her?" Marina hooking a thumb at Ophelia. "I can't walk back down here in these." In a move on par with the Soviet gymnasts of the 1970s, Marina lifted her left leg from the floorboard and stuck it out the window, nearly stabbing the guard in the chest with her stiletto heel, her legs now spread at a ninety-degree angle.

"Jesus," he said, taking a step back. "She can follow you up there. Then you guys need to turn around and get out of here."

The gate opened and the bollards lowered. Marina, with Ophelia right behind her, drove up the road and parked in a small gravel lot near the main entrance. Together, the girls lifted David from his seat and helped guide him as he feigned a staggering gait and moved toward the door. "You're an evil genius," he said to Marina, kissing her on the cheek. "You've both been spectacular," now kissing Ophelia on her cheek. "I hope I see you ladies again."

A pair of glass doors served as the entrance. To the right, a kiosk resembling an ATM was mounted on the wall. A list of instructions outlined the entrance requirements: slide your ID through the magnetic strip reader, place your right eye over the small square of glass with the camera lens behind it, push your thumb against the glass square under the retina scanner.

David slid Peter Shen's ID card through the reader, held the respective iPhone QR codes over their readers, and the door buzzed open. He glanced at the girls, relieved that Jim Broderick's spy gear had worked without a hitch.

"Be careful," Marina said.

"Please come back to us," Ophelia added.

David forced a smile and stepped into the lab.

A hundred yards up the road from the main building sat a structure resembling a small warehouse. It contained parking bays for several black Humvees, quarters for twenty security contractors, and, out back, a helipad for a Blackhawk helicopter. Below the building, a subterranean level held offices and rooms full of telecommunications and security monitoring equipment. In one of those rooms, former Navy SEAL Nick Slattery and ex–Army Ranger Paul Oberlein—both clad in desert-camo fatigues with no identifying markings—made cursory glances toward an array of monitors fixed to the wall in front of them. These two men, and the facility in which they resided, were part of Jonathon Neville's handpicked security force, a paramilitary group known as Blackrock Global. BRG was one of several private companies used by the US military as a supplier of human and technological security assets. A subdivision of the company unofficially provided covert security personnel that handled strictly domestic matters.

"We have two vehicles approaching the gate," Slattery said, leaning forward in his chair for a better look.

Oberlein swiveled his chair and moved closer to the monitor receiving the feed from the guardhouse. "Vehicle one contains a female driver and a subject of indeterminate sex slumped against the passenger door. Vehicle two contains a lone female."

Slattery pulled up the log of expected arrivals. "Nothing on the schedule until tomorrow morning."

Both men watched the verbal exchange between the marine sentry and the driver of the first vehicle. The sentry studied the

ID he'd been handed, walked around to the passenger side, then abruptly returned to the driver's side.

"Was that a black stiletto that just came out the car window?" Slattery asked.

"With a long, slender leg attached," Oberlein replied.

The sentry opened the gate and allowed the two cars to pass.

"What's that jarhead doing?" Slattery said.

"My guess is we have a drunk contract worker being hauled home by his girlfriend. If he's able to pass the biometrics, we'll pull him up."

- 82 -

David stood at one end of an uninhabited, dimly lit corridor that was about a hundred yards long. The walls were white cinderblock, the floors black-and-white-streaked linoleum, the doors along the hallway gray metal, with small chicken-wire windows set at eye level. The utilitarianism of the interior of the building matched the generic red brick exterior. The walls were lined with bulletin boards containing notifications, title pages of scientific articles, photos of Gram-stained bacteria, and electron micrographs of viruses and plasmids. He could have been in the biology building of any public university. Along the ceiling was something one would not find in a university corridor—cameras. Domes of smoke-colored glass were mounted at regular intervals down the hall. He'd seen these things all over the Nevada casinos—the eye in the sky, watching the gamblers, looking for cheaters, feeding all their images to a room full of security personnel. He was alone, but that did not mean he wasn't being watched.

David started down the hallway with a slight stagger to his gait, the bumbling, drunken contract worker once again coming in late. He made sure the vomit down the front of his coat was visible but kept his face hidden beneath the hood. He did not try any doorknobs, nor did he peer through any windows. He needed to figure out where he was and where he needed to be. Peter Shen had told Marina he worked in a secret underground laboratory and had a level-one clearance, which he claimed was the highest with four being the lowest. David knew the latter was a fabrication—an attempt to look impressive in the eyes of a perceived girlfriend—but what he didn't know was whether a level-one clearance correlated with working on the first biosafety level, and if that correlated with the first floor and if the first floor was, in fact, underground. To add to the confusion, the numbers outside the doors along this hallway all started with AA.

"He's in. I'm pulling him up," Oberlein said as David stepped into the building. The ex-Ranger tapped a keyboard. The name matching the biometric data came up, accompanied by a photo and a bullet list of information. "Peter Shen. Contract worker. Cleared for level one only. Came in about a month ago in a similar condition—inebriated, staggering."

"What is that?" Slattery pointing at the screen.

Oberlein moved closer to the monitor. "I think it's puke. Christ, he's covered in it."

"Fucking lightweight," Slattery said.

Oberlein looked over at his partner. "And you've never heaved after drinking too much?"

"Not all over myself."

"All right. Let's just keep an eye on him, make sure he gets to his quarters."

Halfway down the corridor, David encountered a passageway branching to the right. A sign hanging overhead said ELEVATORS. He had to believe level 1 was the first subterranean floor. He turned right.

Unlike the main corridor, the walkway leading to the elevators was lined with windows, and what David saw was straight out of a Sci Fi movie. Farther up the canyon stood two massive boxlike structures. Closely spaced floodlights lined the roofs, shining down on parking lots full of cars and panel trucks backed up against loading docks. Large metal doors were rolled up, revealing pallets stacked with boxes and forklifts moving the pallets into trucks. The vaccine. The monoclonal antibody. Those two buildings were the production centers, and that's why he was alone in the lab. Research and development were complete. Now all efforts were focused on production, and the C-130s Mr. Miller had observed coming and going from NAS Fallon were part of the supply chain. David kept walking, careful not to linger and stare. If he worked here he had seen this before, and other than a passing glimpse it should not garner his attention.

David exited the elevator on level 1, mentally flipped a coin, turned left, and resumed a slight drunken stagger. This hallway was completely different from the one upstairs. Instead of white cinder block, the walls were paneled and painted in muted earth tones. Tall, narrow windows stretched from floor to ceiling, allowing David glimpses into small offices and support labs. Larger windows revealed sizable laboratories with ventilation hoods along the walls, workbenches filling the middle of the room, centrifuges, autoclaves, lots of stainless steel, lots of glassware. He did not see spacesuits or air hoses, nor was there double-door access with a Lysol shower chamber interposed. Only a single door separated the hall from the laboratory. This was a level-one biosafety lab, and it was full of computer workstations.

Okay, David thought, *computers are everywhere, but so is the eye in the sky.* If he ducked into a lab, anyone watching would wonder why this drunk guy didn't just go to his quarters and pass out. He needed a reason to enter. But what was it? Outside each laboratory stood a stainless steel refrigerator, probably full of petri dishes, cell cultures, and growth media. That was it. He needed to count colonies and document cell growth. Whomever was on the other end of the camera had surely seen this before. David made a big show of looking at his watch, walked with purpose over to a refrigerator, and opened it.

As he had anticipated, the shelves held bottles of red growth media, amber growth media, and stacks of petri dishes. On the top shelf sat plastic racks containing dozens of glass vials. He picked up one of them and read the label: SARS-CoV-23-mab.

"Holy shit," David whispered loudly.

M-A-B. SARS CoVid23 monoclonal antibodies.

The cure. Nova's cure.

The vial in David's hand was an inch and a half in diameter, contained fifty milliliters, and had a rubber stopper for a top. The solution inside was sterile and ready for injection—ready for human use. Based on his experience with cancer patients and his time on the infectious disease service, David figured one vial equaled one dose for the average-size adult. He took two, slipped them into his coat pocket, then took two more and put them in the other pocket.

Okay.

Now what?

He had four vials of what he'd been desperately trying to find for the past two weeks. He could close the refrigerator, go to the car, and get out.

But what about the world beyond David Aaronson and Nova Featherstone. It needed him to complete his mission, to provide the vaccine, and the antibodies, and the truth behind the greatest mass murder in human history.

And his own country needed him—the West Coast and any other liberal population centers the president regarded as enemies of the state.

David could leave now and tell Jim Broderick what he had seen—warehouses stockpiled with vaccine and monoclonal antibodies—but who would Broderick be able to tell? What proof would he be able to provide? It was all hearsay, and the president's propaganda machine would blow such claims out of the water.

David let his head fall forward, his forehead resting against the cold top shelf. The longer he stayed, the greater the risk of failure—no saving Nova, no saving the world. If he left now, Nova would be saved but not the rest of the world. "Fuck," he muttered under his breath.

He lifted his head out of the refrigerator, stood up straight, carefully picked up a stack of petri dishes, and entered the lab.

"Now what's he doing?" Slattery said as David—Peter Shen—opened one of the refrigerators on level 1. "Why doesn't this guy just go to bed?"

"Probably needs to check something related to his work," Oberlein replied. "Remember back a year ago how this place never slept? Work going on around the clock? The hallways and labs always filled with white coats?"

"Yeah, I remember, but there's something not right about this guy. It bothers me that we haven't seen his face. That coat must reek, and you'd think he'd push back the hood and breathe some fresh air." Slattery looked over at Oberlein. "I think we should go check him out."

"No thanks," Oberlein said. "You know how bad the stench is going to be? It has probably wafted throughout the entire lab by now. Besides, he's passed the biometrics. There's no way to do that unless you are who you're supposed to be."

"I guess," Slattery said, "but I still don't like it. I mean look at him, just standing there with his head in the refrigerator."

"He's probably hoping the cold air will clear his senses."

David found a computer workstation in the back corner, away from the hallway and its ubiquitous cameras. He sat down, spread out the petri dishes on the countertop, and then reached into his pocket for the DARPA flash drive. Both heels drummed the floor like pistons as he slipped the drive into a USB port and waited for something to happen. Finally, it did. A simple box appeared, a progress bar in the middle. A green line started advancing, but it advanced slowly—an intolerable snail's pace. In the likely event he was still being watched, David pretended to type in a series of commands, then he got up and walked over to a small anteroom off the main lab.

The room had a sink, thank Christ. The first thing he did was rinse his mouth and gulp a bunch of water. The ipecac-induced nausea had worn off, but he still had a headache, to which dehydration was no doubt contributing. He then grabbed handfuls of paper towels, wet them, and cleaned the vomit from the coat. The stench had been constant for the past hour, and he could no longer stand it. Anyone watching would see a guy who had sobered up, come to his senses, and needed to clean himself up.

David returned to the workstation to find the progress bar at twenty-five percent. He studied the petri dishes, acting as though he were counting colonies.

The progress bar hit fifty percent. Taking too long. He pretended to type in more commands, went back to the anteroom and splashed cold water on his face, swallowed several mouthfuls.

The bar hit seventy-five percent. "Jesus," he muttered. He jumped up again and took another drink of water in the anteroom. He was losing it, nervousness giving way to panic. He looked suspicious. Was acting suspicious. His heart about to pound through his chest. A security force flooding into the lab any second. He started to pace but forced himself to sit down and relax and stare into more petri dishes.

The bar reached one hundred percent. David slipped the flash drive from the computer and put it in his pocket. If Broderick was right, the thumb-size piece of hardware held the formulas for the vaccine and the antibodies, and—hopefully—evidence the viral plague had not been unleashed upon mankind by careless Chinese but instead by a US president who believed he was above the law, a president who viewed all moral and ethical standards with disdain and who thought the power of the presidency gave him the right to do whatever served him and his constituency. Now all David had to do was get it out of the lab, through the gate, down the road to Fallon, and into the nearest internet-connected USB port. And there was no doubt in his mind that getting out was going to be much harder than getting in.

- 87 -

Oberlein and Slattery watched David leave the level-one lab and walk down the hallway toward the elevators. They expected to see him exit the elevator on zero level and head for his quarters. Instead, he exited on the main level and started moving toward the front entrance, his stagger markedly improved.

"Now what's he doing?" Slattery said.

"I don't know," Oberlein replied. "Maybe he sobered up and he's heading back out to link up with his girlfriend."

"At two in the morning? Bullshit," Slattery said. "And anyway, he shouldn't be driving. I'm going over there to see what he's up to. Call the gate and tell that jarhead not to let him pass."

- 88 -

David climbed into Peter Shen's car and drove toward the gate. The guard recognized the vehicle and lowered the bollards, as David had hoped. And this time the driver's side was opposite the shack, so David figured it was just a matter of keeping his face hidden and the gate would open. That's what he did, and that's what happened. The gate started to move, but David did not see a light at the end of the tunnel. Instead, he was overcome by a sense of dread. Everything had gone as planned. It had been too easy. He was sure the other shoe was going to drop, and drop it did.

The guard's phone rang. He answered it, his gaze turning toward the approaching car, his demeanor changing from accommodating to alarmed. He hit the switch reversing the gate, then stepped out of the shack into David's path. He drew his sidearm, cranked a shell into the chamber, and aimed the gun at the car's windshield—at David's head.

David stomped the accelerator.

The guard fired multiple shots while jumping out of the way.

David ducked below the dashboard, the windshield exploding into a spiderweb of holes, cracks, and fissures. Seconds later the Audi smashed through the gate, the car skidding sideways, dust flying, gravel pelting the undercarriage. David sat up, regained control, and sped down the hill. It wouldn't be long before a squad of black ops mercenaries in Humvees would be on his tail.

He was right. Headlights flickered in the rearview mirror, the beams cutting through the dust, falling and rising with the undulations of the road. With each turn the rear tires broke loose, sending David into slides that pushed the limits of control. Every rise launched the car into the air, even if only for a moment, but long enough to further diminish his control of the vehicle. He glanced at the speedometer—sixty miles per hour. He grasped the wheel tighter and focused on the road ahead instead of the lights gaining from behind. More turns. More fishtailing. Airborne again. Dust roiling. Gravel pelting.

Then he saw the black ribbon of Highway 50 at the base of the hill, the hospital only fifteen miles up the road, and there'd be security at the entrance who would let him pass, while hopefully blocking the entrance of heavily armed men who had no reason to storm a hospital.

David tried to finesse a right-hand turn as he approached the highway, but he was going too fast. All four tires broke loose, the car sliding sideways, and when the rubber gripped the asphalt the Audi flipped and rolled, once, twice, and a third time down the shoulder and into the sagebrush, glass shattering, metal crumpling, airbags exploding.

The car came to rest on its top, David suspended by the lap belt, the shoulder harness cutting into his clavicle. The left side of his body ached and throbbed, and every breath met with a stab of pain. He released the belt, fell onto the ceiling of the car, and wormed his way out the driver's side window. He leaned against the wrecked Audi, caught his breath, and palpated the left side of his skull. It was exquisitely tender to the touch, his fingertips covered in blood.

A black Humvee stopped on the shoulder of the highway. Two bulky figures jumped out, locking and loading their weapons no more than twenty yards away. They resembled the private security force that had rescued David and Mr. White from the Connecticut woods—unmarked camo fatigues, heavily armed—but now they were trying to kill him instead of help him. David needed to hide the flash drive and vials.

He spotted a Coke can among the broken glass, papers, Air Jordans, and other debris that had been jettisoned from the rolling car. He grabbed the can, shoved the flash drive through the hole in the top, tried doing the same with one of the antibody vials. Too big. He stomped the can flat and threw it like a Frisbee into the desert at a right angle to the highway.

"Hands on your head, fingers laced!"

David turned toward the voice, now ten yards away, his hands on his head.

Two red dots flickered on his sternum.

While the two mercenaries held their laser sights on David's chest, a second Humvee pulled off the highway, and a black Escalade drove up behind them. Two men climbed out of each vehicle and weaved their way through the sagebrush over to David and the upside-down car.

Three of the new arrivals added their laser sights to the other two already darting around David's chest. The fourth man did not have a weapon. He didn't need one. He was in charge. A patch on the right breast of his camo fatigues read, "Neville."

"Where is it?" the colonel said.

"Where's what?" David replied.

"The classified material you stole from the United States government. You realize you have committed an act of espionage, which is punishable by death."

And David knew if he handed over the drive, the death sentence would be carried out right here, right now. No judge, no jury, just a single shot to the back of the head while he cowered on his hands and knees. "I'm sorry, but I don't know—"

"Wrong!" Neville shouted. He turned toward the two men who had arrived first. "Grab the girl. If the father gets in the way, kill him."

"Wait," David said. "It was in my pocket. It must have come out during the crash."

"Go," Neville said to the men. "You," Neville pointing at two others, "zip-tie him and search him, and get rid of that rancid coat. I can smell it from here."

While one of the mercenaries aimed a laser sight at David's forehead, a second removed Peter Shen's coat, rifled through the pockets, and came out with the four vials of monoclonal antibody.

"Well, well," Neville said as he was handed the vials. He held one of them up to the moonlight. "The magic elixir that will save your girlfriend. Now, if you'll hand over the flash drive, we can all go home."

David said nothing.

"Okay," Neville said. He set one of the vials on a flat rock and crushed it with his boot. "Finish searching him, rip the car apart, and scour the surrounding area if you need to."

They did not find the flash drive on David, in the car, or in the brush, and the longer they searched, the more agitated Neville became.

"Goddammit," he finally blurted out. "This is taking too long. We need to get off this road." To the two men executing the search, he said, "Go back to the lab." To his driver, "We'll take him to Salt Wells and wait for the girl." To David, "When your pretty girlfriend gets here, you are going to sorely regret this act of heroism."

89

Jenny Hightower awoke to bright lights shining through the gauzy curtains of her bedroom. She didn't think much of it. She lived in a circle, was a light sleeper, and was often awakened by the after-dark activities over at Billy Jack Featherstone's place. But then she heard the muffled pleas of a young woman, and a male voice talking in a threatening tone. She climbed out of her bed, went to the window, and pulled back the corner of the curtain. It was Nova—beautiful young Nova—being shoved into a black Humvee by a couple of white men wearing military gear. As the car pulled away, Jenny threw on a robe, grabbed her keys and phone, and headed for the garage.

From Jenny's subdivision, two streets led to Reservation Road— the main road leading off the rez and into Fallon. If she used whatever street they didn't, and she timed it just right, she would already be driving down Reservation Road when the SUV pulled out of her subdivision. That's what she did, and it worked. She was now several car lengths behind them, and pretty much inconspicuous in her little Subaru. She grabbed her phone and dialed Billy.

It rang once, then twice.

"C'mon, c'mon, answer," she said.

Two more rings. He answered. "Jenny, I'm busy. What is it?"

"Somebody just grabbed Nova. White men in a black Hummer, and they looked like soldiers with helmets and vests and big machine guns."

"Slow down," Two Feathers said. "They took her from the house? Soldiers?"

"Yes. They were all decked out like you see on TV, like those guys in Afghanistan and Iraq. I'm behind them now, Billy. We're driving down Reservation Road toward Fallon."

"Don't lose them, but don't get too close. They'll spot you."

"Okay, but I'm really nervous."

"I'm leaving now. Just stay on the phone and tell me where they're going."

The Humvee followed Reservation Road to the junction of Highway 50 and turned left. It was three in the morning, the highway deserted. Jenny hung back at least five or six car lengths but was nervous as hell. They were leaving town and heading into uninhabited desert. If they wanted to run her off the road and kill her, they could.

About ten miles later, the SUV slowed and made a right turn onto an unmarked dirt road. Jenny did not follow. She didn't need to. She knew where the road led.

"Billy, you still there?" Jenny said into her phone.

"Yes. I'm on the outskirts of town," Two Feathers replied.

"They just turned off the highway. They're going to Salt Wells."

90

Neville rode in the front passenger seat of the Escalade, with David in the middle row, sitting on his zip-tied hands. They drove east on Highway 50 for a few miles, away from Fallon, then turned onto an unmarked dirt road. David knew where they were going.

While familiarizing himself with his adopted home, he had come across the story of Salt Wells, a burned-out brothel someone had torched a few years back. It sat above the valley at the end of a dirt road about a mile off the highway, and all that remained was the burnt shell of the brick structure that once housed the bar and lounge area. The mobile homes that had served as bedrooms for the girls were now piles of scorched, twisted aluminum. A couple of minutes later they pulled up to what was left of the place.

The headlights gave the wreckage an otherworldly feel. The lone remaining structure was a small single-story building made of white cinder block. The door was gone, the windows blown out. Scorch marks blackened the walls around the doorway and above the window frames. Beyond the building were the scattered remains of the mobile homes—piles of warped aluminum siding, steel chairs, metal doors, and other scrap that escaped the flames.

The Escalade turned off. The wreckage went dark. David was led into the shell of the lounge by flashlight. Neville's driver found an intact chair among the debris, turned it upright, and pushed David toward it. Neville found a second chair and sat down across from David, the two men staring at each other for a moment, then Neville said, "Who is helping you?"

"Nobody," David replied.

"The device you used to steal everything on our servers and wipe them clean, it was designed by DARPA—my agency—and there's no way you could have acquired it without high-level help, like military intelligence or NSA."

"I still don't—"

"Drop the 'dumb' act, Doctor. There are factions in Washington that want to bring down the president and his deep state conspiracy, but guess what, they are now the deep state. They've been forced into the shadows. Anybody who matters is on board with the president. And why wouldn't they be? A chance to rid the geopolitical landscape of all Muslim states, all Arab states, all Communist states, without firing a single shot, launching a single missile, or exploding a single warhead? If the roles were reversed and China or the Russians or the Muslims had this capability, they would not hesitate to use it."

"Look," David said, "I just need the antibody. The rest of you can do whatever you want."

Neville leaned back and folded his arms across his chest. "Who is helping you?"

"Why does it matter? You've accomplished your mission. Even if the US is exposed as the source of the virus, nobody can fuck with us now."

"As you know, our president cares very much about how he is regarded. He wants history to remember him as the savior of the world, not a destroyer of nations, so, by proxy, I am authorized to do whatever it takes to keep the true source of the virus hidden."

"Does that include the murder of Mark Wallace, a kid named Andy, and about twenty people in a bar?"

"Yes, so one more time—who helped you?"

David said nothing.

Neville gave the remaining three antibody vials to his driver. "Line them up in the windowsill over there, hand me your sidearm, and shine the flashlight on them." The man did so, and when he had stepped back, Neville raised the pistol and fired a round.

The boom was deafening, David flinching as the first vial turned into a cloud of mist.

Neville crossed his arms over his chest and stared at David.

David stared back.

Neville fired again, David flinching as the second vial disappeared.

"Only one left," Neville nodding toward the window sill, "but it contains billions of antibodies, more than enough to kill every viral particle in your girlfriend's body and reverse the massive inflammatory response inside her chest. It truly is a miracle drug."

The sound of a groaning engine caught both men's attention.

Neville reached out and fired another round, exploding the last vial, then he walked over and peered through a blown-out window. "Your girlfriend is here," he said, turning back toward David. "Last chance to save her from something infinitely more painful than a ruptured spleen."

Car doors opened and closed. Gravel crunched under multiple sets of feet.

Nova was pushed through the doorway by one of Neville's mercenaries. She'd been gagged with a cloth and her hands zip-tied behind her. She tried to move toward David but was intercepted by Neville's driver.

- 91 -

As Two Feathers sped down Highway 50 in his Ford Bronco, he tried to figure out who would kidnap Nova. He had a long-standing truce with the southern Nevada suppliers, and if the Sinaloa cartel had decided to break that truce and take over his operation, they would just kill him. They would not abduct his daughter. And the Mexicans did not run around in full-body armor. Black SUVs, yes. Battle gear, no.

Two Feathers did not take the road to Salt Wells. Instead, he drove another two miles and turned onto a different dirt road. This one skirted the edge of a salt-crusted dry lake that stretched between him and Salt Wells and gave the brothel its name. He parked a few hundred yards from the highway, and as he climbed out he grabbed the heavy canvas hunting coat and binoculars from the passenger seat, and a pint of Jack Daniel's from the glove box. After taking a large swig, he slipped the bottle into the back pocket of his jeans and tapped "Dangerous Dan" on his phone.

"Five minutes out," Dan said.

"I'm going up the hill to take a look," Two Feathers replied. "Meet me up there."

Two Feathers needed one last thing before heading out. He went around to the back of the Bronco and opened the tailgate. A forty-two-inch hard-sided tactical gun case lay in the cargo area. Inside, an AK-47. He removed the assault weapon, strapped it over his shoulder, put four clips of ammunition in his coat pockets, and started up the road. After a few steps he felt for the Buck knife hanging from his belt. It was there. It was always there.

An icy wind buffeted Two Feathers as he climbed up to a high ridge. From there he could see the derelict brothel, the bed of the dry lake, and the occasional headlights on Highway 50. He flipped up his collar, took another swig of Jack Daniel's, and put the binoculars to his eyes. The sky was clear with a three-quarter moon overhead, but there wasn't enough light to give him much detail. He could make out the wreckage of the mobile homes, the shell of the main building, and two SUVs, but that was all. "Fuck!" he said into the wind, and he took another swig of Jack.

Moments later, Two Feathers spotted headlights turning onto the dirt road he had taken. He peered through the binoculars. Dan's Pontiac Grand Am. Two Feathers finished off the whisky and threw the empty bottle into the sagebrush.

Dangerous Dan joined Two Feathers on the ridge. He had a long, thin, soft-sided carrying case and a small backpack strapped over his shoulders. "What the hell's going on?" Dan asked as he approached.

"Jenny Hightower saw two men in battle gear take Nova out of the house and followed them here. Motherfuckers. I'll kill every one of 'em—military, cartel, whatever, they're all dead."

"And it's just the two of us?"

"Nobody moves as quietly as me and you. Anyone else would be a liability. You got your night vision scope?"

"My thermal imager is gonna work better." Dan slipped off his backpack, removed what looked like a rifle scope, and held it up to his right eye.

"See anything?" Two Feathers asked impatiently.

"Two SUVs, engines still warm, and two men in the parking lot."

"Weapons?"

"We're too far away for any detail, but fully automatic, I'm sure. Probably M16s or M4s. We'll definitely need the element of surprise."

"All right. Let's drop down to the dry lake and follow the shoreline. The lake ends a couple hundred yards from the parking lot. From there we can use the sagebrush for cover."

The two men left the road, exhaling frosty breaths as they worked their way down a steep hill, and fifteen minutes later they were crouched in the high brush about fifty yards from the brothel. Faint light shone through the broken-out windows of the old lounge. "Flashlights," Two Feather's said. "Nova's gonna be in there."

Dan peered through the thermal-imaging scope. "Still only two men out front—automatic weapons, helmets, body armor." He removed a pair of headsets from his backpack and handed one of them to Two Feathers. "You go around back. I'll move closer, take out the guards, and try to get a look inside. Don't make a move until I know how many hostiles we're dealing with."

Neville gestured for one of the mercenaries to hand over his assault weapon. "When I was a medical student," Neville said, taking the rifle in his hands, "the surgery residents were adamant that the postsurgical patients avoid any activity that might stress the abdominal-wall closure." He turned toward Nova, who was still in the grasp of his driver. "When a stressed surgical wound rips open and can no longer contain the structures within the abdominal cavity, that's called a dehiscence." Neville looked over at David. "If I were to plant the butt of my associate's weapon into this young woman's abdomen, would it not result in a wound dehiscence, Doctor?"

"Really?" David said. "You'd lower yourself to the level of a sadistic animal to get what you want? You're a doctor. You took the Hippocratic oath. At some point in your life you must have had at least a modicum of compassion toward your fellow man."

"I think you lack the capacity for clear insight," Neville said. "This is a momentous time, when great men of destiny are changing history, and we're doing it specifically for our fellow man. Yes, there have been and will be many deaths, but the safety and stability of a new world order will more than justify the sacrifice."

"And you're proud to be a part of this xenophobic genocide?"

"When I was a college freshman, I vowed to change the world in a way that would resonate with humankind far into the future. Then fate brought me together with men of similar ideas and ambitions who helped me fulfill that goal. So yes, I am proud. Now"—Neville motioned for his driver to pull on Nova's arms, fully exposing her abdomen—"back to business."

He positioned the rifle so the butt end of the stock was pointed toward her.

She squirmed, screamed through the gag, tears streaming from her eyes.

The man tightened his grip.

"What type of closure did you use for the fascia, Dr. Aaronson? A running stitch that when cut or broken allows the entire suture to unravel? Or did you use the more reliable method of placing interrupted sutures? In other words, am I going to have to hit her only once, or am I going to have to hit her multiple times?"

Neville moved the rifle away from Nova, then started to thrust it toward her.

"Okay!" David said. "I know where the flash drive is. By the car in a flattened Coke can."

"Very good." Neville turned to his driver. "Accompany the doctor down to the wreck and have him find the can for you. When you return"—Neville was now speaking to David—"you will tell me who has been helping you."

- 93 -

Dan knelt in the sagebrush a few yards from the parking lot and no more than twenty yards from the two guards. They stood near the front of the main building, and the contrast between their dark bulky figures and the light-colored cinder block of the brothel would allow him to take his shots without using a night vision scope or thermal-imaging camera. After quietly removing his compound bow from its case, he slipped an arrow from the bow-mounted quiver, clicked the nock of the arrow onto the bow string, laid the shaft onto the arrow rest, and drew back the string to his anchor point—his right cheek. He then aligned the peep site on the string with the pin sight of the bow and—knowing that the 402-grain arrow tipped with a broadhead was capable of penetrating Kevlar, Dyneema, and Spectra body armor—he aimed the pin site to the right of the target's sternum, slowly exhaled, and when his lungs emptied, he released the string. The man silently dropped to the ground. His partner, disoriented by the sight of an arrow protruding from the man's heart, hesitated just long enough to give Dan time to slip another arrow out of the quiver, mount it, and shoot. The second man went down as cleanly and quietly as the first.

Dan mounted a third arrow, stood, and slowly made his way toward the building. Into the headset, he whispered, "Both targets are down. I'm advancing toward the entrance. Stand by for a head count and Nova's position."

Neville's driver pushed David out the door of the brothel. David stumbled forward, almost tripping over a body lying on the ground. Two bodies on the ground. The men standing guard, arrows protruding from their chests, their hearts.

"Men down," yelled Neville's man. "Both men are down."

A figure emerged from the darkness, raised a bow, aimed it right at David and fired. The arrow passed by David's ear with a hiss and struck Neville's driver in the throat, dropping the man where he stood.

"Holy shit," was all David could manage.

The man came at him, another arrow loaded on the bow and pointed at David's head. Then they recognized each other from the aborted assassination two nights ago.

Two Feathers leaned against the cinder block wall of the building, quieted his breathing, and was about to slip in through the back door when he heard, "Men down. Both men are down." It came from the parking lot, but it wasn't Dan's voice. From inside the building he heard, "This is Salt Wells. Send in another team. The surgeon has the upper hand."

Two Feathers stepped over the charred remains of the door and quickly but quietly moved down the hallway toward the front room, dodging blackened chunks of wood, metal, and other debris as he went. He came to the end of the hall and peered around the corner. Nova was sitting in a chair, hands zip-tied behind her, her back to him. Behind Nova stood a man in desert camo fatigues, and he was raising a walkie-talkie to his mouth. "And put a chopper in the air," he said.

In one swift move Two Feathers moved behind the man, wrapped his massive left arm around the man's head, hyperextended his neck, and pressed his razor-sharp Buck knife into the skin just below the Adam's apple.

"Drop the radio," Two Feathers said.

Nova turned around and mumbled, "Daddy," through the gag.

Two Feathers' grip tightened, slightly cutting the skin of the man's neck and drawing blood. "You okay, baby?" he said.

At that moment, David walked through the front door with Dan right behind him.

"What the fuck are you doing here?" Two Feathers said, glaring at David.

David turned slightly, revealing his zip-tied hands.

"Cut 'em both loose," Two Feathers said to Dan.

Dan returned his arrow to the quiver, set down the bow, and cut the zip ties with a large Buck knife that flipped open like a switchblade. Both David and Nova rubbed their wrists.

Neville said, "This family reunion is touching, but you should know there's a team of commandos on the way."

Two Feathers dug the knife deeper. "Who is this guy?" he asked David.

"Colonel Jonathan Neville. He created the virus that caused Nova's spleen to rupture."

Two Feathers jerked Neville's head back. "Surgeon, you take Nova outside. Dan, see if anyone is coming up the road, and watch for a chopper."

Neville tensed and wiggled in a feeble attempt to break loose.

Two Feathers clamped Neville's head tighter, extended his neck farther, dug the knife deeper.

"This is a big mistake," Neville said, his voice strained and coarse from the extreme angle of his neck. "I'm a colonel in the United States Army. My mission has the backing of the president of the United States."

Dan grabbed his bow and walked out.

David put his arm around Nova, and they followed Dan through the door.

96

Two Feathers joined the others in the parking lot. Both hands, both arms, and the front of his coat were drenched in steaming blood. Quarter-size drops of blood spatter dotted his face and neck. Nova gasped and covered her mouth, a fresh round of tears welling up. David shuddered as he imagined the violence that had just taken place. Of all the vessels in the human neck, only the carotid arteries bled with such force. The Buck knife, which Two Feathers was wiping clean on his pants leg, must have been driven right down to the cervical vertebrae. Even Dan—the guy who had just fired arrows into the hearts of two men and the throat of a third—looked unnerved.

While Two Feathers slipped the Buck knife back into its sheath, he glanced at the three dead men lying on the ground. "Dan, get your arrows out of these guys and let's drag them inside." He looked over at David. "Surgeon, you help us. Nova, watch for headlights coming up the road or anything in the sky that looks like a chopper."

With steady traction, Dan was able to slip the arrow out of the first man's heart without leaving the broadhead tip inside the chest. And while Dan went to work on the second arrow, Two Feathers and David grabbed the first man's arms and legs and started dragging him.

"Daddy," Nova said. "Headlights just turned off the highway."

Everyone looked up. Another Humvee. Barreling up the road.

"You brought the C-4, right?" Two Feathers said to Dan.

"Six bricks."

"Plant one on each of these guys. I'll put the other three on the colonel. I don't want them to find anything but teeth."

"Daddy." Nova was now pointing down the valley.

A chopper. A couple of miles away.

Two Feathers disappeared into the brothel.

Dan laid bricks of C-4 explosive on top of each of the dead men, then inserted a radio-controlled blasting cap into each one.

David rifled through the pockets of Neville's driver, found the keys to the Escalade.

Two Feathers emerged from the brothel. To David and Nova: "Our cars are by the dry lake two miles east of here. If we stay low in the brush, they won't see us."

David: "I have to get back to the highway."

Two Feathers: "What for?"

"The cure for Nova, it's on a flash drive near the highway. I have to get it."

Two Feathers to Dan: "Can you help him?"

The Humvee was now a half mile away. The chopper had cut its distance in half as well.

Dan: "Yeah."

Two Feathers handed his AK-47 and ammo clips to Dan and disappeared with Nova into the sagebrush.

Dan took the keys from David, and they jumped into Neville's Escalade.

97

The Escalade flew down the dirt road at sixty miles per hour, while the Humvee flew up the hill at the same speed, the two vehicles blowing past each other a quarter mile from the brothel. The chopper came out of nowhere, passing overhead a hundred feet off the desert floor, the *whump whump whump* of its blades shaking the Escalade, its spotlight turning night into day and illuminating the swirling clouds of dust blanketing the road. David looked back to see what the Humvee was going to do. Its brake lights lit up. "They're turning around," he said.

"What about the chopper?"

David lowered the window, stuck his head out and looked up. "Circling the building, searching it with a spotlight."

Dan handed David an old flip phone. "Hit the dial button."

"What?" David said.

"The number on the screen, hit dial."

David did.

A huge fireball erupted. The blast jolted the Escalade like a thunderclap.

"Christ," David said.

"Is the chopper still airborne?"

David stuck his head out the window again. "Yes, but it's all over the place, spinning and weaving. Wait a minute. It just disappeared behind a hill."

"Did it crash?"

"I didn't see an explosion."

Headlights flooded the interior of the Escalade, the Humvee now two hundred yards back.

"The highway, left or right?" Dan said.

"Left. There's a wrecked car across from the turnoff to the military lab."

Dan slowed down and turned onto Highway 50, the Humvee now one hundred yards away, no sign of the chopper. "This flash drive we're after, where is it?"

"I put it in a Coke can and threw it away from the car. I'll need a flashlight to find it."

"No flashlight. You'll draw fire," Dan said. "There's a night vision scope in my backpack. Scan the ground with it. The contrast between the can and the dirt will be very sharp."

Dan checked the rearview mirror.

The Humvee turned onto the highway.

He pressed on the accelerator, the Escalade bumping up to a hundred miles per hour.

David dug through the pack and came out with two scopes, black and gray.

"The black one," Dan said. "The other one is a thermal imager. It won't see a cold aluminum can. And once we have this flash drive, then what?"

"I need to get to the hospital and—"

The rear window exploded.

Automatic weapon fire pelted the vehicle.

Both men ducked.

"Where's the AK?" David shouted over the road noise and machine guns.

"Not yet. Save the ammo," Dan hollered back. "That Humvee is probably armor plated. The only way to buy you time is to keep them pinned inside."

"How? When we stop, they'll drive right up our ass."

"I'm gonna fly off the road into the brush, jump out, and start shooting while you look for the can. Stay low and move fast."

"There," David pointing at the wrecked car to the left of the highway.

Dan hit the brakes and cranked the wheel.

The Escalade careened down the shoulder, fishtailing right and then left, clumps of sagebrush bouncing and rocking them. Dan stomped the brakes and brought them to a standstill twenty yards past the wreck.

"Go," Dan said as he jumped out and grabbed the AK-47.

Both men ran to the overturned Audi.

Dan ducked behind it and locked and loaded the assault rifle as the Humvee drove off the other side of the road.

David crouched and moved away from the car, scanning the desert floor with the night vision scope.

Dan fired the AK, filling the air with the *pop-pop, pop-pop-pop* of the semiautomatic weapon.

David kept low to the ground, moving the scope back and forth in a systematic fashion, then stopped short and yelled, "Fuck!" as a big fat, ghostly green scorpion scampered through his field of vision. The magnification made it seem like the fucker was a foot long.

The continuous barrage of fully automatic machine guns drowned out Dan's *pop-pop-pops*. The commandos had exited their vehicle.

Spits of dirt erupted near David. Bullets whistled above and around him. Tracer rounds ripped through the darkness like falling stars. He dropped to his hands and knees, aiming his scope between the clumps of sagebrush, looking for a solid-green object among the stippled greens of the soil and vegetation. Nothing. He needed to stand and visually draw a line from the lab access road, across the highway, and through the wrecked car. He did so and found he was left of where he should be. He dropped back to ground level and moved to the right.

David crawled around a clump of sagebrush, and there it was, the flattened can he'd thrown like a Frisbee. He grabbed it and tore it open. The flash drive fell to the dirt. He picked it up and put it in his pocket, raised his head above the brush to reorient himself, and started back toward the Escalade.

98

The Humvee had stopped on the far side of the highway, down off the shoulder, its lower half hidden below the road. The commandos were shielded by the vehicle, one popping up above the hood, the other two leaning around the rear, all taking turns showering Dan and the Audi with automatic weapons fire. Flames spit from all three muzzles, the smell of burning gunpowder filling the air, the noise deafening.

David crouched near the driver's side door of the Escalade, waved at Dan, and held up the flash drive.

"Go!" Dan hollered. "I'll buy you as much time as I can."

David did not want to leave the guy behind, but if they both jumped in and took off, the commandos would follow, and David wouldn't have the time needed to get into the hospital and up to the third floor. There was no other way.

David climbed into the vehicle and started it.

The passenger-side windows exploded, spraying shards of glass everywhere.

Bullets clinked and clanked as they pelted the steel body.

David lay across the console and blindly stomped the gas pedal.

The vehicle lurched, bounced and rocked, front to back and side to side as he plowed through the stout, unyielding clumps of sagebrush. But he didn't want to drive up and onto the highway too quickly, thus giving the commandos an opportunity to shoot out his tires.

And as suddenly as it had started, the fusillade of bullets ended. David sat up and looked out the shattered rear window. No flames spitting from muzzles. No audible bursts of gunfire. No human movement. Just an eerie calm. *Dan*, he thought, but he pushed the worst-case scenario out of his mind.

David drove up onto the road and floored the accelerator. This stretch of Highway 50 had recently been repaved and was mostly straight, with the occasional gentle curve. He ran the Escalade up to 110 miles per hour. The hospital was fifteen miles up the road. He'd be there in less than ten minutes.

- 99 -

Eight minutes later, David hit the edge of town and a thirty-five-mile-per-hour speed limit. He slowed to sixty. In a hundred yards, a quick right and a quick left would take him to the hospital. He glanced in the rearview mirror. No headlights. He had made it.

Then everything lit up—the cab of the Escalade, the highway, road signs, trees, and bushes. A chopper roared overhead, flew past him, banked a hard turn and came back at him, blinding David with its spotlight.

He cranked the steering wheel to the right, the Escalade's tires screeching as he turned onto Harrigan, then cranked a left, tires screeching again as he made the sharp turn into the parking lot. He blew through the mostly empty lot, stopped in front of the ER entrance, and jumped out of the vehicle. Jesse, the graveyard-shift security guard, met David inside the sliding glass doors. He looked David up and down, glanced at the bullet-riddled SUV.

"What the fuck, Doc. You all right?"

The chopper swooped in, hovered thirty feet off the ground, dropped a pair of ropes.

Two commandos leaned backward out the door, then rappelled down to the pavement. When their boots hit the ground, two more followed.

An infant sitting on its mother's lap in the waiting area started crying.

An octogenarian facing the window said, "God Almighty, it's D-day out there."

"Don't let these guys in," David said. "They're trying to kill me. Has to do with the pandemic." And he took off down the hall.

- 100 -

The first commandos reached the ER entrance just in time to see David enter the stairwell. The rest quickly caught up to them. Captain Rick Honeycutt, the ranking officer, pulled his Glock 19 from its holster, cranked the slide, and buried the muzzle into the security guard's neck.

"Where's he going?" the captain said.

"I don't—"

The captain jammed the pistol deeper.

"He didn't say," Jesse said, his voice faltering with fear. "He just told me not to let you in, then ran down the hall."

"And up the stairs," one of the commandos added.

"He's a surgeon, right?" the captain said. "What floor is surgery on?"

Jesse hesitated.

"Which floor, goddammit?"

"Third."

The captain turned toward his men. "Doyle and I will go to three. Baker, you and Smith are with us. I want two teams of two to go to the second floor. The rest of you cover all stairwells and set up an exterior perimeter to watch the exits. This is a small place. Find him, shoot him, get the hard drive—in that order."

101

David ran up three flights of stairs and sprinted down the corridor toward the OR. The third floor was in night mode, with two thirds of the fluorescent bars turned off, casting the hallway in islands of light. To his left, the recovery room was fully illuminated. He glanced through the open doors. A lone nurse was preparing for the arrival of a patient.

At the OR entrance, David hit the plate on the wall, the electric motor emanating a grinding noise as the doors slowly opened. In front of room four, bright light shone through the window into the hallway. David peered inside. The surgical team was performing a case. Pennington looked up. Their eyes met briefly, then David hurried around the corner into the surgeon's lounge.

Thomas Pennington was finishing an emergency appendectomy on a twelve-year-old girl when he thought he saw someone in the OR window. He looked up to find David Aaronson peering into the room, then David vanished. Even though he'd caught only a glimpse, something about David didn't seem right. His hair was askew, perhaps matted on one side, and he appeared disheveled and anxious. Thomas Pennington had never seen David Aaronson exhibit anything other than complete self-possession. And what was he doing here at three in the morning?

On the second floor, four commandos entered the main corridor. Two of them went left toward the medicine ward, two went right toward the surgery ward. The remaining four continued up the stairs to the third-floor corridor. Baker and Smith went left toward the ICU. Honeycutt and Doyle went right toward the operating rooms and surgical recovery area.

The surgeon's lounge television was on. The computer wasn't. David sat down and hit the start button. The machine was old and slow. His heels drummed the floor as he waited, knowing he had no more than a minute, maybe two, to pull this off.

The screen turned on.

The Windows icon came into view.

The ticking circle went round and round.

Honeycutt and Doyle moved quickly but quietly along the dimly lit hallway, peering into windows and checking doors as they advanced. Everything was locked and dark except for a pair of double doors farther down on the left. Backs against the wall, the commandos silently moved toward them until Honeycutt could see inside. A young woman in scrubs was turning on a heart monitor. The men slipped past and continued on to another set of doors on the right side of the hall. These were marked OPERATING ROOMS, AUTHORIZED PERSONNEL ONLY, SCRUB ATTIRE REQUIRED. Doyle pushed the plate on the wall. The doors opened with a metallic groan.

This hallway was also dimly lit. Large windows sat above stainless steel sinks, two on the left and two on the right. Beside each sink, a door, the nearest one marked OR 1. From the next window, light flooded the hall. The commandos approached and peered inside—a surgical team performing an operation. The surgeon looked up at them. They moved on.

The sight of armed soldiers in full battle gear standing outside his operating room, only moments after a panicked David Aaronson had passed by, alarmed Thomas Pennington. He finished taping the dressing over the appendectomy wound, stripped off his gown and gloves, and headed for the surgeon's lounge.

The ticking circle was relentless. David's heels drummed the floor. He took the flash drive from his pocket, his hands shaking as he removed the cap. Just insert it into the USB port, wait for the connection and hit Enter, Broderick had said. Simple enough, if the fucking machine would start.

The ticking circle went away.

The home screen appeared.

David inserted the drive into the port.

The screen went blank, then a dialogue box opened. *Searching for 84.51.500.01* was all it said. The IP address for Broderick's supercomputer? But nothing was happening, no ticking circle, no blinking dots. "Goddammit. Hurry up," he said through clenched teeth.

The door behind him burst open. "Hands over your head, now!"

The dialogue box flickered: *Connection to 84.51.500.01 established.*

David reached for the Enter key, his fingertip inches away.

Through the doorway Pennington yelled David's name, but the simultaneous discharge of two M16 rounds blotted out his words. Then, nothing but black.

"What the hell is this?" Pennington screamed at the soldiers as they lowered their weapons. He rushed over to David, who lay in a heap on the floor.

While Pennington dug his fingers into David's neck, trying to find a carotid pulse, one of the soldiers walked over to the computer, studied the screen for a moment, plucked the flash drive from the USB port, and said, "We're done here. Radio the others to stand down and move out."

102

Searing pain in his right chest lifted David out of a semiconscious state and thrust him into a swirl of confusion, disorientation, and harsh fluorescent light. The pain, along with a throbbing headache, filled his eyes with tears and blurred his vision. He blinked, focused, and found himself propped up in a bed, IVs in both arms, a hissing oxygen mask covering his nose and mouth, a heart monitor beeping in concert with the throb in his head—*chirp-throb-chirp-throb-chirp-throb*.

The room became familiar, as did the circumstances—the lab, the crash, Salt Wells and Nova, the firefight in the desert, and the chase through the hospital—all culminating right here, the intensive care unit of the Fallon-Churchill Community Hospital. He shifted his weight to get comfortable. Big mistake. The movement sent stabbing pains through his ribs. He carefully lifted the sheets to find bloody dressings taped to the right side of his chest and a 40-French chest tube protruding from his lateral chest wall. French was a unit of diameter, and forty was the biggest, about the size of an adult thumb and most commonly used for evacuating blood from the pleural space. Where was the nurse? He needed to know what happened. Did he get shot? Go to the OR for a thoracotomy? What was the extent of his injuries? As if he had silently summoned her, Jeannie—who'd been on duty the night Nova came in—walked through the door. "Dr. Aaronson," she said. "Glad to see you're awake."

David slipped the oxygen mask off his face. "What happened last night? Did I go to the operating room?" His voice was dry-throated and raspy.

"You had a hemothorax. No surgery. Dr. Pennington will give you the details. He asked me to page him as soon as you awakened."

"And this?" David touching the layers of gauze wrapped around his head.

"Nothing too serious. Let me page Dr. Pennington."

"Wait," David said as Jeannie walked toward the nurse's station. "Have you seen Nova?"

"She was here this morning, but her father wouldn't let her stay."

"But she looked okay?"

"Yes. She was worried about you but otherwise seemed fine."

David checked the clock on the wall. Three p.m. Top of the hour. "Jeannie, sorry, one more thing. Will you turn on the television? CNN?"

Hello. I'm Wolf Blitzer, and welcome to The Situation Room. *We have breaking news coming into CNN, and to say it has significant global implications would be an understatement. I'm referring, of course, to the worldwide pandemic that has now killed one hundred million people. CNN has learned that just a few hours ago, the Centers for Disease Control and Prevention received an anonymous email containing the formulas for a vaccine that might stop the spread of both CoVid19 and CoVid23, and a treatment—an antibody drug—for those who have contracted the highly lethal and contagious CoVid 23. It was only five days ago during his Sunday-morning address that President Bell vowed to fast-track the development of a vaccine for the new strain of coronavirus, but it seems as though a vaccine and treatment already exists. For more on this we go to Jim Avala, who is standing by at the Centers for Disease Control in Atlanta.*

The studio shot cut away to a reporter standing in front of the familiar blue-and-white CDC sign. In a voiceover, Wolf Blitzer said:

Jim, it is quite bizarre that a vaccine and cure for a disease of biblical proportions shows up as an anonymous email sent to the director of the CDC, and even more puzzling that the president had assembled a team to develop these drugs when, apparently, they already exist.

Jim Avala: *It is confusing, Wolf, but the scientists here are not concerned with anything the president has to say. Instead, they plan to fast-track the development, testing, and manufacture of the—quote—email vaccine, and widely distribute it as quickly as possible, if it is indeed the real thing.*

Wolf Blitzer: *The email is reportedly anonymous, but does the director have any idea who may have sent it?*

Jim Avala: *He does not, Wolf. In fact, to add to the mystery, the director received a text message alerting him to the presence of the email and instructing him to open it immediately. The number associated with the text was traced to a disposable TracFone.*

Wolf Blitzer: *Quite the mystery indeed, Jim. We will, of course, watch this story closely, and we'll try to determine why the president was unaware of the existence of a drug with the potential to save millions of lives.*

The shot returned to the studio, but David tuned out, closed his eyes, and allowed his head to sink into the pillow. He had done it. They had done it—Marina, Ophelia, Andy, Vince Strahan, and Ruby Mae Parker. And, of course, Two Feathers and his friend Dan.

Moments later, Pennington entered the ICU and came over to David's bedside.

"Welcome back to the land of the living," Pennington said.

"Seems like I've heard that before," David replied.

"I'm sorry?"

"Nothing," David said, shaking his head as he recalled his visit to the Tombs infirmary.

Pennington glanced at the television, then gave David a wink and smile. "Mission accomplished," he said, "but not without some cost."

"Yeah, there are a few blanks that need to be filled in."

Thomas Pennington explained how he had come up behind two soldiers in the doorway of the surgeon's lounge, "And as the red dots were settling on your head and back, I hollered your name and pushed into them, throwing off their aim, but only by inches. The headshot grazed your right occipital bone. The second bullet entered your right chest under the tip of the scapula and exited below the right nipple. A couple of ribs were shattered, and you sustained a hemopneumothorax and pulmonary contusion. I placed a forty-French chest tube to drain the blood and reexpand the lung, then scanned your head in anticipation of transferring you to the trauma center in Reno, but only the outer table of the skull was fractured. The inner table was intact, there was no brain hemorrhage, and by then the bleeding from your chest had slowed to a trickle, so I saw no reason to transfer you."

"Jesus," David said. "What happened to the shooters?"

"After you hit the floor, one of them walked over to the computer, removed a flash drive, and they left."

"How do you know I'm responsible for the email they're talking about?" David asked, nodding toward the TV.

"Armed men chase you through the hospital, try to kill you while you're sitting at a computer, and twelve hours later the CDC has a CoVid vaccine from an anonymous source. And now there's an FBI agent guarding the door and a government spook in the waiting area who wants to see you. Elementary, Dr. Aaronson."

103

Jim Broderick moved a chair next to David's bed, and for a moment he just sat there in his overcoat and fedora, smiling and shaking his head. Then, "You did it. I told you you'd be able to do it."

"I had plenty of help," David said, "but that's not important." He told Broderick about the vials of monoclonal antibodies in the refrigerator on level 1, and the two warehouses up the road from the lab where pallets full of boxes were being loaded onto trucks. "They must be the manufacturing plants for the vaccine and the antibody."

"The lab is swarming with federal agents, and a CDC team just landed at the naval air station. I'll relay your observations and make sure Nova is their top priority."

"Okay, good," David said, and he found himself relaxing and sinking into the softness of the bed. Then, "Wolf Blitzer says the director of the CDC does not know who sent the email."

"Actually, he does know, but he has agreed to protect my identity for as long as he can."

"Any chance I'll be able to keep my anonymity?"

"I'd say no. As we speak, local, state, and federal investigators are combing through the wreckage of Salt Wells, the site of your car accident, and the hospital's CCTV security system. They've linked the mercenaries to Jonathan Neville, and as soon as Dr. Pennington gives them the green light, the FBI will want to question you."

David glanced past Broderick to see if Jeannie was nearby, then quietly said, "What about my true identity—David McBride?"

"I'm going to say no to that as well. I've seen everything on the flash drive, and I can tell you the scope of the president's network of conspirators reaches far and wide. He has abused the power of the presidency. He has broken domestic and international laws. He has participated in genocide. And he has sanctioned the murders of US citizens. I'll be questioned by the FBI and other intelligence agencies, and there will be testimony in front of multiple senate and house committees. I can try to solicit whistleblower protections for you, but ultimately, I'll be subpoenaed to reveal your identity. Then the NSA will want to talk to you about Richard Whitestone and the dead Russian, and the NYPD still has an open case with David McBride's name on it."

104

After Jim Broderick left, Jeannie and her assistant moved David from his bed to a chair. As painful as it was, David knew the importance of sitting upright after suffering broken ribs, a hemothorax, and a pulmonary contusion. If he laid in bed and continued to take shallow breaths, he would absolutely develop pneumonia. He needed to sit for extended periods, and he needed to work out with his incentive spirometer, both of which would be more tolerable when the patient-controlled anesthesia device arrived from the pharmacy.

"While we're waiting," Jeannie said, "I'll give you two milligrams of morphine."

Once she had infused the IV pain medicine and covered David with warm blankets, Jeannie motioned toward the nightstand near the headboard, which he'd been unable to see while in the bed. "Nova left those for you," she said.

On the stand sat a large medallion and maroon velvet pouch, the same Shoshone talisman and medicine bag Nova's tribal sisters had given to her following her surgery.

"She wanted to stay," Jeannie continued, "but her father has her on lockdown. There's even some guy named Dangerous Dan sitting by the front door with a crossbow. She'll try to come see you tonight after her father chills a little."

David felt a rush of relief to hear Dan had made it out of the firefight alive.

Jeannie handed Nova's gifts to David. He held the talisman in his palm and admired the inlaid gems of black, white, yellow, and red, and the corresponding bear, wolf, buffalo, and eagle engraved along the periphery of each quadrant, representing spiritual, emotional, physical, and mental health, Nova had told him. The pair of sterling silver feathers hanging from the bottom of the medallion brought to mind the feathers that so often adorned Nova's hair, and now he could smell the lilac scent of her freshly washed hair, and feel her soft bronze skin, and see her radiant smile framed by her exquisite face. God how he ached to see her, to hold her, to sit next to her while eating Chinese takeout and drinking iced tea. And as his heart filled with love and hope and optimism, the soothing warmth of the blankets and the neuronal depression of the morphine induced within David a euphoric peace, and he drifted into a deep sleep.

- 105 -

Two months after the Salt Wells incident
Third floor, Fallon-Churchill Community Hospital
The unoccupied surgeon's lounge

From the always-on-and-always-tuned-to-CNN flat-screen television mounted on the wall, *The Situation Room with Wolf Blitzer*:

Hello, I'm Wolf Blitzer, and welcome to The Situation Room. *We have breaking news that, if you are my age or close to it, will induce a sense of déjà vu. The president has announced that he will address the nation from the Oval Office at nine p.m. Eastern Standard Time. Much like Richard Nixon did in 1974, it is widely believed President Bell will use this occasion to announce his resignation. Facing certain impeachment by the Democrat-controlled House of Representatives, the president met today with ranking members of the Republican-led Senate, where he was told they will no longer support him. Rather than face an impeachment hearing in the House, and the inevitable removal from office by the Senate, President Bell, it is believed, has decided to resign. This will not bring an end to the president's troubles, however. He still faces a multitude of criminal charges here at home, along with forty-one of his co-conspirators, which include his closest advisors, other top government officials, high-ranking members of the military, and nongovernment civilians. In addition, countries around the world are calling for the International Criminal Court in*

The Hague, Netherlands, to indict the president and try him for crimes against humanity, not only for genocide but also for knowingly withholding a life-saving vaccine from the world while secretly vaccinating his own country. Vice President Joe Spence has given no indication that he will pardon the president should he step down.

- 106 -

One month after the resignation of the president
Third floor, Fallon-Churchill Community Hospital
The unoccupied surgeon's lounge

From the always-on-and-always-tuned-to-CNN flat-screen television mounted on the wall, *The Situation Room with Wolf Blitzer*:

> *Hello, I'm Wolf Blitzer in* The Situation Room. *We have major breaking news coming into CNN right now. As you know, during his first month in office, President Joe Spence has reopened the borders, widely distributed the supervirus vaccine and treatment, both here and abroad, and has delivered humanitarian aid to all countries impacted by the pandemic. Today he turned his attention to related domestic affairs and this morning announced that he will grant a full presidential pardon to Dr. David McBride—also known as Dr. David Aaronson—the Fallon, Nevada, surgeon who exposed the former president of the United States as the true perpetrator behind the viral plague that has decimated much of the world. Dr. McBride faced charges of espionage after breaking into a US Army biosafety lab and stealing state and military secrets. During the investigation following these actions, it was revealed that McBride was also wanted in the state of New York for his role in the murders of two men and the forcible removal of human organs from three others. In an exhaustive review of the circumstances surrounding those crimes, it has been*

determined that McBride was forced to surgically remove the kidneys from the three victims and only then resorted to murder in retaliation for the loss of his pregnant wife, his father, and a close associate. Given McBride's highly charged emotional state at the time, and his subsequent heroic actions and service to the country and the world, President Spence was unequivocal in granting McBride's pardon.

- 107 -

Four months after the Salt Wells incident and the harrowing investigations that followed, David finally felt comfortable stepping into the public eye. He had testified in front of multiple congressional committees, had been interrogated by numerous law enforcement and national security agencies, and his current and past transgressions had been exposed, picked apart, scrutinized, and judged. The president of the United States granted him a full pardon for all alleged crimes, the news media had treated him fairly, and the nation generally regarded him as a hero.

On this night he sat across from Nova at a small table in the steakhouse just off the main floor of the Stockman's casino. All his soft-tissue wounds, contusions, abrasions, and broken ribs were healed. Nova was fully recovered from her abdominal surgery and splenectomy, and the enlarged lymph nodes in her chest had regressed to normal size. His work environment had normalized, and the mass of reporters and journalists who'd been following him for four months returned home. Even his relationship with Two Feathers had settled into an uneasy peace. He understood that David had been grilled relentlessly about Salt Wells and hadn't revealed anything. And, David figured, as long as he did not try to move Nova away from Fallon, Two Feathers would accept the inevitable.

But none of that mattered on this crisp winter evening. The beautiful, the exquisite, the magnificent Nova Featherstone sat across from David, her hand holding his as she read the menu. The soft ambient light and flickering candle in the middle of the table added a lustrous sheen to her silky black hair and a warm glow to her bronze skin. She wore a simple black dress with a deep-V neckline, which provided the perfect backdrop for the gold chains adorning her neck. David's favorite, the gold-lace dream catcher with a topaz stone in the center and three tiny golden feathers dangling from the bottom, perfectly complemented the feathers clipped into her hair. He reached for his tumbler of Maker's Mark with his free hand, took a sip, and marveled at her beauty and his good fortune. After two years of doubt and insecurity, of tragedy and loss, and loneliness and violence, and running and hiding and lying, his world had finally righted itself. He believed he had atoned for past transgressions and had redeemed himself for the murders of two men and the pain and suffering he'd inflicted on three others. And as he gazed at Nova he felt nothing but love, and renewal, and optimism, and he anticipated a beautiful life together.

A middle-aged, weather-beaten man and his wife timidly approached the table. His jeans, snap-button shirt, cowboy boots, hat, and leather belt gave him away as either a farmer or a rancher.

"Good evening, Dr. Aaronson—sorry—I mean Dr. McBride," the man said as he removed his hat and held it deferentially near his waist. "I apologize for interrupting your dinner, but I've been hoping to see you so I could tell you that you saved my son's life. He got the screening CAT scan they did on everybody in town, and they found the enlarged nodes and were able to treat them and get them to go away. So my wife and I, well, we wanted to thank you."

"I had a lot of help," David said as he stood and shook hands with the man. "I'm just happy to hear your son is doing well."

The couple thanked David again, then turned and walked away.

David looked across the table at Nova, who had a big grin on her face. "You're gonna have to get used to that," she said.

"Yeah, well, public adoration isn't really my thing."

David was sipping his drink when a younger man approached. He looked like one of the regulars from the Beaver—rumpled jeans and shirt, billed cap, work boots, sheathed Buck knife hitched to his belt. He planted both hands on the edge of the table and leaned down so close to David and Nova that David could smell the cheap whisky on the guy's breath.

"Hey, Doc," he said. "I been wantin' to talk to you also. I just want you to know there's a lot of us that liked what our president was doin' and wished you'd a kept your nose out of it, so on behalf of all those good Americans who would like to see you dead, I say *take your fucking squaw and go live on the reservation. We don't want you around here no more.*" The guy stood, spit on the floor, and with a stupid smirk on his face, he said, "Enjoy your dinner, Doctor."

David just sat there dumbfounded as the asshole stumbled out to the casino. Then he turned toward Nova. "You know," he said, "for as smart as we humans are, we're really stupid."

Acknowledgements

Writing and publishing a novel is a long and arduous process, requiring many contributors along the way. The following individuals deserve my immense gratitude:

Franco Audia, Kathleen Isdith, and Jackson Streeter for their early reads and feedback.

The developmental and copyeditors at Kirkus editorial services.

Kate Race at Artitudes Design for her cover and marketing platform designs.

Chris O'Byrne and the staff at Jet Launch Strategic Publishing for their design expertise.

Claire McKinney at Claire McKinneyPR, LLC for her expert marketing and publicity.

About the Author

Richard Van Anderson is a former heart surgeon turned fiction writer. His surgery training took him from the "knife and gun club" of LSU Medical Center in Shreveport, Louisiana, to the famed Bellevue Hospital in Midtown Manhattan. His education as a writer includes an MFA in creative writing from Pine Manor College in Boston, Massachusetts. He currently lives in Seattle, Washington with his wife and two sons.

To learn more about Richard Van Anderson visit rvananderson.com.

And finally, the best way for a book to find its audience has always been, and still is, word of mouth recommendations. If you liked the story, please consider telling others about it, either person to person, using social media, or (and this is the most effective way) posting reviews at your favorite review site. Thank you.